Felony

NORMA WYMAN

Enjoy!

Norma Wyman

PAGE PUBLISHING, INC.
New York, NY

First originally published by Page Publishing, Inc. 2015

ISBN 978-1-68213-123-7 (pbk)
ISBN 978-1-68213-124-4 (digital)

Printed in the United States of America

To my wonderful husband, Wayne, who has supported me throughout this entire process.

Chapter 1

"I wanted to get that bastard before I retired," Sam Jacobs told his partner, Sue Patnode, as he perused the file on Max Bertolini.

Sam was a typical cop. He was heavyset, but regular workouts had kept him fit. His gray hair was tightly curled, and most women considered him handsome. He was sixty years old and due to retire from the New Rochelle Police Department in two weeks.

His partner was thirty years his junior. They had worked together for five years and shared a mutual respect. Sue was naturally slim, attractive, and had an outgoing personality. She had married recently and was pregnant with twins. She would soon be taking an extended leave of absence to care for her children.

"This would not be a good time to go after Max," she told Sam. "Even if we could prove he was selling drugs and was probably the cause of his wife's death, a jury would be sympathetic to him."

"He wouldn't go on trial for months."

"Yeah, but a smart lawyer would play up to what he was going through at the time of his arrest."

"You are right. I guess I will have to let it go."

"Sam, I will go after him when the time is right," Sue promised. "I will get him for dealing drugs, and I will find out what happened to his baby and his sister-in-law."

"I doubt they will be able to be found. Max would see to that."

"What would be Max's motivation for harming them?"

"Max doesn't need motivation. Anyway, let's go over what we have in the file."

"Max owns a small import business in the center of town. Most of his imports come from Central and South America and Mexico. He supposedly imports coffee, Macadamia nuts, and fruit, but most believe there are other things imported he does not want inspectors to know about. He reports an income of about fifty to seventy-five thousand dollars a year on his income tax returns. There is no way that income can support his lavish lifestyle. He claims he inherited money from his paternal grandfather, but there is no evidence of that. His younger brother does not seem to have benefited from such an inheritance. Max and his brother come from a rough background. There is nothing to suggest that either his father's or his mother's family had money."

"The Bertolini family was intact until the father was killed when Max and his brother were in their late teens. He was killed by gunfire, and it was determined that he was in the wrong place at the wrong time. However, given his abusive nature toward his boys, there was always suspicion that there was more to the story than was told. I always believed he was set up somehow but could never prove it."

"Do you think Max set him up?"

"Probably Max and his brother."

"We believe that the boys suffered a lot of physical and emotional abuse at the hands of their father, and the mother did little to protect them. The family is not very close. The mother travels around the world with a new, rich boyfriend. The brother lives in California, trying to become an actor. I think he has a bit part in one of the soaps. He attended college for a while but partied a lot and quit. He probably flunked out."

"Both the brother and the mother flew in for Max's wife's funeral. But neither stayed around very long after the services. The mother was obviously not very concerned about her new granddaughter. I don't believe either of them know anything about Max's business or anything about the disappearance of the baby or sister-in-law. Hell, they probably don't even know they are missing."

"The only useful information we have about the time they disappeared is that the wife's car was found at the airport. A shuttle van driver noticed it was parked in the same spot for a couple of weeks and called security. After checking the license number, they discovered it was registered to Max and called him. He told some weak story about loaning the car to an associate who had unexpectedly had his business trip prolonged. He picked it up, had it cleaned, and sold it."

"So much for evidence."

"If there was any evidence in the first place."

"We also learned that five hundred dollars was taken from the wife's bank account and that her debit card was used at a local pharmacy. Lana, the wife, had several thousand dollars in her account that was never touched, so robbery was not the reason for the withdrawal."

"Sam, you know I am going to be on leave for an extended period. I want to raise my children myself until they are old enough to go to school. If this case has not been solved when I return, I promise I will make the investigation a priority."

"Well, by that time it will be a cold case, so good luck."

"I'll see you later. I need to go home and get spruced up for my surprise retirement party."

Sue grinned. She had to go home and get ready for the party too. *I'm going to really miss this guy*, she thought. *He thinks I will not be able to solve this case, but I will show him.*

She had no idea of the events she would precipitate in a few years when she returned to work and attempted to keep her promise to Sam.

Chapter 2

Max Bertolini and his brother Larry were the envy of their classmates when they attended New Rochelle High School in the nineties.

They seemed to have it all. They performed well in their classes and were star athletes in all school sports. They lived in a big expensive house, had their own cars to drive, and had money to spend. They had no trouble getting dates. They intrigued all the girls at school.

No one guessed what the boys' lives were really like. Their father abused them physically, verbally, and emotionally. He never gave them recognition for their academic success or athletic triumphs. The physical abuse occurred with the slightest provocation. Their mother, though sickened by the sight and sounds of their cries while being hurt, was not strong enough to help them. She would go to her bedroom, close the door, and cover her ears to block out the sounds of their cries. Max never forgave her for being so weak.

Max started using drugs when he was in high school. It helped him deal with his father's abuse. It also gave him the courage to confront his father. Eventually, as he got older and larger, the physical abuse stopped. His father was afraid to touch either Max or his brother. When Max's father died of a gunshot wound when he was a senior in high school, he did not mourn the loss. He was relieved not to have to worry about his brother's safety once he moved out of the house.

He was careful to keep his drug use both limited and a secret. He did not want his use to adversely affect his performance in class and on the athletic field. He did not want his brother to know about it and start using. He never became an addict.

His use of drugs did not hurt his performance in school but did have a profound effect on his life in the future. He recognized the amount of money that could be made dealing drugs and began to plot a way to take the business over from his supplier.

He was ruthless in that endeavor. The only thing he cared about was his brother. Threats from other dealers who suspected he was trying to take over their territory had little effect. They soon learned not to threaten his brother. Those who did paid dearly. He wasn't worried about what the drugs did to his "clients." It was their decision to use. If they didn't get their supply from him, they would get it somewhere else. He might as well be the one to make the money.

After graduating high school, Max realized he would need to start a legitimate business to serve as a front for his drug business. He was able to get a business loan from the local bank to start an import business. His former girlfriend's father was president of this bank. That fact plus his reputation as a good student and athlete helped him.

He had been smart enough not to touch Becky, the bank president's only daughter, when he was dating her in high school. He was a perfect gentleman. He knew he might need help from her father later. He satisfied his prurient needs with girls who lived in another part of town. Even then he was discreet.

He was lucky that Becky's parents didn't know the real reason for their breakup. They thought it was just high school behavior and that their relationship couldn't survive the separation when she left for college. Only Bart's brother suspected what happened.

That would eventually be Max's undoing.

Bart Hamilton was a rival of Max's all through high school. They often vied for the same positions. Sometimes Max won; sometimes Bart won. They both wanted the same girl. Becky was with Max, but he knew that could easily change. The only other person who came close to Max's accomplishments was Joe Boccia. Joe could always be beaten; Bart couldn't.

Max's girl, Becky Barker, was blonde, blue eyed, and had a figure that could stop a freight train. Her father was a wealthy banker, and the family lived in a beautiful house. He loved being with Becky and loved being with her family. He thought they might be useful to him sometime in the future. He wasn't about to let Bart Hamilton spoil that for him.

Becky had begun talking a lot about Bart. She said he was good-looking and smart. She enjoyed his prowess on the football field. Max didn't like the looks that passed between Becky and Bart when they were in the same room.

He decided he had to take steps to resolve the problem before it got out of hand. He had drugs available. He had taken the local drug trade from Bobby Durand. It had been easy enough. A few well-timed phone calls led Bobby's supplier to believe Bobby was skimming drugs and selling them for his own profit. He was Bobby's lieutenant, and Bobby confided in him that his supplier was accusing him of skimming. He was scared for his life. Max helped him get away. No one in New Rochelle ever heard from him again. Max now had easy access to a variety of drugs.

Bart Hamilton did not drink, but at a party after a pep rally and bonfire heralding the start of the football season, Max bullied him so unmercifully that he consented to trying a beer. Max had him where he wanted him. He slipped drugs into the beer. He thought everyone would laugh at Bart for not being able to handle a drink when he started to behave erratically. He didn't expect Bart to insist on leaving for home when he began to feel ill. He didn't expect Bart to crash his car and die.

Becky was never able to forgive Max for insisting that Bart drink that night. Their relationship ended. No one ever knew about the drugs. Bart's heartbroken parents demanded that that never be made public. Only Bart's older brother suspected what really happened. At the grave site, he promised Bart redemption.

Max successfully ran his drug distribution business for several years before he met and married Lana Mitchell.

In October 2001, against his better judgment, Max accepted his brother's invitation to a college fraternity party. Hell, he was paying his tuition, he might as we get something out of it.

He spotted her the moment he walked into the room.

Why he ever got involved with her he could never figure out. He certainly never intended to get married or have a kid. Lana had promised him that she was protected and wouldn't get pregnant.

He knew that marriage was a mistake, but god, he wanted her. He just did not want the legal complications that marriage brought.

But she was so beautiful and sexy and so excited about planning the island wedding she wanted that he allowed things to get out of hand. Next thing he knew, he was married.

Lana's untimely death solved the problem of marriage, but now there was a kid, and everyone knew it was his.

The aunt may have solved that problem. He was sure she and the kid were hiding out somewhere. He didn't try to find them because he didn't want to be focused on by anyone, especially the police.

Friends and family were satisfied when he told them that Laura had returned to school in New England and Barbara Jean had been adopted. Everyone understood that it wouldn't be good for Max to raise a child alone. They also understood why Laura would want to return to New England and not have contact with Max.

Only Joe Boccia and Ruth Carter knew the truth. For now, he believed they could trust them. If not, they could be dealt with.

Chapter 3

Joe Boccia did not often think about his past. It was too painful. His legal name was Joseph Lee Boccia II. He never knew whom the *II* referred to. He never knew the father who left him, his mother, and infant sisters as soon as the newborn was brought home from the hospital. The other child was just thirteen months old. Joe was three.

His mother, overwhelmed by the responsibility of raising three young children alone, put the two girls up for adoption. She felt the girls were young enough to adjust to new homes. Joe was very close to her, and she knew he would have a difficult time adjusting to a new home. She felt she could handle raising just one child. She was adamant that the girls stay together and was involved with choosing the couple they would be placed with. She always knew that the girls were loved and well cared for. She never talked about them to Joe, and he never knew what happened to them.

Joe knew his mother loved him, but she had loved his sisters too. He always feared that circumstances would force his mother to give him up as she had his sisters. As a result, he strived to be the best he could be. He wanted to make things easy for his mother and make her proud of him. He often wondered what she would think of him now if she were still alive.

Growing up, Joe was always in second place both athletically and academically. He should have been proud to be in that position. His size was a disadvantage. He was both short and thin. No matter what he did, he could not seem to bulk up. Classes did not come easy either. He had to study more than most to get good grades.

To make matters worse, it was always Max Bertolini and Bart Hamilton that he was second to. The three boys grew up together in New Rochelle. They went to elementary and middle school together. In high school, if Max and Bart got an A- on an algebra test, he got a B+. He could never quite catch up. On the athletic field, if Max and Bart were first-string players, Joe was second string. When he became an adult, he never got higher in a business than an assistant manager.

As a grown man, he was still short and thin. He had olive skin and black eyes that seemed to dart all over the place as if he were constantly searching for something. He had black hair and black bushy eyebrows.

Now, Joe was Max's right-hand man. He was still in second place. Only Lenny Butler took orders from him. They were the only regulars Max hired. People who transported drugs were contracted out. Max wanted as few people as possible to know about his operation. In that way, if anyone were arrested, they would not be able to finger him.

This type of operation gave Joe some leverage. He was easily able to change orders. He was very familiar with Max's operation and hoped to use this information to his advantage someday.

He was glad when Max met and married Lana Mitchell. Having a kid was a bonus. Max would be preoccupied with family matters, leaving Joe to run the operation.

However, everything changed when Lana died and the kid disappeared. Max handled his grief by investing his energy in the business.

His threat concerning Lana's sister was just so many words. He didn't really care what happened to her or his kid.

He did lose ten grand when he was not able put the kid up for adoption, but he is wealthy man and the money was not all that important to him. Joe, however, was disappointed to lose what would have been his cut.

But that is all water over the dam, Joe thought. *I think I am close to taking over this business. The cops are beginning to give Max a hard time, but that is nothing compared to what I have planned. And he won't even know what hit him. I have been patient. Now is the time for me to make a move.*

Chapter 4

August 2007

Laura McKenzie quickly turned off her television. She didn't want to hear the breaking news story about a mother who was charged with a felony for failing to return her children to their father after a weekend visit. The mother was charged with kidnapping. The story brought reality too close to home.

Laura was excited about her new endeavor, but at the same time was gripped with fear as she prepared to leave for school. After graduating from college, she knew she could not have stayed at the shelter much longer. But is she making the right move, or is she putting herself and her daughter, Benjii, in danger? Could she lose everything including Benjii?

She could hardly believe her good fortune when she was offered a teaching position at the middle school in Mapleton, New Hampshire. She was finally going to realize her lifelong dream of becoming a teacher and in a setting that was ideal for her situation. The town itself was rustic and beautiful. The center of town had a square with a small white church, three schools, and police and fire departments staffed mostly by volunteers. Most important of all was the fact that the town prided itself in providing its children with an excellent educational system.

Laura would be a special education teacher for grade eight in the middle school. Her daughter, Benjii, would attend an all-day kindergarten in the elementary school across the street. She knew that having an all-day kindergarten was a new concept for the people in this small New England town.

Providing an all-day kindergarten had been hotly debated. Budget-conscious townspeople felt an all-day kindergarten was nothing more than a high-cost day care. Others believed it was too long a day for five-year-olds. However, the more liberal thinkers in town believed that the children would benefit from attending the all-day program. They knew more time could be provided for art, music, physical education, and development of social skills. The children would benefit from this program as long as ample time was provided for play, snack, rest.

The school also had a before- and after-school program for children of school district employees and other parents whose work schedule did not coordinate with school hours. Laura's school will start an hour before Benjii's so the child will attend the morning program before her school starts. Laura will have an hour after school to prepare for her classes the next day before picking Benjii up to go home. If she has meetings or other obligations, Benjii will stay for the afternoon program until Laura is ready to go home. She hopes this will not happen often. It will be a long day for the child and she is not used to being separated from Laura for long periods. It will be a long day for Laura too.

Correcting and grading papers and doing planning will have to be completed evenings after Benjii goes to bed as well as on weekends. Most people do not realize that a teacher's day does not end when he/she leaves school in the afternoon.

Laura had been able to find a small affordable two-bedroom apartment in a gated complex. It was close to the school, and the security and privacy was very important to her.

Laura McKenzie looks a lot different from the way she did when she was known as Laura Mitchell. She is still thin and petite, but her hair is now short and strawberry blond. She wears blue tinted glasses that she does not need for vision. She wears boots or shoes that make her look taller than she really is.

The shelter she and Benjii had lived in for several years had helped her establish a new identity for both of them. She had relinquished her New York driver's license so a new license would reflect her new appearance without having questions asked. She had completed her education and earned her teaching degree while living at the shelter. She and other mothers there had looked after each other's children while they worked or went to school.

She owed a huge debt of gratitude to everyone at the shelter and deeply regretted not being completely truthful with everyone there about her real situation. She hoped that someday she would be able to find a way to repay them and tell them her true story. That may alleviate her guilt.

Still, she is not able to alleviate her fear. She knows it is right to work and support herself and Benjii without being dependent on others. Leaving the shelter made room for other women and children who needed help, and she was excited about providing a more normal life for her and her daughter. She hopes her true identity will never be revealed. The problem is that she will not be living far from where she had lived for so long and where her troubles started.

Tears stung her eyes as she thought about these things. She had lost so much. These thoughts led her back to the event that took place several years ago.

She had no idea of the events that were currently going on that would devastate her life.

Chapter 5

Tragedies

June 2001

The door closed softly behind the last guest, and Laura Mitchell turned quietly to her twin sister. Her eyes were moist with grief.

As Laura hugged her sister, she said, "At least they're together. Neither will have to live without the other. That is a comfort. They were very much in love."

"I suppose," Lana said. "But this has not been easy."

"Death is never easy, Lana."

Lana shrugged then said, "Well, what on earth are we going to do with all this food and all these damn flowers? We should have had people take them before they left."

"I am not sure that would have been good manners. They would be the same people who brought the food and sent the flowers to show their concern for us. I asked the caterer to take the food to the community kitchen. The funeral directors are going to give the flowers that were not left at the cemetery to the hospital and nursing homes."

"Well, aren't you little Miss Efficient?"

"No, I asked John Breen to make those arrangements."

"I don't remember you consulting me."

"I tried to. You told me to do whatever I wanted. Don't you remember?"

"Yea, I guess I do."

Laura stared at her sister. She was worried about her. Sometimes she seemed zoned out. She thought about the past and how things have suddenly changed.

Laura and Lana Mitchell had grown up in a small community outside New Rochelle, New York.

They had led a charmed life. Their father was a successful businessman, and their mother was a stay-at-home mom who did volunteer work in the community when the girls were in school.

Laura and Lana were fraternal twins, but except for the life their parents provided them they shared nothing in common.

Laura had brown eyes and brown hair like her father. She was petite in all sense of the word. She was short and weighed just 105 pounds. She was very serious about her education and did well in school.

Lana was beautiful like her mother. She was statuesque with large, well-formed breasts and had a sleek athletic body. She was intelligent like her sister but did not take her education seriously. She did the minimum to pass her classes to graduate high school. She was a constant concern for her parents.

After graduating high school, both girls enrolled in college. Laura attended a small college in southwestern New Hampshire which offered a strong curriculum in education. She had wanted to be a teacher as long as she could remember.

Lana had no idea what she wanted to do with her life, so she enrolled in the state university and took liberal arts courses. She did not take these classes very seriously. She spent most of her time partying.

The girls were just completing their first year in college when tragedy struck. Their parents had died in a small plane crash while island hopping in Hawaii. They were celebrating their twenty-fifth wedding anniversary with this second honeymoon on the islands.

Both girls had returned home as soon as they heard the news. They had the task of notifying friends and family and planning the funeral. They did not have many extended family members, but their parents had many friends and associates, their father from his business and their mother from the various charitable organizations she served. Therefore, many people had attended the services. The calling hours and funeral services were held concurrently with visiting hours two hours before the funeral service. The twins did not feel that they could handle two days of condolences. During the days before the services, there was a stream of visitors to their home bringing food and flowers and offering any assistance needed. These visitors couldn't help but notice the difference in attitude between the two girls. Laura was sad and misty-eyed. Lana was stoic.

Laura and Lana spent some time resting after the stress from the services, then they had the difficult task deciding what they would do with their parents' belongings. Their father had left them well provided for. He had a lawyer that would be sure the legalities of the estate would be settled before the twins returned to college the end of August. Most of their parents' assets had been put in trust for them until they reached the age of twenty-five. His lawyer, John Breen, would be the executor of the estate. However, they still had to decide what to do with personal items. Some things they gave away, and valuable items, such as their mother's jewelry, were put in a safe-deposit box in the local bank.

They couldn't bear to sell the house or furniture, so John Breen made arrangements to rent it to a young teacher and his family.

Saying good-bye when it was time for them to return to college was very painful for Laura.

She didn't know when she would return to her hometown again. She knew she would miss the holidays at home when that time came around. She and Lana had both been invited to the homes of different friends for Thanksgiving.

"We won't even be together that day," she cried as she and Lana were discussing the holiday plans.

"We'll be together for Christmas," Lana said. "I have an idea about that day, but I want to surprise you if things pan out the way I envision."

Laura was in for a shock.

Chapter 6

Laura spent Thanksgiving break at the home of a friend from college, Marge Spencer. Marge and her family realized that this would be a very difficult holiday for Laura. They did everything they could to make her feel like a member of the family, but they could see the pain in her eyes.

This pain was compounded by the fact that she could not get in touch with Lana. She called Lana's cell phone several times each day but got nothing except voice mail stating that the recipient of the call was either out of the calling area or was not available to take the call.

As much as she had enjoyed being with Marge and the rest of the Spencer family, Laura was happy when it was time to return to college. She had rented a small studio apartment off campus so she could be alone to study and process the grief she was still experiencing over the loss of her parents.

She also had to deal with the fact that she missed Lana awfully.

The apartment, which she was able to rent with money John Breen allowed her for college expenses, had a small living area that served as a living room and kitchenette, one bedroom, and a bath. She had furnished the apartment with furniture from her bedroom at home and other pieces from her parents' house. These pieces of furniture gave her some comfort.

As soon as she returned home to her apartment after attending her classes on the Monday after Thanksgiving, she tried to call Lana again.

When Lana finally answered the phone, Laura said, "Lana, where have you been all weekend?"

"At a friend's house. I thought I told you where I would be. Why?"

"I tried to call you all weekend."

"You did? Why?"

"To wish you a happy Thanksgiving. I really missed you, and I missed Mom and Dad terribly. I needed to talk with you. It's the first Thanksgiving we haven't all been together."

"Oh, sorry. I didn't think to call. I don't understand why your call didn't come through. I had my phone with me all weekend. It never rang."

It never occurred to Lana that someone may have tampered with her phone to prevent her from accepting calls. It would be much later before she realized how she was controlled by the man she was with.

"Maybe you were in an area where service is limited."

"No, I was in New Rochelle."

"New Rochelle? I thought you said you spent Thanksgiving with a friend."

"I did. My friend lives in New Rochelle." Lana gave no further explanation. "Did you go by Mom and Dad's house?

"No, I didn't. I didn't even think of it. Besides, I think John Breen rented it to a young teacher with a family."

"I thought about the house all weekend. I thought of all the wonderful holidays we had there."

"Laura, you have to move on. I have."

"It's only been three months."

"Hey, I've got to go. I'll talk with you again in a few days."

"First, what are your plans for Christmas?"

"We are going to be at the house in New Rochelle that we were at for Thanksgiving. I'll tell you more later."

Laura hung up. She did not ask who Lana was talking about when she said *we*.

Two days before Christmas, Laura rented a car at the airport in Albany and drove to the address in New Rochelle Lana had given her. She was surprised when she realized what part of town she was driving to. It was the part of town where the wealthiest townspeople lived. Neither she nor Lana had frequented that part of town when they were growing up in New Rochelle.

When Laura arrived at her destination, she left her bags and the gifts she had brought for Lana in the trunk of her car and walked up the sidewalk to the front door of a very exclusive home and rang the bell. A woman in her fifties answered the door. The woman was tall and thin with brown hair that was showing signs of growing gray. She had a kind face.

"'Good afternoon, you must be Laura," she said kindly. "I am Ruth Carter, Mr. Bertolini's housekeeper."

"Who is Mr. Bertolini?"

Mrs. Carter looked perplexed. "If you don't know, I had better let your sister explain. Let me show you to your room first."

Laura was just getting settled into the guest room when Lana came bursting in.

"Hi, sis, I didn't realize you had arrived."

Lana's eyes were dull, and her words were slurred. Her hair had always had a bright sheen but was now dull. Her complexion was sallow.

"Lana, whatever is wrong with you? Are you ill?" Laura was shocked by what she saw.

"What do you mean what is wrong? How can anything be wrong when I live in a fabulous place like this?"

"You live here? How can you afford it? It must cost a fortune. John Breen would never give you enough allowance to rent a place like this."

"The hell with John Breen. I hate having him control our money the way he does. He's probably skimming some from the top."

"I don't believe it. John Breen is an honest man. Dad wouldn't have appointed him to handle his financial affairs if he weren't."

At that moment, Laura was glad John did have control of the money. She wouldn't trust Lana with it.

Lana lit a cigarette. Her hand was shaking.

"When did you start smoking?" Laura asked. "Dad would have a fit."

"Dad isn't here. There isn't much he can do about it."

Laura was shocked that Lana could speak so coldly of their dad. He had been a perfect parent and had loved them very much. She decided not to comment further.

"Tell me about this house."

"I live here with my boyfriend."

"Boyfriend?"

"Actually he is much more than a boyfriend. His name is Max Bertolini. You will meet him at dinner tonight."

"I didn't know we would be with other people. I thought there would be just the two of us. We could catch up on what each of us has been doing since college started last August. I thought we would have a quiet holiday."

"How dull."

"Lana, this will be our first Christmas without our parents. I am not sure I will be very good company."

"You don't need to be good company. I can be company enough myself for Max," Lana said suggestively.

"Are you sleeping with him?"

"Of course."

"Lana, you look awful. I am not sure this man is good for you. How did you meet him?"

"I met him at a frat party at school. He paid for his younger brother to go to the university. I think it was love at first sight. He is older than me, but that doesn't make any difference."

"Don't you realize how awful you look? You're still beautiful, you always will be. But your eyes are dull, your hair has lost its sheen, and your hands shake constantly. Are you drinking too much? Are you using drugs?"

"All of the above. No, just kidding. I have a cocktail before dinner and wine with dinner. It's how the rich people live."

Laura knew better. A cocktail and a glass of wine each day would not have that much of an effect on Lana's health, but she decided not to pursue the subject.

Laura met Max Bertolini at dinner later that evening. She took an immediate dislike to him. He was abrupt and cold. He didn't take her hand when she offered it when Lana introduced them. She had the sense that he didn't like having her there. He said no words of welcome. Instead, he leaned over and gave Lana a prurient kiss that made Laura blush with embarrassment. But what bothered Laura most was Max's eyes. They were cold as ice, even when he looked at Lana. Max frightened her.

Dinner conversation was mundane. When Laura tried to turn the conversation to Max's business or family, he put her off and abruptly changed the subject. He did say he had a mother, stepfather, and younger brother. He said no family members would be joining them for Christmas. It would be just the three of them. Mrs. Carter would be there most of the day to see to their needs.

Christmas day was a very painful day for Laura. There were just a few gifts under the tree.

Laura had brought gifts for Lana. She had gone out Christmas Eve to purchase an expensive bottle of wine for Max and a lovely glove and scarf set for Mrs. Carter. Mrs. Carter had seemed shocked and pleased to receive them. Neither Lana nor Max had thought to get gifts for her. Max gave Lana an expensive diamond bracelet.

"For the gems you provide in bed," he said, glancing at Laura.

He was trying to embarrass her again, but by this time she was used to his innuendos, and they no longer bothered her. Lana gave Laura a lovely cashmere sweater. Laura thought her gifts looked shabby in comparison.

Originally, Laura had planned to stay with Lana until after the New Year, but when she learned that Max was planning an elegant New Year's Eve party, she decided to return to her apartment early. She thought things she didn't want to be party to would probably be served at Max's party. If she wanted to be a teacher, she couldn't be found in an environment where drugs were used. Also, she didn't think she would like Max's friends, and it pained her to see how controlling he was over Lana.

Marge Spencer had invited her to a party, so she could go out if she wanted to.

She was unhappy to realize that the party and possible drug use were not the only reason she wanted to go home early. She simply did not want to spend more time with Lana. She was troubled by her behavior; she was afraid that Lana was constantly high. She decided to have it out with her when she told her she was leaving the next day.

"Lan, you need help," she said. "You are an alcoholic and possible a drug addict. You need to get away from Max."

24

"Get away from him? I plan to marry him."

"Does he know that? He doesn't seem to be the marrying kind."

"Not yet, but he will."

"Max is cold and unfeeling. I don't like the people I have seen here. They frighten me. You know very little about Max's background. You don't even know how he makes his money. He may be a crook or a drug dealer. He won't tell you anything about his background or his business, so he must be hiding something. He may be a very dangerous man, and I don't want you getting any more involved with him."

"You know how involved with him I am already. I am twenty-one years old, and I can take care of myself. My love life is none of your business."

Laura returned home with a very heavy heart and a feeling of foreboding. She was brokenhearted when she found out that she and Lana would not be spending more time together. Lana was going to Mexico with Max. She said she may not be returning to school.

Laura spent spring break volunteering at a local middle school.

Chapter 7

Laura did not see Lana after her Christmas visit until the end of the school year late in May. It was then that Lana told her that she and Max had been married in January and that she was expecting a baby in the fall. The baby had been expected before the wedding.

"We had a beautiful island wedding," Lana said. "A lot of Max's friends attended." It never occurred to her that Laura was hurt that she had not been invited to the wedding.

Laura had always dreamed that she and her sister would have traditional weddings with their father walking them down the aisle and with each other serving as a maid or matron of honor.

I guess I have more to worry about than that, Laura thought as she was listening to Lana's description of the wedding. She did not think Lana had made a good choice when she selected Max Bertolini for her husband.

Laura was spending a few days with Lana at her house because Max was away on a business trip. Laura was thankful for that. A couple of days after Lana had bragged about her beautiful wedding, she suddenly became very quiet and introspective. Laura would attempt to converse with her but Lana would not respond to her attempts. It seemed that she had something on her mind but could not bring herself to share it with Laura. Eventually, she began to talk.

She told Laura that shortly after the wedding the dark side of Max began to emerge. He told her he was not happy about the impending birth of a child. He said he did not want to be a father because he knew he would not be a good parent and did not want the responsibility of a child. He told Lana about the abuse he and his brother had suffered at the hands of their father. He told her that their mother did not protect them but protected herself from what observing what was happening then spoiled them to try to make up for what their father did. He would not tell her any more about his life and refused to answer any questions about his business and where he went when he left on business trips. "I give information on a need-to-know basis," he would tell her. "And you don't need to know." He refused to allow her to accompany him on these trips.

"His mother tried to warn me about Max the one time I met her before the wedding. She said that when Max was angry, he lashed out with his fists. I believed Max loved me and would never do anything to hurt me. I was wrong. He is very jealous and always wants his way. He hit me several times when I tried to go against his wishes. The first time he hit me was when I told him I was pregnant and was several weeks along when we got married. He said he had trusted me to take precautions against pregnancy and that he would never trust me again. After each incident he said he was sorry and seemed to regret his actions. He promised it would never happen again. He tried to make up for his actions by being exceptionally loving and buying expensive gifts for me and the baby."

When Lana admitted these things to Laura, she asked her to promise to take care of her baby if anything happened to her.

"Of course I promise, but you need to leave Max before he really hurts you or the baby," Laura answered.

"He would never allow me to do that. I am afraid he would try to take the baby from me. He would be embarrassed that he couldn't keep his wife and would punish me for it. I am not sure he likes being married, and I certainly know he doesn't want to be a father, but a divorce would have to be his idea. In that case, he would probably be generous with a settlement. Isn't this ironic? I just finished telling you about my fabulous wedding, now I am talking about divorce. I guess I should have learned more about Max before rushing into marriage. The problem was, I was pregnant and wanted financial security."

Laura wanted to say "I told you so" but held her tongue.

"Anyway, will you promise to take care of my baby if anything happens to me? I have no one else I can trust."

Laura could not understand why she felt so uneasy when she said those words.

"Of course, I told you I will, but nothing is going to happen to you."

Chapter 8

Laura was busy getting adjusted to her schedule for the fall semester at school when she received the call from Max. Lana was going into labor.

"I don't care if you come or not," he said. "But it is important to Lana that you be here when the kid is born. The doctor said it would be several hours. What should I tell her?"

"Tell her I will be there in traveling time. I need to get things settled here, and it will take me five hours to drive. I will drive right to the hospital unless I hear something different from you.'

"Yeah, whatever."

Max hung up.

Laura quickly packed a bag and called her friend Marge Spencer and asked her to notify her advisor of what was happening and ask him if he would let her professors know that she would not be attending classes for a few days. She did not want to take the chance of being dropped from the enrollment due to absences. She had no idea how long it would be before she was able to return to school. She certainly had no idea she would never be enrolled as Laura Mitchell in that school again.

When she arrived at the hospital several hours later, she found Lana in the final stages of labor. Max was in the waiting room but did not acknowledge her arrival. Lana had been asking for her, and the nurses dressed her quickly into scrubs and ushered her into the labor room. Barbara Jean Bertolini was born at 6:15 p.m. on September 10, 2002.

Laura would always remember the joy she felt while assisting with the birth of this perfect little girl and the first time she was able to hold the baby in her arms. At that time, both the baby and Lana appeared to be in perfect health. They were discharged from the hospital two days later.

Laura agreed to stay at Lana's house for a few days to assist with the baby so Lana could rest.

Max had made arrangements for Lana to be removed from his room to another part of the house where a nursery was set up. Laura had a room next to Lana's and the nursery. She got up with the baby during the night. Lana seemed lethargic and unwell. She took little interest in the care of Barbara Jean. This worried Laura, and she wondered if she should speak to Max about hiring someone to care for the baby when she returned to school. She decided to wait and see if Lana would do better after she rested. Laura did not want any contact with Max if it could be avoided. Max never came to the nursery to see the baby.

Two days after her return home from the hospital, Lana began to hemorrhage and was rushed to the hospital by ambulance. Laura, carrying Barbara Jean with her, followed the ambulance to the hospital with Max in his car.

The doctors worked for hours to save Lana's life, but the years of drug and alcohol abuse had taken its toll on her body. It simply could not fight of the assault of an infection. Lana passed away September 15, 2002.

When Max was informed of Lana's death, he came to his child, who was sleeping peacefully in Laura's arms, and looked at her with intense hatred.

"This is your fault," he said to the sleeping child. Then he snapped his fingers on the chest of the infant so hard that she woke up howling.

Chapter 9

Stunned by her sister's death, Laura agreed to delay her return to school long enough to help with funeral arrangements and the care of the baby, Barbara Jean, until the services were over. She remembered her promise to her sister and wanted to be sure Max could find a suitable nanny to care for the infant. She would visit as often as she could. She wanted the baby to grow up recognizing her as her aunt who loved her dearly.

The days following Lana's death were a blur of horror. Laura was in deep, deep mourning. In less than two years she had lost her entire family. Somehow, without really being aware of what was happening, she managed to complete the tasks required of her.

The first order of business was to make an appointment to take Barbara Jean to her pediatrician to determine if the formula given to them at the hospital was the correct one for her. Lana had planned to nurse the baby, so the formula they had was a temporary one. The hospital personnel had advised them to visit the pediatrician as soon as the services were over. This proved to be Laura's salvation.

Services were well attended by Max's family and friends. Some of Laura parents' friends attended also, expressing their grief and shock over Lana's death. Max allowed Lana to be buried next to her parents at the New Rochelle Cemetery. After the burial services John Breen spoke to her briefly asking her to contact him as soon as she felt emotionally able.

Following the services a reception was held at Max's house. Mourner's remained late into the afternoon and some into the early evening. Laura was happy to see the last guest leave. She wanted nothing more than to see to Barbara Jean's needs and to tumble into bed.

As she was preparing to retire, Mrs. Carter knocked on her door and told her Max wanted to see her in his study. The minute she walked into the room, she realized Max was drunk. She also suspected the use of other substances as well. Little wonder, she thought.

He spoke to her before she even had a chance to sit down.

"I don't know how to break this to you." Max smirked. "So I will come right out with it. I am putting Barbara Jean up for adoption!"

Laura fought down her rising panic, knowing she needed to sound calm and sensible.

"I know how upset you are right now," she said. "But there are other options. I will help with the care of the baby, and you have your mother, brother, and his girlfriend, Tina. I know Mrs. Carter has been hired only as a housekeeper, but I am sure she would also help with the care of the baby until you can find a suitable nanny."

"You attend college, my brother and Tina are always drunk or high on pot. My mother wouldn't want to be tied down with a grandchild. She hardly gave Barbara Jean a glance when she was here for the services. She doesn't want people to know she is a grandmother. Right now, she is on her way to the Cayman Islands with her new, rich boyfriend. She couldn't even bother to come to the house for the reception after the services. She doesn't want anything to do with me or my brother. She doesn't want to be reminded of the past. Mrs. Carter has her hand full running the house."

Laura recognized that all this was true.

"What about your plans to hire a nanny? You can certainly afford to hire someone who would be responsible and take excellent care of Barbara Jean. It would be easy to find someone by going through a respectable agency."

"Look," Max said, "I didn't call you down here to discuss the issue. Barbara Jean will be out of here by Friday. Joe Boccia is picking her up and taking her to a private adoption agency. She will be with someone who really wants a kid."

"Joe Boccia," Laura cried, "I think he is a crook. You can't be sure the agency he brings the baby to is reliable enough to find suitable parents for her."

"Who cares," Max sneered. "The agency is giving me ten grand for her. I told you she will be with someone who wants a kid of their own."

"You are selling your own child. You can't do that. She is Lana's child too."

"Lana is dead. I'm not selling the kid. I am just getting reimbursed for my expenses. By the way, I said the kid would be out of here by Friday. I want you out of here tomorrow. Now get out of here and leave me alone."

Laura went to her room but did not sleep. She now knew she needed to formulate a plan to save Barbara Jean. She had promised her sister she would take care of the child if it became necessary, and somehow she was going to keep that promise.

The next morning Laura tried to appear nonchalant when she went down stairs to face Mrs. Carter.

"Good morning, Laura. You look exhausted. Didn't you sleep well last night? Would you like breakfast?"

"Just coffee, thank you. No, I didn't sleep well last night," Laura admitted truthfully. "Max wants me to leave today, but there are several things I have to do first."

"You should eat something," Mrs. Carter advised. "You need to regain your strength."

Laura knew she was right. She did not know when she would eat again, but now was no time to be thinking of food. Her stomach was tied up in knots. She doubted she could get anything down, much less keep it down.

"Before I leave today, I have to take Barbara Jean to her pediatrician," she said casually. "He needs to assess her formula to be sure it is right for her."

"Good," said Mrs. Carter. "Max has left for the day, and I don't have much time to do it. I hope he doesn't expect me to care for the child with all the other duties I have. I hope he gets a nanny soon. I wish you could stay but I know you have to return to school."

Laura was pleased when she heard Max had left for the day. It would make it easier for her to carry out her plans.

"By the way," she said casually, "is there a one-hour dry cleaner near here? I need to get some things cleaned before I head back to school later."

"There should be one listed in the phone book," Mrs. Carter replied.

Laura did not need a dry cleaner, but she did need an excuse for carrying out garment bags to her car. When she left with the baby, she would pack as many of their things in the bags that she could without arousing suspicion. She would also pack as much as possible in a diaper bag. Everything else would have to be left at the house. She would leave the navy blue shift she had worn to Lana's funeral. She doubted she would ever be able to put it on again.

Laura had taken an ATM card from Lana's purse. She left the savings book. She knew she would not be able to withdraw money from inside the bank. They probably would require ID. *Is it really stealing*, she wondered, *if your sister is gone and the money is to be used to save her child from an unknown fate?*

She found Lana's pin number taped in the pocket of the purse. Lana could not remember such things since she started using drugs. Laura also took Barbara Jean's birth certificate that had been left in the bureau in the nursery.

After placing these items in her purse, Laura took the garment bags and diaper bag out to the car and carefully hooked the baby seat in the back of her car. She hooked the baby in the carrier that connected to the car seat and said a casual "See you in a while" to Mrs. Carter. She hoped the housekeeper would not notice all the bulky blankets she had placed around the baby to get them out of the house. It was a warn day for September. She would stop and remove the blankets once she was far enough from the house to feel safe doing so.

Her first stop was at a large pharmacy where she could pick up baby supplies without getting too much attention. She hoped the number she found in Lana's purse was indeed the correct pin number for that debit card. It was the number of the month and day of their mother's birth, so she suspected it was the correct one. Lana left little to chance when it came to memory. Laura decided if she had trouble with the pin number, she would make a lame excuse and use cash.

The transaction at the pharmacy went smoothly, so she knew she could use Lana's card at the drive up ATM at the bank. She would withdraw $500, the limit allowed by the bank, then destroy the card. It would be of no further use to her.

After completing these transactions, she left town and drove south in the interstate to the airport's long-term parking lot. There, she left Lana's car and boarded the shuttle to the airport. She hoped the garment bags and diaper bag she was carrying were enough to make her look like a legitimate traveler. When the shuttle bus driver asked her which airline, she quickly looked at the signs ahead and said, "Continental."

"Do you have other luggage?" the porter asked as she left the shuttle bus.

"No," she replied. "My husband is taking a later flight and has the rest of the luggage. I have all I can handle here." She smiled, hoping he would not notice the lack of a wedding ring.

She walked to the ladies' room hoping not to receive too much attention and changed the baby's diaper. "From now on, you will be known as Benjii," she told the sleeping infant. When she exited the ladies' room, she walked directly to the taxi stand. She picked a driver who appeared to be kind and got into the cab.

When he asked her her destination, she said, "Can you take me to a shelter for battered women?"

"That I can," he said sympathetically.

The people in the shelter in New Rochelle listened carefully as she explained that she needed to leave the area. They had found a shelter for her that was about seventy-five miles south of New Rochelle and provided transportation for her and Benjii to their new home.

Laura and Benjii would live in this shelter for over five years. She often wondered if Max was trying to locate them. Perhaps not; maybe he was content to be rid of them and get on with his life.

As a rule, Mrs. Carter was not afraid of Max. However, today she could sense his anger and felt herself trembling as she answered inquiries from him and Joe Boccia about where Laura and Benjii could be.

"Why didn't you notify me when Laura did not return with Barbara Jean?"

"I have been busy making sure everything is in order after yesterday's events." She did not want to use the word *funeral*. "I didn't realize how late it was getting."

"Okay," said Max, "you may return to your duties, Mrs. Carter."

"What are you going to do?" asked Joe Boccia. "You don't want the kid, why don't you just leave well enough alone?"

"Because no woman is going to make a fool of me," said Max. "I will have to make an example of her."

"What about the kid?"

"I'll put her up for adoption as planned. Her aunt will be in no condition to care for her when I find her."

"It may take a while to locate them."

"I am a very patient man."

Chapter 10

Sue Patnode sighed as she read through Sam Jacob's notes on the Max Bertolini Case. *I guess I'm out of touch*, she thought. She had just returned to her job as a detective in the New Rochelle Police Department after taking five years off to raise her children. They were now enrolled in school, so she was able to come back to the job she loved.

She was now ready to keep the promise she had made to Sam Jacobs several years earlier. She and Sam Jacobs were both sure that Max Bertolini had something to do with the disappearance of his baby daughter and sister-in-law, but she could not come up with any leads or reasons for Max to hurt his family members. Sam had not been able to find a reason either.

There has to be clues in these notes, she thought. *But I sure can't come up with anything.*

"You look perplexed, Sue."

A fellow detective, Bill McDermott, walked into the room. Bill was handsome in a childish way. His skin was smooth and he had an impish twinkle in his eyes even when he was serious. He and his wife had became friends with Sue and her husband when he and Sue became partners. They had a great social and professional relationship.

"I'm looking over the Max Bertolini file. I promised Sam Jacob I would try to get Max on drug charges and try to find out if he had anything to do with the disappearance of his baby daughter and sister-in-law, Laura Mitchell. They disappeared right after his wife Lana passed away. That seems pretty suspicious to me."

"Then let's visit with Mr. Bertolini to see what he has to say for himself," Bill suggested.

"No, I don't think so. I don't want Max to know right now I am investigating him. He will know something is up if I suddenly call after six years and begin to ask questions about his family. We did not investigate the disappearance of his family at the time."

"Why not?"

"I would like to say it was because no complaint was ever filed, but in actuality we dropped the ball. Two people disappeared and we should have found out what happened to them. I think I will see if I can interview the housekeeper when Max is not at home. She will probably inform him that I have spoken to her, but at least I may be able to catch her off guard and can speak with her when Max is not around. If she has any inclination to tell me anything, it will be easier that way."

Sue had read in the local newspaper that Max would be attending a conference in Las Vegas for a few days. To be sure he would not be home, she called the house under the pretense of asking Max to donate to a charity event. Mrs. Carter confirmed the Max would be out of town or several days and would be unavailable until the weekend.

Sue walked up to the door of a beautiful Italian-style mansion, knowing she would find Mrs. Carter alone. She rang the bell several times before Mrs. Carter opened the door.

"May I help you?" she asked.

"I'm Detective Sue Patnode from the New Rochelle Police Department," Sue stated while showing Mrs. Carter her badge.

"I told you on the phone that Mr. Bertolini is out of town until this weekend."

"I know. I came to talk with you, Mrs. Carter."

"Why would you want to talk with me? I am just a housekeeper. I know nothing about Mr. Bertolini's business or personal life."

"I want to talk with you about the disappearance of his daughter and sister-in-law."

"I don't know if they disappeared. We just haven't heard from them for a while."

Mrs. Carter immediate recognized her mistake.

"That 'while' is over five years. Isn't Mr. Bertolini concerned about what has happened to his daughter? It seems incomprehensible that he is not or has not been frantic about the welfare of his daughter."

"As I said before, I don't know anything. I am just a housekeeper, and I don't ask questions. You will have to wait and talk with Mr. B."

"Look," Sue bluffed, "we can do this informally here at the house, or we can have this conversation at the police station. The choice is yours."

Mrs. Carter was visibly upset.

"Come in and ask your questions. I won't promise to answer."

That's a step in the right direction, Sue thought.

Mrs. Carter refused to answer about Max's relationship with either Lana or Laura.

She was cautious not to answer questions about his business or daily routine or any questions about how he reacted when Barbara Jean and Laura left without explanation. She was shocked when Sue suggested Max had been responsible for their disappearance.

"He was away with a business associate the day Laura left with Barbara Jean. He didn't think it would look right for him to go to his office in town the day after his wife's funeral."

"'Do you think he was grieving?" Sue asked.

"Mr. Bertolini doesn't grieve," Mrs. Carter answered.

When Sue asked Mrs. Carter about the last time she or Max saw Laura, she recounted the conversation they had had about a dry cleaner and the pediatrician.

"Laura was obviously upset that day. But after all, she had just lost her sister. Also, Max had ordered her out of the house, and she was concerned about who would care for Barbara Jean. I think Max was going to put Barbara Jean up for adoption, but I have no real knowledge of that. Just an impression from things I had heard said. He did vow to search for them, but I think that was just a smoke screen. I don't think he ever did anything to find them."

"Would she have been upset enough to kidnap the child?" Sue asked.

"It wouldn't be kidnapping. She is family and just wants to care for the child."

"When someone takes a child from the parents and doesn't return, it is kidnapping, and that is punishable by many years in jail."

Chapter 11

Bill had promised Sue he would do some investigation of his own while she was interviewing Mrs. Carter. He filled her in on what he found out as soon as they both returned to the office.

"I went to the airport first but did not learn much more that we know already. I spoke to the shuttle bus drivers who were working at that time. Of course, memory would be a problem, so I knew it would be a long shot. One of the shuttle drivers thought he remembered picking up a woman with an infant from the long-term parking lot at about the time Laura Mitchell and the baby disappeared, but he could not be 100 percent sure of the date. He said he thought the infant was not more than a few days old, and he believed he had taken them to the drop off terminal for Continental Airlines. He remembered because she did not seem to have any luggage except a diaper bag, garment bags, and her purse. He thought it was strange that she packed garment bags instead of suitcases, which would have been much easier to handle. He heard him tell a porter that her husband was meeting her with the other luggage, but she was not wearing a wedding ring.

"I visited the taxi office that services the airport. The dispatcher for the office called in the drivers who he thought might have been working at that time. He encouraged them to tell me anything that they might remember that would help the investigation. No one seemed to recall anything helpful. I had a feeling one of the drivers might be holding something back, but I could not be sure. After the drivers left the dispatcher did tell me something that is a little puzzling, and might be helpful. He said he had a private investigator in recently asking the same questions I was asking. He said he did not trust the guy, so did not call in the drivers. He simply said the company did not have any information that would be useful to him.

"Next I called the bank where Lana Mitchell had her checking and saving accounts. They were reluctant to speak to me, but the manager did give me a small amount of information, most of it we already know. On the day Ms. Mitchell and the infant disappeared there was a withdrawal at the ATM and at a CVS pharmacy. He would not tell me the amounts of the transactions but did say a significant balance remained and was untouched. There was no withdrawal from the savings account. Max eventually closed both accounts. The withdrawals I mentioned may have just been a case of theft."

"Maybe not. Laura Mitchell may have borrowed money from the account to help her get the baby from Max."

She then relayed the fact that Mrs. Carter believed that infant was going to be put up for adoption.

"If that is true, Laura Mitchell's actions were noble. I wonder what the course of action should be if we find her."

"We'll find her."

"Maybe Max is not guilty of causing the disappearance of Laura and Barbara Jean. Maybe Laura wanted to disappear and take the infant with her. That would put a whole new twist on the Max Bertolini case. I guess we need to concentrate on the drug and money laundering case instead of the case of the disappearance of Laura and Barbara Jean."

"Our move to put Alex Hamilton under cover was the right one," Sue remarked. I had questioned the move when the captain suggested it right after I asked to review Max Bertolini's files. Alex's personal interest in this case makes him an ideal candidate for the job but may also influence his judgment when he has decisions to make."

Chapter 12

Reggie Palmer was a simple man. He had worked in a glassmaking factory on northern New York for nearly forty years. When he reached retirement age, he and his wife agreed that he should take his small pension and work just part time. He loved to drive, and he loved meeting people, so working as a cab driver was perfect for him.

The route he drove included runs to the airport in Albany. He often met fares that he would remember for a long time. One of those fares was a woman he picked up at the airport about six years ago. He knew right off that she was running from something or someone. She looked fearful. Her eyes kept darting around as if as if she was searching for something. He was not surprised when she asked him to drive her to a shelter for battered women. He had figured that she was in flight because she left the airport with no baggage except a garment bag and a diaper bag. The only thing that bothered him was that there were no bruises or sign of battering, and she wore no wedding band. He had no doubt that the child was hers. He didn't think anyone could look at a child with such love and tenderness if the child did not belong to them. Must be it is some boyfriend she is running from instead of a husband, he thought. It's the way of the world these days.

Reggie drove Laura and the baby to a shelter run by the local family service center. When they arrived, he helped her carry the garment and diaper bags inside. He wondered how such a tiny thing had managed to juggle everything alone. He introduced her to a social worker who was a friend of his wife.

"You had better take good care of this little girl, Pricilla, or I will have Abby get after you."

Pricilla Marsh and Reggie's wife, Abby, had been friends since elementary school. Pricilla smiled. She trusted Reggie, and knew that he would never discuss this event to anyone, not even his wife.

Reggie remembered that when he turned to leave the shelter, the young woman shook his hand and thanked him warmly. He learned later that she called his taxi company, praising him for his help and professionalism. That call resulted in a fifteen-cent-per-hour pay raise as well as job security.

Six years later, Reggie recalled all these things when the sleazy guy claiming to be a private investigator came into the taxi office asking if anyone had picked up a college age kid with an infant and drove them to the airport during the month of April about six years ago.

I didn't take anyone to the airport, he thought. *I wouldn't tell him if I did.*

He was a little concerned when Bill McDermott from the New Rochelle Police Department came in a few days later asking the same question. Why so much interest in that little girl now? he wondered. He listened quietly as Bill explained that the department was investigating an old missing person case. He recalled the concern—no, not concern—fear in that young woman's eyes. He knew there was no way that woman would harm that infant she had with her.

Infant, he thought, *the child must be near school age now.*

It was obvious to him that the young woman was deeply concerned about the safety of both of them. He decided to keep his mouth shut until he had more information.

Chapter 13

Alex Hamilton returned to the cheap rent-a-room motel he was living in after a day working on the docks. The desk clerks at these motels paid little attention to the guests as they came and went as long as they paid their bill in a timely fashion. For this reason he felt reasonably safe, but he still moved often to prevent recognition. There were several such motels in the area, so he had plenty of choices. He was dressed like other dock workers, some who rented a room for just an hour to carry on certain activities.

This night, he tossed and turned on the lumpy mattress, trying not to wonder if the sheets had been changed after the last occupant of the room vacated it.

He needed to find a way to investigate Max's unit. By three in the morning he had devised a plan. He searched through his meager belongings and found what he needed. After that, he was able to sleep for about two hours.

When Alex awoke, he dressed in khakis, an open-necked, blue-striped shirt, blue blazer, and loafers. He left by a side door to avoid the desk clerk and went to rent a car. He needed the car to look official. He paid with a credit card issued to a Tony Jordan. The charge would go directly to the NRPD.

Alex figured someone would be working at the unit when he arrived. There were usually deliveries at that time. As soon as the delivery truck left, Alex banged on the door. He was right in assuming that the worker would be busy processing the merchandise that had just arrived.

"Who is it?"

"Inspector."

"Go away, I'm busy."

"Can't. I have a job to do, but I can get a cop to assist me if that is what you want."

The door was opened by a tall, thin man with a long goatee flowing from his chin.

"I don't ever remember an inspector coming here."

Alex showed him the ID provided to him by the NRPD.

"You probably haven't. The federal government talks a good game about protecting consumers, but the truth is there are not enough of us guys to check businesses as often as they should be checked. I was told to cover this area. I have a lot of other places to visit today, and I want to get home early enough to attend my kid's school play, so let's get going. I don't have a lot of time to take crap from you."

"Okay, let's get this shit over. I don't have any more time than you do."

Alex took out an official-looking pad and started looking around. He noticed that some of the cartons containing coffee ended in a two instead of a three. It seemed that all cartons from the same delivery should end in the same number. He checked the fruits and nuts for verification and noted they all had the same numbers. He noted the differences on his pad but did not comment to the worker.

When Alex was finished, he said thank you and asked the worker's name.

"Leonard Butler. People call me Lenny."

"Who is the owner of this business?"

"Max Bertolini."

"You work for him?"

"Appears that way, don't it?"

"Any other employees?"

"Probably, but I don't see them. My job is to accept shipments and be sure they are ready to be shipped to the proper retailer.

"Do you have the names of the retailers?"

"I'll give you a list. Most are small convenience stores and specialty shops." Lenny knew that certain names would be left off the list.

How accommodating, Alex thought.

After having inspected the items for about an hour, Alex had Lenny sign the "inspection" form and left. He was disappointed that he had not learned more. Except for the change in the last lot number, he had not found much useful information. He did notice that cartons of coffee going to one merchant had different last numbers.

I wonder how significant that is, he thought.

It must be important since all the other information on each carton was the same.

Time for the drunk to visit the docks again, he said to himself. *If I can figure out what is going on, the NRPD will have lots of cartons of coffee sitting around. I hope the stuff is good.*

Chapter 14

When Max returned home from his export/import conference in Las Vegas, Ruth Carter told him about the visit from Sue Patnode.

"I told her I don't know anything about your personal or business affairs, that I serve as your housekeeper, not your secretary. I did tell her about Laura Mitchell's last day here. I told her about our conversation about a dry cleaner and about her plans to take Barbara Jean to a pediatrician to get the correct formula for her feeding. I hope I didn't say too much."

"All you did, Mrs. Carter, was to tell the truth. That is exactly what I would expect of you. Thank you for filling me in. You may return to your duties now."

Max closed the door after Ruth left and dialed Joe Boccia.

"Yea?"

"I think we have a problem. Someone from NRPD was here last week while I was away and questioned Ruth Carter about my business and about Laura Mitchell and the kid."

"Who was it?"

"A detective named Sue Patnode."

"Then I don't think there will be a problem. She's practically a rookie. She worked with Sam Jacob for a while before he retired. During that time she got married then left to have a couple of kids. She just came back. The department is a little short of personnel right now due to budget cuts, so she has her hands full. With kids and a busy job, she won't have time to investigate us. She will have her hands full with priority cases. If it was Sam Jacobs, I would be worried, but I am not worried about this gal."

"Well, I'll get a chance to size her up this weekend. I made a big contribution to the NRPD, so I got an invite to the Policeman's Ball Saturday night. You never know when you might need a friend in the police department."

"What did she want anyway?"

"She asked a lot of questions about my business, personal life, and about Barbara Jean and my ex sister-in law, Laura Mitchell."

"What did Carter tell her?"

"That she was just a housekeeper and knew nothing about my business or personal life. She did tell her about Laura's last day here."

"Maybe it's time to start a little investigation ourselves. We could switch the cop's interest from your business to the tragic loss of your child. That ought to interest a new mom. Patnode will get involved with the search for the child and will forget about your business."

"We could take care of Laura Mitchell at the same time. I don't know what Lana might have told her. She knew very little about my business, but I think she had her suspicions. She may have expressed concerns to her sister. Maybe we can throw a little kidnapping charge her way. That is worth a lot of jail time. Do you know anyone who could start an investigation for us?"

"I do. I'll get back to you."

"By the way, did the shipment come in?"

"Yeah, you are a richer man today than you were yesterday."

Max hung up.

And maybe so am I, Joe thought. *I think my time has come.*

Chapter 15

The Saturday after Max's conversation with Joe regarding Sue Patnode, the New Rochelle Police Department held its annual charity ball, giving Max the chance he wanted to check her out.

Max cut a very handsome figure when he entered the New Rochelle Country Club for this event. He had received an invitation because of the ample contribution he had made to the department's fund-raiser. Some in the department questioned if the donation should be accepted because of Max's dubious reputation. People in the department wondered if the money being donated came from illegal means. They solved the problem by endorsing the check over to the children's hospital to help families who could not afford the medical treatment their children required.

Max did not have a date. Since the fiasco of his marriage to Lana, he steered clear of serious relationships. He did not have trouble finding dance partners or companionship. Many women were more than ready to accommodate him. He could always find someone to go home with him and share his bed if he so desired.

He asked an acquaintance to point out Sue Patnode to him. As he approached Sue and her husband, he couldn't help but notice how attractive she was. She and her handsome husband made a striking pair.

He introduced himself and shook hands with Rick Patnode then turned to Sue.

"I understand you made a visit to my home last week," he said.

"I did. I wanted to talk with Mrs. Carter."

"About what?"

"Confidential police business."

"Well, if you have any more confidential police business to discuss with my employees, it needs to be done in my presence or the presence of my lawyer."

"Are you paranoid, Max? I did not say that the business I discussed with Mrs. Carter had anything to do with you."

"Mrs. Carter did. Remember, no lawyer, no warrant, no conversation."

"Why, Max, do you have something to hide?"

Sue and her husband started to walk away.

"By the way, Detective Patnode, I thought I should tell you that those little twins of yours are real cute."

Sue felt a chill and moved closer to her husband as he turned to Max and said, "If I ever see you near one of my kids, you will be sorry."

"Don't forget," Sue interjected, "I have the entire police department behind me. That includes the state police. You had better heed my husband's warning."

Maybe that detective is more dangerous than Joe thinks, Max thought. *She'll bear watching. I better not antagonize her any more than I have already. I need to try to get back on her good side.*

Maybe I will ask her to investigate the disappearance of my daughter and sister-in-law. I will wait and see what Joe is able to come up with. I won't discuss any plans I make with him. I will keep them to myself.

Chapter 16

Big Jake Turner's office is in a rundown building in a poor section of New Rochelle.

I can barely pay the rent on this dump, he thought. *I gotta get a high-class client who can afford to pay big fees and cover a lot of expenses. I'm sick of this dump, but how can I get that kind of client? Anyone with class is going hire a PI with a classy office in the high-rent district in town. I'll never be able to dig myself out of this hole.*

The phone rang, a rare event during the past few weeks.

"Turner Investigation."

"Jake, it's Joe Boccia."

"What can I do for you, Joe?"

"I got a job for ya."

"A paying job?"

"Don't be a wiseass. I'm not your client. Max Bertolini is."

Big Jake tried to hide his excitement. He was thinking he could probably charge double his regular rate and really pad his expenses. Bertolini had the kind of money he had been dreaming about just a few moments ago.

"What's the assignment?"

"To find his kid and his wife's sister, Laura Mitchell."

"Why now? Haven't they been gone for several years?"

"Don't ask questions. Max's reasons are his own. Do you want the job?"

"I'm pretty busy, but I guess I can squeeze the job in."

"Don't screw with me, Jake. I know how busy you are."

"Fee is two hundred a day plus expenses."

"Okay, just don't pad the expenses. Max doesn't take kindly to being cheated."

"Hey, would I do that?"

"You would."

"Okay, what can you tell me about this Mitchell woman and the kid? Are they still alive?"

"I don't know, but both Max and I think so. The woman might not be if Max finds her. He thinks the sister-in-law took the kid and hid her to prevent him from putting her up for adoption. He lost ten grand on that deal and he is not happy. He's been seething for six years."

"Hey, I don't want no part of murder. I ain't going to the pen."

"I don't think anything will really happen to her. If she's smart, she will give up the kid and disappear."

"Why didn't he call the cops six years ago?"

"Hey, I said don't ask questions. Do you want the job or not?"

"When do I start?' How do I report to him?"

"You don't. You report to me. And get to me as soon as you find any information about the woman. I will see to it that you are paid in a timely fashion."

"I'll see what I can find out."

"Here is some information that might help you get started. Laura Mitchell was attending a small teaching university somewhere in New England. That may be a good place to start."

"Okay, I'll get right on it."

Joe smiled as he hung up the phone.

I got it made, he thought. *Big Jake's doing the footwork, and Max will pay for it. Then I'll move in.*

After talking with Joe, Big Jake drove into town and went to a cafe that caters to college students. Inside the cafe was a room with computers that had access to the Internet. Several people were at the cubicles with computers and were hard at work.

Jake walked to the back of the cafe and knocked lightly on a door.

"Who is it?"

"It's Jake Turner."

"Come in, Jake."

Jim Fallon sat behind a large wooden desk that had several computers, copiers, fax machines, and printers. He looked like a typical computer geek. He was tall with thinning brown hair. He wore glasses with thick lenses.

"I have a job for you, Jim."

"Jobs cost money, Jake. Sometimes you have trouble paying."

"No problem this time. I'm working for Joe Boccia. Max Bertolini is picking up the tab."

Jim tried to hide his excitement.

If Jake is looking for the information I hope he is looking for, it will be just the break I need. I'll get paid double, no one will be the wiser.

"Well, what do you need?" he said nonchalantly.

"I need to find Max's sister-in-law. She disappeared six years ago with Max's kid."

"Why is he looking for her now?"

"Joe wouldn't tell me why, but I bet it has something to do with his business."

"Why would he be concerned about that? What kind of business is he in? I don't want to cause myself trouble."

"I don't know. Joe was pretty tight-lipped when I asked the same questions."

"Maybe he cheats on his taxes."

Or maybe he is dealing drugs, Jim thought.

"Okay, where do I start? What do you know about this woman?"

"She was attending a small teachers' college somewhere in New England before her sister died. Joe thinks she may have gone back to school."

"You just made my job easy. I can hack into college records easy enough. Just give me a few days. I'll get back to you."

"Hey, have a beer and sandwich on the house before you leave. I can afford it. I'll send Joe a whopper of a bill."

"You send it to me. I'll get it to Joe."

As soon as Jake left, Jim picked up the phone.

"I just got a visit from a private eye named Big Jake. He gave me some information that will help me find what you are looking for. I'll get back to you."

Chapter 17

A few days later, Jim called Jake with the information he had gathered about Laura Mitchell. It was the second time he had called and relayed this information, but Joe had no way of knowing that.

"Laura Mitchell was enrolled in a small college in Southwestern New Hampshire before her sister died, but she never returned to that school under that name. It appears that her records were removed from the school's data base. However, several months later, someone named Laura McKenzie began taking classes at that same school. Even though there does not seem to be any record of this Laura McKenzie attending the college earlier, two years of courses and grades were transferred into her records. Of course, they could have been transferred in from another college, but there is no record of that happening. Laura McKenzie took classes part time for about a year then matriculated full time to complete course work then completed an internship. She graduated with honors with a Bachelor of Education. Her major was special education."

"She received her teaching certificate from the New Hampshire Department of Education. I checked special education teaching vacancies in New Hampshire and checked to see if they had been filled. In August, Laura McKenzie signed a contract to teach special education students at the middle school in Mapleton, New Hampshire."

"Great work! I'll contact Joe and see that you get paid immediately."

After hearing from Jake, Joe immediately contacted Max.

"I think we have found Laura Mitchell," he told Max. "She is teaching at a middle school in Southwestern New Hampshire. The woman we found looks a little different. The picture on her New Hampshire license shows her hair lighter and cut very short, and she wears glasses. She lists her weight as 110 and her height as 5' 3", which is taller than Laura Mitchell. Records show that she has a daughter enrolled in kindergarten in a school across from the one where she will be teaching. That would be about the right age for your kid."

"How did you get all that information?"

"I hired a private eye named Big Jake Turner. He in turn had records researched by a guy who can hack into any college or other school records."

Joe relayed all the information Jake received from Jim Fallon to Max. Neither Joe nor Max knew who the researcher was.

"Okay, have Big Jake case the area to see if he can find this woman and kid. See if he can harass her, scare her a little in case we want to take further steps to see if she is Laura Mitchell. We won't do anything more right now. We don't want any attention paid to us until we complete this month's business. We need to get the deal completed and our shipment in. I don't want any cops around."

Ruth Carter carefully hung up the phone. She was shocked and sickened over what she just heard. She couldn't believe Max would do anything to hurt Laura and Barbara Jean, if indeed the people Joe Boccia was talking about was them.

That's what I get for eavesdropping, she thought. *But I am worried about what Max may be into. I don't like the way Joe Boccia comes around all the time. He walks right into the house even when Max is gone, scaring me to death. If the situation here becomes dangerous, I will leave my position. I'm glad I told Max that I was developing some medical issues even though I am not. In that way he won't be suspicious if I suddenly resign.*

Chapter 18

Ruth Carter carefully hung up the extension in the kitchen. It wouldn't do to have Max find out that she listened to his conversations, but it was for her own protection.

She was confused about what she heard regarding Laura Mitchell. Could it be that she really had been located?

She decided to call her sister Pat. Pat has always been her sounding board.

Besides, if she has to leave her job with Max, she will need to stay with her sister and her family until she finds another job and a place to stay. And her sister lives in Mapleton, New Hampshire. It sounds a little like the town Joe Boccia describing to Max. Ruth dialed the phone.

"Hi, Pat, how are things going?"

"Oh about the same. Tom is still struggling in school. There is a new teacher at his school that I may try to contact. She just started a few weeks ago when the new year started, but I hear she is a good teacher. I may try to get in touch with her and see if she can help Tom. I will wait a while though. She is a single mom and probably needs time to get into a routine."

"How many kids does this teacher have?"

"Just one. She is very young, probably about twenty-five years old. Her little girl is in kindergarten."

"Boy, I hope I don't know who she is. I hope this is just a coincidence. What does she look like?"

"How could you know her? She just moved into the area, I believe."

"Just tell me what she looks like."

"She is petite and very pretty. She has very short strawberry blond hair. She wears large colored glasses, so I don't know what color her eyes are."

"What is her name?"

"Laura McKenzie."

"Pat, she is the right age and size of someone I may know. That person may have a child of kindergarten age. If I am right, she is not someone to be trusted. Be very careful around her."

"What are you talking about? You must be crazy."

"She may be Max Bertolini's sister-in-law. If she is, she is a kidnapper. An associate of Max's found Laura Mitchell. He said she is a special education teacher in a small New England town. The person you are talking about has got to be her. Everything is too much of a coincidence for it not to be her."

"Ruth, you are absolutely wrong. Don't go causing trouble. I hear this woman is a wonderful person. She certainly is not a kidnapper. I have to go get dinner for my kids. Tom will be home soon from his paper route, and Jim will be home from practice. Talk to you later."

Pat hung up.

Ruth is crazy, she thought. *She is putting two and two together and getting five. But I guess I won't contact that teacher right now.*

Chapter 19

Max decided to call the NRPD as soon as he hung up from talking to Joe. He hadn't committed to the phone call when talking to him. Sometimes it is best to keep information to oneself, he thought. He dialed the phone.

The call was answered by Sergeant Russ Parker.

"Police Department."

Russ tended to be a little terse. He hated this desk job, but he knew he was lucky to have a job at all after his injury. Sam Jacob knew that Russ would never be able to work in the field again, but he had made sure before he retired that Russ would never be out of work. Sue felt fortunate to have someone of Russ's caliber on the desk.

"I need to report a missing person, two people actually."

"You should come in and file a missing persons report. How long have they been missing?"

"About five years."

"Excuse me?"

"Look, my sister-in-law and infant daughter disappeared a little over five years ago. I want to find out what happened to them. I don't suspect foul play. I just got some new information."

Russ felt like saying, "What's your rush?" but he didn't want to antagonize the caller. He believed something important was going on.

He did say, "You must have been really worried about them if you waited five years to call. I'll talk with Lieutenant Patnode and have her call you when she comes in. What is your name?"

"Max Bertolini."

Later that morning, Sue returned Max's call.

"What can I do for you, Mr. Bertolini?"

Her voice was cold. She remembered her encounter with him at the policemen's charity ball. In addition, she was suspicious of the call. He probably knew by now of her and Bill's activities in relation to his business. She was sure he did not know about Alex's undercover work.

"I want you to investigate the disappearance of my kid and sister-in-law."

"Why now, Max? It has been over five years. It would be a cold case."

"I hired a PI. New information came up."

"It seems a little late for you to be concerned about you missing daughter. What brought this on?"

"Look, you're a cop. You're supposed to handle this kind of case without wise comments. Are you going to investigate the case?"

"I'll review my files and get back to you."

"What files? You never looked into this before."

"The files we have on you, Max."

Sue didn't want to discuss this matter with Max any more until she had time to think.

Chapter 20

Big Jake parked the semi outside the convenience store and soda shop that he knew was a hangout for middle school kids.

He hoped he didn't look too conspicuous or out of place at a hangout for a bunch of kids.

Maybe if they looked at his 6' 2", 250-pound bulk they would think he was just a hungry truck driver stopping at the first place he came to for lunch. He ordered a hamburger, fries, and a large Coke to be sure he looked the part. He knew he would have to eat and drink slowly so no one would wonder why he was hanging around. Only one man looked at him in a questioning manner. He had bought a newspaper to help hide his face. Reading it would also give him more time to hang around and observe those around him.

He noticed two couples sitting in one booth. The guys were obviously from affluent families. They wore expensive Red Sox jackets and Nikes. The girls with them were cheerleader types who also looked like they were from affluent families. He knew they were not what he was looking for.

In the second booth were two boys who were shabbily dressed. Jake sat at the booth across from them, being careful to stay at the end of the seat so he was closest to the two boys. He put the newspaper close to his face and tried to hear their conversation.

"I dread starting school tomorrow," one of the boys said. "It's going to be just like last year. Look at Beth and Amy drooling over

Scott and Tony. I really like Beth, but she won't even look at me. Why should she when she can have Tony McLean. He's captain of the football and baseball teams and his older brother drives him around in an old Cadillac convertible."

"Yea," the other boy said. "It is tough to compete with guys who can afford designer clothes and whose families have classy cars."

"I'm sick of being poor," the first boy said. "My mom's great. She works very hard, but she barely makes enough money to pay the rent and put food on the table. The old clunker she drives costs a mint for repairs, but she can't afford to buy another one. I have to give her whatever I make after school and weekends to help pay the bills. It doesn't leave any money for me to buy decent clothes, say nothing about the stuff the guys sitting over there can afford. I wish I could think of a way to make some fast money."

"Be careful what you do, Dodie. You don't want to do anything that will make you end up in juvie."

"I don't intend to do anything illegal, Tom, you know that. I give my mom a hard enough time with my attitude and performance at school. She doesn't need any more grief."

"Why don't you do better in school?"

"'Cause I got an image to keep."

I think I found my pigeon, Jake thought. *I better get out in my truck. I hope the kid goes home from here so I can get his address and phone number.*

Luckily for Jake, Dodie Mcintire obliged.

Wearily, Jane Mcintire picked up the phone just shortly after Dodie arrived home.

"I hope that is not the light or phone company," she said half to herself, half to Dodie. "I can't pay them until I get paid next week."

"Hello, yes, he is here. It's for you," she said with relief. "I am going downstairs to start the laundry while you take the call, then I will start dinner."

Dodie picked up the phone.

"Hello."

"Hello, Dodie, I am calling to offer you a job. It will pay quite well."

"Uh, who is this? How do you know my nickname?"

"I know a lot about you, but that is not important. How would you like to earn fifty or one hundred dollars a week by working just a few minutes a day?"

"How? Who is this?"

"My name is not important, but I am a private investigator, and I need help gathering information. Do you go to Mapleton Middle School, and will you be at school tomorrow?"

"Yes."

"There is a new teacher there named Laura McKenzie. She has some information I need, and she refuses to share it with me."

Jake had decided to use this technique with Dodie. It was as near to the truth he could get. He thought he sounded credible.

"I want to do some things that will make her nervous, and I need your help. All you have to do tomorrow is to get into her classroom before school starts. Can you do that?"

"Sure, I guess so."

Dodie knew that on the first day of school the teachers met in the cafeteria to finalize procedures so the first day of classes would go smoothly. He doubted anyone would notice him coming into the building. He knew where her room was; he had been assigned to her homeroom. It was no way near the cafeteria. He was already planning on giving her a hard time that first day.

"When you do, you need to write something on the board. Get a paper and pencil and write this down. The words have to be exact."

When he had written down what was said, he said, "This makes no sense."

"It doesn't to you, but it will to her. After today I want you to hassle Mrs. McKenzie about the fact that she has a little girl in any way you can think of, just do it often."

"I don't want to do anything that will get anyone hurt, especially a kid."

"No one will get hurt. I just want to make Mrs. McKenzie nervous so she will share the information I need."

"Can't you get the cops or someone to help?"

"No, this is not a criminal mater, it is a private matter. Now let's talk about how we will communicate and how you will get paid. Do you know where the UPS store is in town?"

"Yeah."

"It has individual mailboxes. You can leave information for me there, and I will leave you an envelope with cash. I'll give you fifty bucks every time I am happy with what you tell me you accomplished. Just don't try to mess with me. I will be able to tell if you are accomplishing what I want you to accomplish."

"I can't get into the boxes."

"I will leave you a key in your mailbox tonight. Just be sure you get it before your mother goes to the box. And don't go to the mail drop at the same time every day. I don't want someone to see you there on a regular basis. Different people work different shifts, so if you vary your visits, you should be okay. Wear different jackets and hats."

"You don't know where I live."

"I know everything about you. How do you think I got this phone number? As I said, don't try to mess with me. It won't be safe for you or your mother."

The phone clicked.

"Who was that on the phone?"

"Tom, he wanted to talk about school tomorrow."

"It didn't sound like Tom, it sounded like an older man."

"You calling me a liar, Mom?"

"No, if you say it was Tom, it was Tom," Jane Mcintire said wearily.

Dodie left the kitchen and went to turn on the TV. He didn't want his mom to see how nervous he was. He was scared. He wanted the money offered by the man making the mysterious requests, but he didn't want anyone to get hurt. He didn't want to get in trouble.

The guy promised no one would get hurt. He knew how to harass someone and act tough. He had done it all his life to cover up how he was really feeling. If the guy was watching him, he wouldn't be suspicious if he saw Dodie around Mrs. McKenzie a lot. He would expect that, so Dodie would know if she was okay. He could always make an anonymous call to the cops if he thought she or her kid were in danger. The cops were always encouraging people to contact them if they saw anything suspicious. The police chief was always talking about the community working together.

Well, now it was time to call Tom and lie to him about how he couldn't walk to school with him tomorrow. He couldn't wait to see what this Mrs. McKenzie was like. Time to practice his tough image.

Chapter 21

Starting School

The middle school where Laura would teach and Benjii's elementary school were across the road from each other. The approach was steep and the hill they climbed was tree lined. The setting was lovely and reminded one of an old country road. Laura drove first to the elementary school.

Laura and Benjii reported to the principal's office first, and they were greeted warmly by Mrs. Price, the school secretary.

Mrs. Price was a stunning blonde. She had brown eyes and an attractive figure.

She wore a blue business suit, but Laura bet she did not wear that kind of attire when she was away from her job.

"Good morning, Ms. McKenzie and Benjii." Tammy Price looked questioningly at Laura. "Is Ms. correct, or should you be addressed as Mrs.? We need to be sure all our information is correct."

"Ms. is fine."

"Also, will you please check your registration form to be sure all the information is correct. We do not have anyone other than yourself listed on our emergency notification card. Is there another person we could add in case you are not available if Benjii should become sick or be injured?"

Laura perused the registration form and found all in order.

"The form is correct, and no, there is no one to add to the emergency card."

"We would really prefer to have a backup person if we cannot reach you Ms. McKenzie."

"I will be teaching right across the street. I will always be available."

"Well, we can leave it at that for now," said Mrs. Price. "But you may not be able to leave your classes if something occurs."

"I hope nothing will occur. Our teacher's contract provides ten sick days. These days can be used for family illness as well as our own. I am sure I can handle any problem that arises."

Mrs. Ashton, the school principal entered the office and heard the last part of the conversation. She had steel gray hair, was in her fifties, and was cool and businesslike.

"I would not like to have my teachers feel they could attend to a sick child during the school day," she stated. "You really should provide us with options if there is a problem while classes are in session. We would like to have the names of other family members or friends we could call if it became necessary."

"Mrs. Ashton, I have just moved to this community and have not made anyone's acquaintance. I have reasons for not wanting to divulge information about family. Benjii and I have been residing in a shelter for battered women. I am sure you will understand why I do not want to reveal past history."

As Laura left the office to take Benjii to the day care area, Mrs. Price followed her closely with her eyes.

"There is a story there," she said. "But I can't imagine what it is."

Mrs. Ashton nodded solemnly then said, "That mystery caller was right. There is something unusual about these two, but I can't imagine what it is. Tammy, I don't like to give credibility to anonymous phone calls, but please tell me again exactly what this person said."

"Well, first they asked if this is the Mapleton, New Hampshire elementary school, and I affirmed that it was. Then the caller asked if a child named Benjii McKenzie was enrolled in school. I told him I couldn't give out that information. Then the caller said, 'I believe that that child is enrolled in your school, and that her mother is using the name Laura McKenzie. That family will bear watching.' Then he hung up."

"Ms. McKenzie will be teaching grade 8 special education, am I correct?"

"Yes."

"Please keep this phone call under your hat. Carol Denver is the science teacher on the team Ms. McKenzie will be working with. She is a close friend of mine. I am going to call her and give her a heads-up. I know I can trust her to keep quiet about the call. At the same time, she can watch for anything unusual about Laura McKenzie."

Yeah right, Tammy thought, *I am sure she won't divulge any information.*

Little did Tammy Price realize how much she would be involved in Laura's story later on.

Chapter 22

Carol Denver was getting ready to meet with her team members when the phone rang.

Oh darn, who is calling now? she thought. *I don't have time to talk on the phone. I need to meet with the others, so we can continue discussing the change in our program. We need to figure out what to do about having a special education teacher and students on our team. We don't want it to cause us extra work. The teacher is just a kid right out of college. We should have been given someone on the team that is more experienced.*

She picked up the phone.

"Hello, this is Carol Denver."

"Hi, Carol, it is Lila."

"Morning, Lila, what's up?"

"I am calling about the new special education teacher on your team. I am sure you met her during the workshop days."

"We did. Why do you ask?"

"She just dropped off her daughter to meet her kindergarten teacher and day care personnel. The child will attend kindergarten here as well as the before and after-school programs while Ms. McKenzie teaches at your school. The child is sweet, and Ms. McKenzie seems nice and very concerned about the welfare of her child, but there is something very strange about the pair. Ms. McKenzie refuses to give information about their past or her family other than they have been living in a shelter for battered women for several years. I guess I can understand that, but there is something else I need to tell you. But for the time being you must keep this information to yourself."

"Of course."

"We recently received an anonymous call stating that Laura McKenzie and the child would bear watching, that Laura McKenzie is not what she seems to be. The person calling would not elaborate and hung up when being questioned by Tammy Price. I wanted you to know this so you can watch for anything unusual about Ms. McKenzie. We will be watching the child closely here. Remember, I don't want you to tell anyone else about this phone call right now. I don't want Ms. McKenzie or the child, Benjii, hurt if this call was just a cruel prank."

"Lila, don't worry, you can trust me."

Carol hung up and walked into the room next door where the other members of the grade 8 team Laura would be working with were already meeting.

"Wait until you hear the latest about our new team member," she told the others. "I may have a way to be sure we get a more experienced teacher working with us. Laura is a young, single mother, which we already knew, but what we didn't know is that she might have some secrets in her background that she does not want to have divulged."

She told the team under the promise of secrecy about the call from Lila Ashton.

"I think we can work with this information. We will try to get her to think we know more about her background than we actually do. That will cause her stress and may affect her performance. We can report any issues we have about her ability to function adequately to Barry Knight. Maybe we can work on the parents and students with innuendos, but we will have to be careful with that one. Well, let's discuss this more later. Laura should be here at school shortly."

Chapter 23

After leaving Benjii in the capable hands of the day care providers, Laura drove across the street to the middle school. She was feeling very good about starting the school year. She was pleased with Benjii's kindergarten teacher and the day care providers. They were very professional but at the same time warm and loving. They greeted Benjii with open arms, and Benjii did not seem to mind when Laura told her she had to leave her to go to her school. She was excited about her role as a special education teacher at the middle school. Her role would be to support her students in their classrooms as well as in small group classes. She would be free to modify her student's work so they could be successful. She could not wait to start work. Her euphoria would not last long.

Before going to her classroom, she went to the office to pick up her mail and the forms the students always had to complete the first day of each school year. As she was going into the office, she met Mitzi Dodge, the other grade 8 special education teacher.

"Hi, Mitzi."

"Good Morning, Laura, are you excited about starting your new job?'

"I am."

"Well, I don't want to burst your bubble, but there is something I need to say to you. I just reviewed the team assignments for each special education teacher in this school this year. I see you are assigned to team 6 in the eighth grade."

"That's right."

"The rest of us in the special education department are feeling a little guilty. You see, we asked the administration for particular assignments so we wouldn't be assigned to team 6. The four core teachers on this team are a very formidable group of women. They tend to be inflexible and want things to always go their way. I am afraid you are in for a difficult year. It would be difficult for an experienced teacher to work with these people. I don't know how a new teacher will deal with them. I wish you luck."

Mitzi Dodge had no idea how difficult Laura's first year will be.

Laura tried to shake off the impact of this warning as she walked to the third floor, where her classroom was located.

It can't be that bad, she thought. *I get along well with all sorts of people. I should be just fine.*

When she walked into her classroom she was in for an even more troubling encounter. She nearly fainted over what she saw. Scrawled across the chalkboard in back of her desk were the words "Is Benjii Barbara Jean?" It took several minutes to get over the dizziness she felt and gain her composure. She barely had time to erase the words before her homeroom students began to file into the classroom. She did not notice that one of her students was paying particular attention to the chalkboard.

I have to deal with this later, she thought. *My first consideration now is my students. I must see to it that their first day at school runs smoothly.*

She turned her attention to her homeroom class.

"Good morning, I am Ms. McKenzie," she said.

Her homeroom was a mixture of regular and special education students. Some she will only see in homeroom. Others she will assist during the entire school day.

The first hour of the day was used for housekeeping duties such as completing forms, assigning lockers, and getting acquainted. Somehow Laura managed to get through this hour successfully.

At nine forty-five the students left Laura's classroom to meet the teachers teaching special classes such as foreign language, PE, art, band, and chorus. It was time for her to attend a meeting with her core teachers. Teachers of the special classes would join the team meeting when they could. This would happen for about forty-five minutes each school day. Laura had met briefly with these teachers on each workshop day prior to the opening of school. Her team, as all other teams in the school, was comprised of an English, math, science, and social studies teacher. Most teams also had a special education teacher as well as teachers from the special programs. She had found the teachers on her team to be cold and not at all interested in what she had to say. She thought it was because they were busy thinking about getting their own programs going for the school year. Because of her warning from Mitzi Dodge, Laura was a little nervous as she walked down the hall to the room where the meeting would be held. She was also having difficulty pushing the note that been on her chalkboard to the back of her mind.

She smiled brightly as she entered the room.

"Good Morning," she said. She hoped her nervousness didn't show.

Mrs. Lewis, the English teacher, was the first to greet her.

"Good morning, Laura," she said. "We welcome you, but we are not sure how you will fit into our team. We certainly hope you are willing and able to take on a substantial workload. Not only must you do your own job, but you must be willing to take on one-fifth of the workload of this team. Do you think you can do that?"

"That is the best way you can be accepted as a member of this group," said Mrs. Hunt, the social studies teacher."

Mrs. Denver, the science teacher, and Mrs. Woodman, the math teacher, nodded in agreement. Laura had noticed another faculty member entering the room as this conversation was going on. He smiled at her and rolled his eyes sympathetically. Later he would introduce himself as Tim Atwood, the physical education teacher.

"I am sure I can handle any workload that comes my way. I will do my duties as well as one-fifth of this team's responsibilities." She emphasized the one-fifth.

"We certainly hope that your personal life will not interfere with your professional duties, Laura, and we hope you are worthy of your position as a member of the faculty at this school," said Carol Denver.

Laura was puzzled by this comment.

"I will be a productive member of this faculty, I assure you, and my personal life will not interfere with my professional duties any more than yours would, Mrs. Denver," she said sweetly.

The physical education teacher, Tim Atwood, smiled at her and gave her a thumbs-up. And to her relief, the subject was changed to the business of the morning.

When the meeting ended, Tim Atwood walked out of the room with her.

"I think you will soon get used to the abrasive attitude. Just don't take it personally."

Boy, I hope I can deal with all of this, she thought.

After the meeting, all grade eight students met in the school's auditorium for a meeting with the principal. He gave a short talk about academic and behavioral expectations for the school year and ended with a pep talk designed to excite the students about the coming school year.

Laura couldn't help but notice that one of her homeroom students, Roger Mcintire, appeared to be making snide remarks about the principal's talk to the people sitting around him. What unnerved her the most was that he seemed to be constantly staring at her.

That's probably because I am a new teacher, she thought. *I hope he is not going to create problems.*

Laura was happy when the first day of school ended. She was anxious to see how Benjii's day went and head home.

Laura and Benjii lived within three miles of the school. She felt safe in the condo she had rented in the secure, gated complex, but she was unsettled by the message on her chalkboard and the comment made by Mrs. Denver. She didn't really think that anyone was looking for her, but at the same time she was not so naive that she didn't realize that anyone who wanted to badly enough could probably get into her condo. She hoped the guard, security system, and lighting would be a deterrent. When she entered her apartment she checked the messages on her message machine. She didn't really expect any calls since she had not made any acquaintances in the community. There were two telemarketing calls and two hang-ups. She wondered briefly about the hang-ups then quickly forgot them.

Laura was happy to find that Benjii enjoyed her first day at school. She was already discussing some of the students with whom she was becoming friendly. Laura quickly explained the routine they would be following after each school day. There would be time to relax and go over the day's events. They would go outside for fresh air when the weather allowed then complete any homework Benjii had.

After dinner it would be bath and bedtime with a story. Once Benjii was asleep, Laura would get clothes ready for the next day then do lesson planning, correct papers, and so on.

She was done early this evening because there were no papers to grade. She checked to be sure all windows and doors were locked. When she closed the drapes, she thought she saw a shadow in the trees but decided it was just her imagination.

I am a little nervous, she thought. *From now on, I will close the drapes before it gets dark.*

Someone watched as she pulled the drapes then walked away.

In the morning, when Laura and Benjii left for school, she realized that the shadow had not been just her imagination. Sprawled across her front door in block letters were the words, "Benjii is Barbara Jean."

"Why did someone write on our door? I can read my name."

Laura was glad Benjii could not yet read the rest of the message.

"I don't know," Laura said casually. "I think someone must have mistaken our door for someone else's. I don't know what the message means."

Chapter 24

He had paid dearly for someone to assist in the search for the information he needed. For years he had been patient. Now his patience had finally paid off.

He moved into a motel in Mapleton, New Hampshire, and paid for the room a month in advance. He had told the clerk he did not know how long his business would keep him in the area, and that was true. He surely did not tell the clerk exactly what his business was.

He was plump, looked forty, and had graying hair. With the help of contacts, his eyes were a deep blue. He looked little like he did when he was younger. His ID and credit cards said he was a computer software salesman whose name was John Hebert. His picture ID matched his current appearance.

First the woman and the kid, he thought, *then on to New Rochelle.*

He watched the house carefully as well as the teenage kid who was hanging around it. Then he saw the kid write something on the door.

That's strange, he thought. *I'd like to see what he wrote, but I can't take a chance being seen. I wonder what Joe is trying to pull.*

He wasn't sure if watching the woman and kid would help, but he had to get Max one way or another. They were a wild card. *I don't want to hurt them, but if it's necessary, it's necessary.*

He saw the woman close her drapes. She looked a little startled.

I'll have to be more careful in the future, he thought. *And I need to watch the teenager. I wonder what happened to Alex Hamilton. He inadvertently helped me get the information I needed then he seems to have disappeared off the face of the earth.*

It may not be important. Things are better than I thought. Joe's trying to screw Max out of his business. He hired Big Jake to find this woman, and Big Jake hired the kid. I will have to watch that situation.

He had not trashed the house when he went was inside this morning, just moved things around a little. She would wonder what was going on and would be nervous. She would realize she couldn't be totally confident in this gated and secure community.

The call to the school would help too. Schools are concerned about protecting the kids. They will take any anonymous call seriously.

This poor woman doesn't have a chance. She'll soon realize she is being watched, that someone is getting into her house, the kid is hassling her, and the school doesn't completely trust her.

Chapter 25

After dropping Benjii off at school the next morning, Laura was thinking about how easy it had been to lie to her. She knew it would be necessary to tell Benjii the truth someday. She just was not sure Benjii was old enough right now to understand what Laura would have to tell her.

The most important thing would be sure Benjii understood how much she was loved and that Laura would always take care of her. Would she really be able to? she wondered.

As she drove into the parking lot she saw the homeroom student she had been aware of in the back of the auditorium the day before. He appeared to be hanging around the lot. She had asked one of the seventh grade teachers about him as they left the meeting yesterday. She was told that at times he could be a troublemaker; he was often sullen, impolite, and refused to complete in school and homeroom assignments.

Now she realized she had seen him in the parking lot yesterday in the morning.

He was also there when she left school in the afternoon.

I wonder why he is always hanging around here, she thought.

Most students enter the building as soon as they arrive at school in the morning, and they have no reason to be in the staff parking lot. Middle school students do not drive to school, and if they are dropped off by their parents, they are dropped off at the front door and immediately enter the building.

"Hey, Mrs. M. How was your evening?"

"Good morning, Roger, perhaps you already know that." She wondered if he was curious about her and was outside her window the night before.

Could he have painted these words on my door? How would he know her secret?

"Call me Dodie. All my friends do."

"Okay, Dodie."

Dodie walked close enough to her to push her against the car.

"Move away right now," she said.

"Come on, Ms. M., aren't you interested in someone who wants to show you what life is like? You have *Ms.* in front of your name. I don't know how you got a kid, but I bet it was not in the usual way."

Laura was beginning to panic. Roger was pressing closer and closer to her, and she was not able to push him away. She did not want to scream and make a scene.

Tim Atwood drove into the parking lot at that point.

"Is there a problem here?"

"I think Roger was just going into school. Am I right, Roger?"

"We'll finish this conversation later, Ms. M.," he said.

"What was that about? Was he threatening you?" Tim asked. "This should be reported."

"No, everything is okay. He was just being wise. I handled it."

Another lie, she thought.

Tim walked her into school. She was shocked at the electricity that shot through her body when he lightly touched her arm.

What on earth is going on, she thought. *I hardly know this man.*

Chapter 26

When Friday afternoon finally arrived, Laura was anxious to pick Benjii up from school and get home to relax. It had been a trying week for both of them. Benjii had been excited about her first week at school, and it had been difficult to get her to go to sleep at night. That made it late before Laura could get started on her lesson plans. The plans had to be adjusted each evening to correlate with the student's performance in class that day. Sometimes she found it difficult to concentrate on her plans when she had so many other things to think about. Why was her team of teachers so negative? Who wrote the messages she found on her chalkboard at school and her door at home? What was going on with Dodie Mcintire? Why was he hassling her?

As she headed for her car in the parking lot, she was met again by Dodie Mcintire. She had been a little troubled earlier in the week to learn that his schedule had been changed, and he would be attending some of her classes as well as being in her homeroom. She wondered if he had somehow maneuvered the change so he could give her a hard time. He did not seem interested in receiving an education. He sat sprawled in the back of the room, paying little attention to the lessons being taught. He was rude and disruptive. She could control much of this behavior by threatening after-school detentions. For some reason, this prospect upset him, and he would at least be quiet, if not engaged in the lessons.

"Yo, Ms. McKenzie," he said, accenting the *Ms.*, "I hear your kid is over at Edwards Elementary."

"Yes, Roger, she is." Laura saw no reason to dispute what he was saying since he seemed sure he had that information.

"Hey, remember to call me Dodie, all my friends do."

"Thank you, Rog—Dodie, I will."

"How come you got a kid? You ain't married. You don't have a ring."

"Dodie, I don't discuss my personal life with my students."

"Have a great weekend."

Laura was shaken as she got into her car and drove across the road to Benjii's school. She could not for the life of her understand why this student was so interested in her personal life, but she was sure it was connected to the messages she had received earlier that week. She would have been even more shaken if she had noticed how many people were paying attention to this exchange.

When Benjii spotted her as she walked into the school activity room where the after-school program was held, she quickly ran into Laura's arms.

"Mommy, Mommy, I missed you," she said.

This was the same greeting Laura received every day when she arrived to get Benjii. Her heart swelled with love.

I couldn't love her more if she were actually my own child, she thought.

"I missed you too, babe," she said.

Tammy Price and Lila Ashton witnessed this exchange.

"Well, one thing is certain," Tammy said. "These two may have a questionable background, but the child certainly seems happy and well adjusted."

"Yes," Lila said. "Maybe we are concerned about nothing, but we still need to continue to watch them carefully."

When Laura and Benjii arrived home, Laura was perplexed. Something seemed not quite right, but she could not put her finger on what it was. Had the vase of flowers on the table been moved?

How could it have been? She must have moved it last night when she was sitting there doing her plans and correcting. But why hadn't she moved it back like she always did? She must have been tired.

And she must have been tired when she folded the clothes she removed from the small-size dryer. They were in disarray sitting on the top of the small washer.

I can't believe I left them so untidy, she thought. *Oh well, it was not important.*

Benjii wanted to go to the park and play for a while before dinner. Maybe the fresh air will help clear my head she thought. And it will be good for Benjii to have time to play with the other children there. She did not realize she and Benjii were being carefully watched by the man sitting on the bench with the newspaper.

After getting Benjii to bed that night, Laura was tempted to forget about her schoolwork for the night. She knew that her first year would be the most difficult. Many of the lessons and materials she prepared this year would be able to be used other years with a few modifications to fit the students with whom she would be working. The work would be saved on both her computer at home and at school.

Next year will be easier, she thought. *But right now I have to keep up with all I have to do. I owe it to my students.*

With a sigh, she got out her briefcase and laptop and sat down at the table.

I know planning will be a little easier next year, but will my team of teachers be more accepting of me and be kinder? Will Dodie Mcintire stop hassling me?

Chapter 27

Soon after Sue's encounter with Max at the charity ball and Alex's "inspection" of Max's storage unit, Sue, Alex, and Bill met in a little out of the way cafe about ten miles from New Rochelle. They did not want to take the chance of being seen together in town. Even with this precaution, Alex wore dark, heavy clothes, dark glasses, and a baseball cap pulled down over his eyes. They did not want his cover to be blown.

"Okay," Sue said, "let's see what we've got."

Alex spoke first. "There is currently a lot of activity at Max's storage unit, but Joe Boccia is the one creating most of the buzz. He goes in and out several times a week, but there is really nothing I can put my finger on that is suspicious. After all, he does work there."

"I told you earlier about my visit as an inspector."

"There is probably a connection between that visit, your visit to Ruth Carter, and the current heightened activity. I just don't know what it is."

"Is there any way we can get into those units?" Bill asked.

"No, we would need a warrant and we have no basis for one. We need to do everything by the book, or the case, if we ever have one, will never fly in court. We can't take any chance of blowing it."

"When I went to the unit under the guise of an inspector, a guy there named Lenny Butler showed me several cartons of fruit, nuts, and coffee. They seemed legit, but I was intrigued by the numbers on the cartons containing coffee. All cartons from the same shipment should have had the same numbers, but there were some discrepancies. I have a record of those numbers, but right now I don't know what to do with that information."

"Who picked out the cartons for you to inspect?"

"Lenny Butler did."

"That is probably why they were all legit."

"Here is a new twist, Alex. Max called me a couple of days ago, asking me if I would begin an investigation into the disappearance of his daughter and sister-in-law."

"Huh?" said Alex. "After all these years?"

"I asked the same thing. He said he has a private detective on the case and he has some new information that will make the investigation easier for us."

"Did you buy that?"

"It might be true, but I doubt he hired anyone five years ago. I think he wants to divert our attention from his business to his personal problems."

"So what so we do now?"

"I decided to call him back and tell him we will do some investigation. The more we are involved with Max, the more excuses we have to contact him and be near his home and business."

"Where do we go from here?'

"I am going to visit the Edwards Elementary School in Mapleton, New Hampshire."

Both men were surprised.

"Why there?" they asked in unison.

"Because of a strange phone call I recently received. Someone called and said that Max Bertolini had hired a private eye of questionable repute named Big Jake Turner. They said he found Max's kid and sister-in-law in a small New Hampshire town called Mapleton. He said, 'You better move fast if you want to find them before Max gets to them,' then the caller hung up. I need to go to Mapleton to verify that information."

"Alex, you keep seeing what you can learn from working on the docks. Bill will keep up his surveillance of Max and Joe."

Chapter 28

The police force in Mapleton, New Hampshire, was staffed mostly by volunteer officers who patrolled the streets at nights and weekends. They also answered emergency calls. There was, however, a full-time police chief. Sue knew she would need the support of the chief before she would be able to extract the information she needed from the school.

Bob Cochoran was a rotund fifty-year-old officer who had been appointed chief five years earlier after the previous chief resigned in favor of a more-challenging, better-paying job in another community. Bob was content to stay in Mapleton. He was happy with his eight-to-five job. He seldom had to go out nights or weekends. His force was able to handle the traffic violations, DUIs, and accidents that occurred. There was little crime in Mapleton, and he reported only to very serious events.

He was surprised to get a call from a detective from New Rochelle, New York. He was even more surprised to hear that it was in reference to a possible kidnapping.

"Detective Patnode," he said, "this is a very small town. I know everyone who lives here, knew when they got married, knew when their kids were born, and know when they die. My wife is in charge of the school lunch program at the elementary and middle schools, and she knows all the kids. No one in my town has been kidnapped. No one in my town is a kidnapper."

"We believe a child enrolled in your elementary school may have been kidnapped from her home in New Rochelle about five years ago. I want to talk to your school personnel, but of course, I have no jurisdiction in your town. I am asking your permission to do that and for you to pave the way for me to see the school principal and anyone else who may be helpful."

"You can come if you want. I'll go to the interview with you, but if I am not comfortable with what is happening, I will put an end to it. No one in my town has been kidnapped."

"Will next Tuesday at ten in the morning be satisfactory?"

"Let me check my calendar."

Bob looked at the nearly blank planner in front of him on his desk.

"I can move things around and see you at ten next Tuesday, but I'll only have a short time to give you."

"See you then."

Sue arrived for her meeting in Mapleton right on time. She introduced herself to the desk sergeant and was immediately brought into Chief Cochoran's office. After introductions and pleasantries, she got right to the point.

"As I told you on the phone, I am here to meet with your school personnel about a student in your elementary school that may have possibly been a kidnap victim. I would like your permission to conduct some interviews."

"Could you show me a picture of the child."

"That is not possible. The child was taken when she was less than two weeks old. No pictures are available."

"That makes things a little more problematic. As I told you before, I don't believe any child in my community is a kidnap victim, but as courtesy to a fellow police officer, I will introduce you to the appropriate school personnel. I intend to stay and listen to what you have to say."

"I have no problem with you being part of the interview. In fact, I think it is an excellent idea."

Bob and Sue were taken to Lila Ashton's office by Tammy Price, who could hardly contain her curiosity. Bob introduced the two women.

"I'll let you explain why you are here, Detective Patnode."

Sue knew she would have to be very careful of how she presented her case. She knew New Englanders were very protective of their own.

"Mrs. Ashton," she said, "we had an infant disappear from New Rochelle about five years ago. We believe she was taken from her father's home by her maternal aunt after the mother of the child passed away. We have reason to believe that the aunt has settled into your community with the child.

"The child may be a student in your school. We have no picture of the child, but we do have a picture of the aunt which was taken over five years ago. Please look at the picture and see if it resembles any of the mothers of your kindergarten or first grade students."

"I doubt that I can help you. I have been a teacher and administrator in Mapleton for nearly thirty years. I know all of the families who have school age children. I am sure none of them are kidnap victims. Both Chief Cochoran and myself know when most of these children were born, and we have watched them grow up."

"Just take a look at the picture please."

Sue pushed the picture of Laura Mitchell over for Mrs. Ashton to view.

Lila tried to disguise her surprise when she saw the picture. The woman she saw looked a little similar to Laura McKenzie. She had heard good things about Laura's skills as a teacher and mentor to the middle school students under her care. She had also observed the deep love and affection between her and Benjii. She did not want to cause them undue trouble. However, she did realize there was something mysterious about their background. She quickly decided to find out more about the case Detective Patnode was investigating.

"This picture does not look like any of our mothers," she said. "I don't believe any of the children in our schools is in any danger. They are mostly all from normal happy families, thank God. What can you tell me about the family of the missing child?"

"I have to be careful about giving out private information, but as I said before, the child's mother passed away shortly after the child was born a little over five years ago. The father still lives in New Rochelle."

"And you have been searching for them for five years?"

"Well, no, we just started searching a couple of weeks ago."

"What took you so long?"

"The father just recently contacted us asking us to begin a search for his daughter. We had heard of the disappearance, but quite frankly, we dropped the ball. The father did have a private investigator on the case, but not until just a few weeks ago. The work of that private investigator brought us here."

"That private investigator never contacted us here at school. Did he contact you, Bob?"

After Bob answered in the negative, Lila said, "He must be some investigator. He didn't contact the most important people who would be knowledgeable about his search."

All this sounds so strange, Lila thought. *Any caring father of a missing newborn would be frantically calling the police when a child disappeared. And why did the mother die? That is very unusual in this day and age. I think I will be quiet, bide my time, and see what happens.*

"I'm sorry. As I said, I cannot help you. I don't recognize the picture. I wish you luck in your search. If that is all, I have another meeting."

There was nothing for Sue to do but end the interview. She was sure Mrs. Ashton knew something. The way she reacted when she first viewed the picture sent up a red flag. She believed she saw something familiar in the picture but did not want to admit it. Perhaps she would come back to Mapleton at a later time.

Tammy Price looked up as Lila left the office where she Bob and Sue had been meeting.

"What was that all about?' she asked.

"Oh just an investigation. As it turns out, it has nothing to do with us."

After saying good-bye to Sue, Bob hung back so he could speak briefly with Tammy.

"Lila knows something about the case we were just discussing but for some reason doesn't want to get involved. The cop showed her a picture of someone I think she recognized but would not acknowledge it."

"I'm surprised to hear that. Lila would want to help any child in trouble."

"Maybe the kid is not in danger. Maybe she is being well cared for."

"She?"

"Yea, the detective is looking for a girl about five or six years old who was taken from her father as an infant. I don't think any kids in our town have a questionable parentage or backgrounds."

"Oh yes, we do. I have been wondering about a teacher at the middle school named Laura McKenzie. She has a daughter enrolled in our kindergarten. She refuses to give the name of anyone to call if there should be an emergency with her daughter. She won't discuss anything about her background except to say that she and the child lived in a shelter for battered women for several years. She says they have no family, and they don't know anyone here. She keeps pretty much to herself. The only friendship she seems to have developed is with Tim Atwood, a PE teacher at the middle school. I have heard that staff members at the middle school have observed them walking together to their cars most every day after school. I think Tim and Laura may be developing some kind of a relationship, but they are being very discreet about it.

"I doubt that they have anything to do with this case. If they did, Lila would have acknowledged it."

I don't want the Price woman to think I suspect anything, he thought. *What a feather it would be in my cap if I could solve this kidnapping case. I think I will go say hello to Tim Atwood and make the acquaintance of Laura McKenzie.*

When Laura left school in the afternoon and walked to her car with Tim, she was surprised to see a police cruiser parked next to her car.

"Who is that?" she asked Tim.

"It appears to be Chief Cochoran. I wonder what he is doing here."

"Oh god, why is he here? I hope Benjii is okay." Laura could feel herself trembling.

"I am sure it is not about Benjii. If she were not okay, the school would have notified you." Tim was surprised at Laura' strong reaction to seeing a police car. "Let's see what he wants."

"Afternoon, Bob," Tim said.

"Afternoon, Tim, who is the pretty lady with you?"

"This is my colleague, Laura McKenzie. Laura, may I introduce you to Mapleton's chief of police, Bob Cochoran."

"Well, ain't that a coincidence. You're the lady I came to see."

"What on earth for?"

"Oh no reason. I just heard you were new in town and came to introduce myself and let you know if you need anything, I will be happy to assist you. Well, I have a busy day, so I will be on my way. Nice to see you, Tim. Nice to meet you, Mrs. McKenzie."

"Does he greet everyone new in town like that? If so, he's a little late. I have been in town for three months."

"Not to my knowledge. Would he have any reason to single you out, Laura?"

"I don't believe so. See you tomorrow, Tim."

"Yes, I'll see you tomorrow. But, Laura, I think you must have a sense of how I feel about you. If you have anything you need to talk about, let me know. I will always be there for you no matter how our feelings for each other develop."

"I am trying not to develop the same feeling about you, Tim. We can't go beyond the stage of friendship. I can never develop a strong, lasting relationship with anyone. I can't explain why. Just understand that I have a problem that can never be resolved."

"There is no such thing a problem that cannot be resolved."

Tim drove away.

Chapter 29

Sue arrived home from Mapleton early enough to pick her twins up from school. When she got outside her children's classroom, she was met by their teacher.

"Mrs. Johnson would like to meet briefly with you in her office. While you do that, I'll get the twins ready to go home with you."

Sue couldn't understand why she should meet with the school's principal.

"Is there a problem?"

"Mrs. Johnson will explain when she sees you. She is expecting you."

As soon as she walked into the office, the school secretary ushered her into Mrs. Johnson's office

"Thank you for coming to meet with me," Mrs. Johnson said. "There is something I wish to discuss with you. The teachers who are out on the playground at the same time as your children have been noticing an unidentified man lingering around the play area. He appears to be working, but the teachers can't quite figure out what he is doing. Sometimes he mows the grass around the sidewalks, sometimes he seems to be working on the light pole or telephone pole. He does not attempt to enter the play area and has not attempted to make contact with children or adults, but still the teachers are concerned. They are certain it is the same man each time. I am speaking to you for two reasons. One is that this man has not been observed any time other than when you children's class is outside. The other is because you are on the police force and would know how to handle this situation. The man might have a perfectly legitimate reason for being there, but I need to know that. If this continues without an explanation, I will have to notify the superintendent and parents of a potential danger. I would prefer not to alarm the parents if it is not absolutely necessary."

Sue was shaken by this news. Was it in any way connected to Max Bertolini's veiled threat at the charity ball? Were her children being put in danger because of her job? She tried to maintain her composure and answer professionally.

"I understand that you have to report this to your superintendent, but I hope you can delay sending a letter home to parents. It could alert the person watching the playground that we are aware of his activities. I can have someone here in a day or two to check out the situation."

When Sue returned to the classroom to get her kids, she felt the need to give them an extra hug.

Chapter 30

The next morning, Sue discussed the school issue with Bill. They had to devise a situation where he could observe the man without being detected. It was also important that Sue's children not see him. They liked him and would immediately ask him why he was at their school if they saw him.

"Give me some time to think," Bill said. "I may have to be around the school for several days before I can figure out what is going on."

The next morning Bill proposed a plan to Sue.

"The high school, middle school complex is right across the street from the elementary school. I see their maintenance van there often when I drop off and pick up my kids from the middle school. If I got permission from school personnel, I could use that van for cover and observe the person in question. I could even help mow the lawn around the bleachers at the football field. That has to be done by hand."

"Good plan. I'll see if I can set it up."

The school superintendent readily agreed with the plan devised by Bill. He had heard from Mrs. Johnson and was anxious to have the mystery of who this person is solved. He was as concerned about the children's safety as Mrs. Johnson and the teachers were.

Bill began his surveillance the next day. It did not take long to identify the man in question. Either he is harmless or stupid, Bill thought. He's trying to look busy, but other than that, he is doing little to hide himself.

During the recess period the next morning, Bill approached the man as he stood on the sidewalk observing the children on the playground.

"May I help you?" he asked, showing his badge.

"No, I am just out for a walk."

"Well, your walk has been bringing you to this playground at this same time for several weeks."

"Yeah, ever since school started."

"You admit it?"

"There is nothing to admit. I just want to see my kids to be sure they are okay, not hurt or anything."

"Why do you need to sneak around to do that? Do you have ID? What is your name?"

"Ben Johnson. Here is my license. To answer your questions, my wife met a new guy and sued for divorce. They accused me of assaulting the kids. There was no evidence of that, and I don't think the judge believed them, but he gave custody of the kids to my wife, and he gave me supervised visits every other weekend until things are resolved. That is why I watch from a distance. I am not supposed to contact them at any other time.

"He also ordered the boyfriend to stay away from the kids. He can see my wife, ex-wife, when the kids are in school or with me. But I don't trust him to stay away. I decided to watch them at school. If they seemed sad or afraid, I would know it."

"I can't let you loiter here every day, Ben. You have aroused the suspicion of the school personnel. They don't recognize you and are concerned about the safety of the children."

"Well, I guess I am glad they are so diligent. It makes me less concerned about my own kids."

"You know I can't just take your story on face value. I'll have to check it out, look for divorce papers, the judge's order."

"I understand that."

"I may be able to help you further. Give me your wife's address."

Ben gave it to him.

"That is close to where I live. I can swing around that way once in a while to see that everything is okay."

The two men shook hands, and Ben walked away from the school, promising he would no longer loiter there.

I hope I can repay that guy someday, Ben thought.

Later that afternoon, Bill reported the incident to Sue. "I checked the court records, and everything he told me is true. Judge Hardy told me he didn't believe a thing the wife said, but his hands were tied. He had to issue both orders to be sure to protect the kids. He doesn't trust the boyfriend at all. He ordered both lawyers to try to get to the truth of the matter."

"I will call Mrs. Johnson and give her this report. She can assure the teachers that all is well and that your surveillance has ended. If this guy shows up again, she can call me right away."

"He won't show up since I told him not to. He is not going to do anything to endanger his time with his kids. He's basically a good guy that is having problems right now."

"I will also have Rick pay attention to the Johnson kids to be sure they seem okay."

"Bill, I really appreciate your doing such a great job on this assignment. It is a relief to know that all the kids at school are safe. I know it took time away from your other cases. I will help you get caught up in any way that I can."

Bill saluted and walked out of the office. He didn't realize he would be hearing from Ben Johnson again in a few months.

Chapter 31

Laura had to will herself to walk down the hall to meet with her grade 8 team. It was the fourth Monday of September, but it seemed she had been working with these people longer. She couldn't understand why, but it appeared that they were doing all they could to make her life miserable. Their actions were subtle, but it was obvious they intended to hurt her whenever possible. She had not attempted to discuss this with anyone because her complaints sounded trivial even to herself, and she feared that her actions would just make matters worse. As she walked, she reminded herself that she was a good person, a professional, and a good teacher. Nothing these women do can change that, she thought.

When she walked into the room, Mrs. Lewis asked her how things were going.

She had a sneer on her face.

"Things are going very well," Laura stated quietly, "since we all understand what is going on here."

Laura did not want these women to think they were getting to her, and in fact some things were going well. She loved her work with the students, and they seemed to like her. When she called parents to discuss an issue with a particular child, they were supportive.

I guess I can handle the rest, she had told herself.

She was relieved when Tim Atwood walked into the room. The women on her team treated her quite differently when other people were in the room.

The chief topic of this morning's meeting was the upcoming open house that was to be held the next week.

Laura had not given much thought to evening meetings. She spent most of the meeting time thinking about how she would provide care for Benjii. She did not know anyone who could babysit and had not planned on needing sitters in the evening.

Tim walked out of the meeting with her. She was suddenly aware of his good looks. He was not tall but was powerfully built. He must work out a lot, she thought. She admired his sandy hair and green eyes.

"You seemed very distracted during the meeting," he said.

"I'm worried about finding a babysitter for my daughter Benjii for the open house. I am new in the area and don't know anyone. I don't want to leave her with strangers."

"I think I can help you with your problem. My daughter, Marcy, is sixteen years old. She can stay with Benjii. I will drive her over and drive you to the meeting. That way you won't have to worry about getting a sitter home after the meeting."

Laura felt very relieved.

"Will that be okay with your wife and daughter?"

"It will be okay with my daughter. I do not have a wife. We have been divorced for about four years now. My daughter lives with me."

Why am I so pleased to learn that Tim is single? thought Laura. *He has only shown a professional interest in me. And I certainly can't get involved with anyone. I would never be able to explain the situation with Benjii. I am going to have to live a celibate life.*

"I really appreciate that offer if your daughter is willing to babysit."

"I am sure she would enjoy the opportunity to earn some extra money. I assure you she will be very reliable. It's settled then, Marcy will babysit, and I will drive you to the meeting."

On the night of the meeting, Tim arrived around six to pick Laura up.

Marcy was a very attractive sixteen-year-old. Laura was relieved to see that she seemed very mature. They discussed Benjii's bedtime routine. Then Laura introduced her to Benjii. This was Benjii's first time with a sitter since Laura graduated from college.

Before that time, the sitters had been other people from the shelter, so they were people she knew. The mothers at the shelter had taken turns sitting for each other so they could work, attend classes, and so on. She seemed a little unsure about how to react to the situation.

"Hi, Benjii," Marcy said. "I bet you are nervous about having me as a babysitter. Well, I'm nervous too. I think we can work this out together. Let's look over the schedule. You can help me find the things we might need."

Laura was impressed.

"You must be very proud of your daughter. She is a very mature sixteen-year-old," she whispered to Tim.

"I am proud of her. She went through a lot when her mother and I separated. At first she spent half her time with her mother and the other half with me. But her mother is a journalist and travels a lot. That interfered with Marcy's schooling, so she stayed with me most of the school year. Now she lives with me permanently, which is what I prefer. Her mother still travels a lot, but Marcy visits her if she is home during a school vacations."

"Where is home?" Laura asked.

"A little town in Upstate New York called New Rochelle. We rented a house from a lawyer who was handling affairs of girls who were away at college," Tim answered.

Laura's gave a little start, and her hands began to sweat.

"Are you okay?" Tim asked with concern.

"Yes. I guess I am a little nervous about this open house."

"You'll do fine. Just be yourself." Tim patted her hand reassuringly.

I hope to God he doesn't feel that jolt of electricity that goes through me whenever he touches me, she thought.

Later that night Laura glowed as she thought about how the evening had gone.

The parents she met at the meetings had been very complimentary about the way she had been working with their children. Even the team of teachers she worked with seemed friendlier than they had in the past.

When she and Tim arrived back home, Benjii was sound asleep, and Marcy was doing her homework. They stayed for cookies and milk and coffee. The conversation between the three of them flowed easily and naturally. Tom suggested that the four of them might go out on an outing some weekend.

The thought of an outing both thrilled and frightened her. She loved being with Tim and Marcy, but getting too close frightened her. It would be too hard to answer what would be natural questions about her and Benjii's past.

After they left for home, Laura continued thinking about Tim and Marcy.

Does this mean I have to go through life without ever having close friends? she wondered. *What about the New Rochelle connection? Surely neither Tim or Marcy could have been responsible for the message written on her chalkboard the first day of school.*

Tim had thoughts later that night, also. I could really go for that girl he thought.

She is intelligent and kind. She is going to be a terrific teacher. She would be a good role model for Marcy. And she is awful cute. As he fell asleep, Tim thought about holding Laura in his arms.

Chapter 32

Jose Sebastian was surprised when he got a phone call at work at the coffee-packing factory. He was worried about his family but knew they would never call him at work unless there was an emergency. His wife, Elena, was in her seventh month of pregnancy and was having problems. He prayed that the problems were not too serious. The baby would be born at the free clinic. He could not afford hospital bills. To make matters worse, the doctor recommended a procedure that would ensure that there would be no further pregnancies. He couldn't afford that either. Elena would not be able to return to work for several months after the baby was born. It was just as well with two other little ones at home. Day care was expensive for two children; paying for care for three would deem work for Elena senseless.

As soon as he had the funds, Jose decided they would defy the orders of the church and take the steps the doctor recommended to be sure there were no more pregnancies. He loved his wife and kids desperately and would do anything to keep them well and keep his family intact. He worked this night shift so he could be home through the day to help his wife.

The phone kept ringing.

"Yeah."

"Jose Santiago?"

"That is me."

"I got a job for you."

"I got a job."

"This is in addition to the job you got. It pays five grand."

Jose gasped. That would nearly pay for his wife's hospital expenses.

"I'm not doing anything illegal."

"You already are."

"What the hell are you talking about? I just work on a conveyer belt at this factory."

"You know the moisturizing enhancement packets you put in the coffee cans before they are sealed?"

"Well, the packets do not contain moisture enhancers."

"What are they?"

"You don't want to know. If you do know, you could be considered an accomplice to whatever is happening. This way, you are just an innocent bystander. All you need to do is make a substitution to the packets you usually put in the cans. New cartons of packets are at the factory. They are near your conveyer belt. The numbers in the new packets end in threes instead of twos. Put these moisturizer packets in the cans instead of the old packets. When the cartons are sealed, put this new number on the outside of the carton."

"I'm not the only one who packs the cans on conveyer 5."

"I know, but you are the only one who works on that conveyer on the eleven-to-seven shift."

Joe was right. The conveyer belt shut down the last two hours of the shift. At that time, Jose packed the coffee cans into cartons, sealed them, and labeled them for shipping. He knew that moisture packets were never added to cans of coffee on the first and second shifts. He never questioned that. He figured his bosses knew what they were doing.

"How do I get paid?"

"Money will be placed in your locker. You will receive the cash in small bills over a period of a couple of weeks. Use it slowly, buying groceries, gas, and so on. You can also deposit some of it into your checking account. Just deposit it slowly and in small amounts so no one will be suspicious."

Jose gave the proposition some thought. He had no way of knowing if anything in the packets was illegal. He was just a laborer doing what he was told, but for his own protection, he would carefully document everything he did as well as this phone call. He had no idea who he was talking to and knew better than to ask.

"Okay, I'll get the job done right."

"Another thing. Just in case you decide to screw up or discuss this phone call with anyone, I know where to find your pregnant wife and adorable little kids."

"I won't do anything that will jeopardize their safety, but if you ever do anything to harm them, I will find you, and you will suffer."

Joe believed Jose. He also knew he wouldn't do anything to hurt a woman or kids, but Jose didn't know that.

"Just do your job, and there won't be any problems."

Joe hung up.

He was ready now to put his plan in place. He would have to locate the correct cartons and be sure they were delivered to the right place then visit Carlos.

Chapter 33

A few days after talking with Jose, Joe reviewed his plan again. It was simple enough to work, he thought. The packets that Jose placed in the cans as ordered and packed in cartons would be part sugar and cornstarch. Joe had spent a lot of his money to bribe dealers to make this substitution. It was a win-win situation for them. Not only did they receive money from Joe, they still had some of their pure drugs to deal. They did not know who their benefactor was, Joe did not want to be identified, but he knew them, and they recognized that fact. They would not dare try to scam him; they did not know if he was dangerous. Joe would keep the cartons of coffee that contained the pure drugs. It was now time to find a buyer for those drugs.

Joe walked into the Blue Fin, a bar in New Rochelle. It was early afternoon, so it was quiet. There were only two customers sitting at the bar. He spoke to the bartender.

"I need to see Carlos."

"Carlos is a busy man."

"Yea, what's he doing, Pete, having a little afternoon recreation with one of his dancers?"

"Carlos is a married man."

"That makes a difference?"

"To an honorable man, yes."

"Well, that lets Carlos out. He's a sleazeball. Anyway, he is expecting me," Joe lied. "He's in the office in the back."

Pete called Carlos from the phone at the bar as Joe ventured back. As he entered the hallway that led to Carlos Rodriguez's office, he was met by a pair of bodyguards who frisked him."

"Careful where you put your hands. Do you think I am stupid enough to come in here armed?"

"Can't be too careful."

Carlos Rodriguez did not look like a typical drug lord. He was fiftyish with a bald head except for a couple of tufts of gray hair over his ears, but Joe knew he could be a very dangerous man.

"What's on your mind, Joe?"

"Business."

"What kind?"

"Drugs."

"What makes you think I know anything about that business? I run a respectable club."

Joe wanted to say that the "club" was a sleaze joint, but he needed to stay on the good side of Carlos.

"Let's just say a little birdie told me. I can provide you with some stuff that is pure as the driven snow, top-grade stuff. So stop screwing around. I want to do business, and I don't have a lot of time."

Joe had plenty of time, but he wanted to get out of there. The atmosphere made him nervous.

"I don't know if I am interested. What do you have?"

"Heroin, coke, ecstasy, you name it. I just have small supplies, but it will bring you big return."

"Why don't you sell it yourself?"

"I don't have a crew of midlevel dealers. I want to do business with someone at the top. That's why I am here."

"You said I could get a big return. What is the street value?"

"It is top-grade stuff, so maybe fifty thousand, give or take."

"How did you get the stuff?"

"None of your business. Are you interested or not?"

"I may be. I have to try the stuff. Where is it?"

"I got it stashed in a safe place." *Or I will*, Joe thought. "Bring it here."

"No way. I am not that stupid. When you decide if you are interested, I will bring it to a mutually agreed upon place. Maybe the Motel 6. I could bring it in luggage, and no one would be the wiser."

"I'll call you when I make up my mind."

When Joe left the Blue Fin, he didn't notice the black truck parked down the street. The driver of the truck dialed his cell phone.

"Joe was in the Blue Fin for about an hour. I looked inside, pretending to read the menu in the window. Joe was nowhere in sight, so I suspect he was meeting with Carlos Rodriguez in his office in the back. Rodriguez is a big drug dealer. I wonder if Joe is double-crossing Max. If he is, he is in big trouble."

He smiled after speaking with the truck driver. Old Joe may be making things easier for me, he thought.

Chapter 34

The secretary in Max's office picked up the phone.

"Bertolini Import and Export. How may I direct your call?"

Carlos smiled at this. He knew Max fielded most incoming call himself. The office was small. Only one secretary worked in the legitimate portion of the business. Max didn't want too many people to be aware of how his business was run.

He must be out or on another call, Carlos thought.

"Mr. Bertolini please."

"I will see if he is available. May I ask who is calling?"

"No, you may not. Just put him on."

The call went through to Max's office.

"Max Bertolini."

"Max, this is Carlos Rodriguez. How ya doin'?"

"Fine. What can I do for you? I'm busy."

Max wondered why he was being contacted by his closest rival. They were covertly competing for business, Max under the guise of his import/export business, Carlos under the guise of his bar and restaurant, the Blue Fin. They kept track of each other's activities but did not interfere with one another. It was a quiet, wary truce, but neither man was comfortable in the presence of the other. Both were making a lot of money, and neither wanted to upset the apple cart.

I bet you are, thought Carlos. "I am calling about your business partner."

"I don't have a business partner."

"Well, your business associate then, Joe Boccia."

"Joe works with me in my import/export business. We deal with coffee, fruit, and nuts. If you need any of those products for your business, you can contact him. I trust him completely."

"Nice pitch, Max, but cut the shit. I want to know about the quality of the drugs he is trying to sell me. I don't want any cheap stuff."

"I don't know what you are talking about. I don't deal with drugs. I don't believe Joe does either. I only have honest people working for me."

Max hung up.

Christ, what is Joe trying to pull? Max wondered. *Where's he getting the drugs? I better be more careful about checking my shipments, but I don't believe Joe would try to stiff me. He knows better. I got to give him credit for going into business on his own. He's a wimp. I didn't think he had the guts to go out on his own. I'm kind of proud of him, but I'll kill him if he's cheating me. I think he and I have to have a talk.*

Chapter 35

Max closed the door to his study before talking to Joe.

"I think," he said as he poured two scotches, "that it is time we enlisted the police department to help find Barbara Jean and her aunt."

Max was not concerned about being less than truthful to Joe about contacting the police. Not after the call he received from Carlos Rodrigues.

"I thought you wanted to wait until the shipment was safely delivered."

"I did, but someone was nosing around the storage unit the other day. He said he was an inspector and needed to check the coffee. Lenny Butler was there, and he was smart enough to give him just the legitimate coffee to inspect."

"I don't believe it was an inspector. I think it was a cop. They suspect we have drugs but can't prove it. They have been nosing around a lot lately. We may have to move the stuff to a different location."

"Also, they think I had something to do with Laura and Barbara Jean's disappearance. Of course, I didn't, so it won't present a problem for me. However, the disappearance of a woman and baby will be a priority for them. They'll think they can get me on a murder charge and will leave my business alone."

"I don't know, Max. I think it is a little early to move the shipment. If the cops are suspicious, they will be watching. Making a move right now may be a little risky."

"I'll think about it further, Joe."

When Joe drove away from Max's house, he had a thought.

Maybe I'll give the cops an anonymous tip about Laura and Barbara Jean being alive in Mapleton. I'll tell them Max hired Big Jake Turner to find them. Then if something happens to Laura or the kid, it will be on his head. If I can talk Max out of moving the stuff for a while, it will give me time to move my drugs. I wish Carlos would get off his ass and agree to buy the stuff.

If all goes right, I can take over Max's business. I could own a big house instead of just visiting Max in his. Hell, I could probably buy his house if he goes to jail.

He picked up his phone to make a call.

Sue dashed into her office to grab the phone.

"New Rochelle Police Department."

"I got some information for you, but I'm gonna say it just once then hang up so you better listen. Max Bertolini hired Big Jake Turner to find his kid and her aunt, the kidnapper. They live in Mapleton, New Hampshire, a small town just over the Mass border. You better move fast if you want to find them before Max gets to them."

The phone clicked.

That's a pretty strange phone call, Sue thought. *Is it just a coincidence that it came soon after Max called? Obviously this caller has no idea that Max called and that I went to Mapleton. And what about the anonymous calls we have received. I don't think this caller knows about the other calls.*

After the call, Sue called Bill into her office.

"Have you ever heard of a Big Jake Turner?"

"Yea, he's a sleazeball private detective. Some of his tactics are questionable, but he always manages to operate within the law. Why do you ask?"

Sue filled Bill in on the phone call she just received.

"I'll pay Big Jake a visit," he said.

I don't know why anyone would ever hire this guy, Bill thought when he walked into Big Jake's shabby office.

There was no receptionist, just a slate gray metal desk with a chair that rolled to a metal file cabinet.

Just one cabinet, Bill thought. *Must not have much business.*

The in/out tray was empty. There were two folding chairs in front of the desk.

Big Jake eyed Bill as he walked in. He could smell a cop miles away.

"Can I help you?"

Bill flashed his badge and introduced himself. "We think you may have some information that will help us with a missing-persons case.

"Is that so? Who's missing?"

"A woman named Laura Mitchell and a little girl about five years old named Barbara Jean Bertolini."

"Never heard of them."

"We have information that says something different."

"From where?"

"I can't reveal my sources."

"Well, I can't reveal mine either, but I don't know these people you say are missing."

"Your private eye license up to date?" Bill asked.

Of course, Big Jake never applied for a license.

"Okay, okay, Max Bertolini contacted me a couple of weeks ago to find them. It's his kid and sister-in-law you are asking about. I went to airports, bus and train stations, and taxi offices asking questions, but I couldn't learn anything. If questioned later, Jake could say he told Bill what he did to investigate. He had no intention of mentioning Jim Fallon. The cops didn't know anything about the computer whiz. Jake was not going to enlighten them."

Bill knew he wouldn't be getting any more information from Turner. Before he left, he gave him his card and instructed him to call if he remembered anything. He knew he would not be receiving any call.

Chapter 36

Two weeks had passed since his talk with Jose. Now that the shipment was in, it was time to act.

He needed to see to it that the correct cartons of coffee were shipped to Kim Lee.

The sound of the alarm startled him out of a sound sleep. He had been keyed up when he went to bed and did not get to sleep until well after midnight. "Shit," he said. He could not believe it was three thirty.

He dressed quickly and made coffee to take with him. He did not bother to shower and shave.

There wouldn't be anyone around where he was going.

He drove an old clunker he had purchased from a kid anxious to get money for college. When he went to meet the kid, he was careful that the kid would not be able to recognize him later if a problem arose. He had worn heavy clothing that would hopefully add weight to his appearance and a baseball cap pulled down over his eyes. He also wore dark sunglasses. He hoped he didn't look too much like a hood and scare the kid. Maybe the kid would think he was someone down on his luck who needed wheels. The kid had asked to be paid in cash, and that was just what Joe had intended to do.

Both he and the kid were happy with the transaction, and Joe doubted the kid would ever give him another thought. Possibly, the kid also had something to hide and would not want to discuss the transaction with anyone else.

Joe pulled into a parking lot a few blocks from the storage unit and walked the rest of the way through back alleys He carried what he needed in a backpack slung over his shoulder. He was dressed in an outfit similar to the one he had worn when he bought the car. He was sure there would not be anyone around at that hour, but why take a chance? He carried the inventory clipboard with him that he used when taking inventory for Max. If someone saw him and he was questioned, he was covered. The only problem was the time of night he was there. If necessary, he would say that the delivery time to the stores has changed and he needed to take inventory before the delivery trucks arrived early the next morning. He looked around carefully before opening the door to the unit but didn't see anyone except a drunk sitting with a bottle on the dock.

These guys are always hanging around, he thought. *Someone ought to do something about them.*

Joe needed to find the cartons that were specially marked by Jose. This was not a difficult task. Jose had done his job well at the plant in Bolivia. He supposed that Jose could be a potential problem, but he doubted it. He could easily solve the problem with a few threats if the problem arose.

Joe kind of patted himself on the back when he thought about how he had managed the switch. After seeing to it that some of the packets were diluted with sugar and cornstarch, he had had a currier deliver the packets to the company at the end of the day shift to be sure that only Jose would receive them. Jose's job had been simply to remove the packets from the coffee cans on the conveyer belt and replace with the ones Joe had delivered to him then pack them for shipment. Both the cartons and the cans were clearly marked with the numbers Joe had given Jose.

I should give this guy a little more money for a job well done. He needs it, and he deserves it. I don't think he will say anything to anyone. He will be too scared. He loves his family and takes threats against them seriously.

Joe carefully separated the cartons that needed to go to Kim Lee and labeled them. Next, he opened other cartons and removed a few drugs to show to Carlos to prove their purity. He put the packets in his backpack and carefully replaced the cans back in the cartons. He labeled these to go to legitimate retailers. The only problem he hadn't solved was how to get more of these drugs when he needed them to sell to Carlos.

I have to see to it that these cartons are not moved from the unit too early, he thought.

Joe walked back to his car without knowing he was being observed.

Chapter 37

Alex looked and acted like a typical dock worker hard on his luck. He was dressed in dark blue and constantly tugged on a bottle. No one paid attention to him or to the fact that the liquid in the bottle never went down. No one noticed what he was paying attention to. He appeared melancholy, and that was exactly how he was feeling.

He wished something would break soon. He had been away from his family too long. He had few opportunities to call and talk with them. He had missed all his kids' soccer games. He had missed school activities and parent conferences. His wife, Meg, he had to do everything on her own. She was finding it difficult to raise their three boys on her own. She was lonely and had been talking about moving to New England, where she could be close to her parents. She did not actually ask for a separation but insisted that their three boys needed a father figure. Her father could fill that role.

Although she had not mentioned the words *separation* or *divorce*, just thinking of the words put Alex in a state of panic. He loved his wife and boys more than anyone could imagine. He couldn't bear the thought of losing them.

The hell with this undercover cop shit, he thought. *When this gig is over, I'm going back to being a regular cop on the beat. Yea, I'll have to be on duty some nights and weekends, even some holidays, but I'll be home most nights. I want to go to my kids' ballgames, school activities, and parent conferences. I want to sleep with my beautiful wife at night.*

He felt a twinge in his groin when he thought of that.

I owe this gig to my parents. That bastard, Max Bertolini, fed Bart the drugs that killed him. He didn't even know what was happening to him. He didn't drink and had never experimented with drugs. I need to avenge his death, but I need to get the job done soon. I can't lose my family for anyone.

Alex had been on the dock for hours and was about ready to call it a night when he saw movement at Max's storage unit.

What is that sleaze bag doing here? he thought as he saw Joe walk up to the unit carrying a clipboard. *Did he really think his clothes and glasses would be a disguise so no one would recognize him?*

He saw Joe look around before he unlocked the door, but knew he hadn't paid any attention to him. He was in the unit close to an hour then came out with nothing but the clipboard he went in with.

That's strange, Alex thought. *What was he doing? If he's stealing from Max, he is in trouble. I'm sure there are drugs in there, but I have not been able to get in there to find proof.*

Alex followed Joe back to his car then called Bill, who was on patrol that night from a pay phone. He gave a description of the car and what he could see of the license number.

Bill called back a few minutes later.

"I checked the license number, but it belongs to some college kid. When I called the parents, they told me the kid had sold the car to some middle-aged guy before going to school. He is at college on the West Coast, so he wasn't driving the car. I guess Joe never registered the car in his name. He probably didn't plan on keeping it long. Anyway, I didn't see anything helpful. He drove straight home. I don't think he will go out again. He closed and locked the garage. The lights have gone out in his house. He's in for the night. I'm going home to get some sleep. You had better do the same."

"Yea, like I can do that."

"Sorry, poor choice of words. Get some rest wherever you are hanging out."

Alex hung up without answering.

Chapter 38

The next few weeks after the open house were very busy at school, so it was easy for Laura to avoid Tim and any situation that would end in a discussion about any outing he might be planning.

Benjii talked constantly about Tim and Marcy. She wanted to see them again soon. Laura was able to appease her by saying that they would see them again soon.

November came quickly, and it was time for the first quarterly reports to parents and for the necessary conferences. Most students were given written reports to take home for parents to sign and return. But time was provided for conferences with parents of students who were experiencing academic or behavioral difficulties.

The conferences Laura participated in at her school were quite revealing. The first meeting was with the mother of a student Laura did not have in her classes. Tom Cook was a boy of average intelligence but was receiving failing grades because he did not complete assignments. Apparently the teachers on her team did not make an effort to see that each student handed in all required work. They simply gave zeros for work not completed.

Tom's mother, Pat Cook, was a large woman with graying hair. Laura though she had probably been attractive when she was younger but know she looked tired and older than her years.

Mrs. Lewis started the discussion by listing a number of assignments that Tom had not completed. The zeros he received for these assignments resulted in a failing grade.

Each teacher on the turn spoke in turn, each listing overdue assignments resulting in failing grades.

"I don't know what to do." Mrs. Cook was visibly upset. "I ask Tom about his assignments every day, and he assures me that they are completed. "

"What would you like us to do to help?" Laura asked.

Mrs. Hunt, the social studies teacher, broke in and said coldly, "I don't believe we need to do more than we are doing now. We have Tom write his assignments in his assignment book, and we give him afternoon appointments, but he does not return for these appointments."

"He has a paper route right after school," Mrs. Cook stated. "If he does not pick up the papers by three o'clock and deliver them in a timely fashion, he will lose his route.

"He spends that money on things I cannot afford and puts half of it in a savings account for college."

"His schoolwork should be a priority," Mrs. Hunt countered.

"Also, you need to sit down with Tom every evening and help him with his assignments."

"I am a single mother and work two jobs to make ends meet. I don't get home from work until after six. I have to cook dinner, drive my children to Scouts and team practices, do household chores. I would like very much to sit down with all my children and help with schoolwork. The reality is that it is just impossible for me to do so."

"Well, Mrs. Cook, I don't know how much more we can do to help," Mrs. Sims replied. "Somehow you need to make your children's schoolwork a priority."

Mrs. Cook rose and said, "Thank you for your time. I'll do my best."

It was obvious she was close to tears. Laura followed her from the room.

"Mrs. Cook, she said, "I am the special education teacher on this team. I don't work with Tom, but I know him. He is in some of the classes I attend with my students. There may be a way I can help you. He can come to my room for small group study periods. That way I can keep him focused on his assignments and can monitor whether or not they have been completed. I also have a few students who come into my room early in the morning for help with assignments. He is welcome to join that group. I just need to write him a pass to come into the building early. Why don't you talk to him and see if he is interested in having those extra study times then get back to me."

"I will talk to him. He gets upset about his assignments. I think he will appreciate any extra assistance he can receive."

Then Mrs. Cook said something that puzzled Laura.

"You seem nicer than I thought you would be," she said.

She doesn't even know me, Laura thought.

When she returned to the room, she could see the teachers were waiting for an explanation for why she left the room with Mrs. Cook.

"Mrs. Cook and I discussed a plan to help Tom that I think will be workable. I will give him a pass that will allow him to come to my room before school starts. That will give him time to complete assignments. He will also come to my room for help during the period 7 study period instead of going into a large group study."

"That class must be getting pretty large," Mrs. Hunt noted disdainfully.

"It is, but it is manageable."

"We don't appreciate you using that time to work with students. It is a free period, and if you spend that time working with students, it reflects negatively on the rest of us."

"I don't think that is true. These kids really need that study time, and I am willing to give it to them. I am able to complete my work after I put Benjii to bed."

Mrs. Lewis spoke up. "What we don't appreciate, Laura, is the fact that you did not include us in this planning. The decision to provide Tom with extra study time was made outside this room between just you and the parent. It should have been a team decision."

"You are right, of course. But the discussion was moving away from team assistance to parent responsibility. I guess I acted impulsively when I saw that Mrs. Cook was upset. I don't regret my actions."

"Well, the rest of us do. Someone in your position should be more careful."

What on earth did she mean when she said "Someone in my position"? Laura asked herself later when recalling the conversation.

Chapter 39

Laura was surprised when she received a notice to attend a conference with Benjii's teachers. She assumed that conferences at the elementary school were planned on an as needed basis as they were at the middle school. She checked Benjii's schoolwork work on a regular basis and knew she was doing very well academically. She was sure there were no behavioral problems. She would have been notified earlier if that were the case.

She was surprised to see four people sitting around the conference table when she entered the room. Sitting at the table were the teacher, Ms. Colson, the school principal, school secretary, and the guidance counselor. Laura had met the teacher and principal on the first day of school. She had never met the counselor but had seen him at meetings before the school year began. Mrs. Price was taking notes.

"Well, this looks like a committee meeting," she stated, trying to hide her nervousness.

"Good afternoon, Ms. McKenzie," Mrs. Ashton said. "You know Ms. Colson and Mrs. Price, of course, but I don't believe you have met our guidance counselor, Mr. Jacobs. Mr. Jacobs, this is Ms. McKenzie."

Bob Jacobs was trying not to notice how cute Laura was. He noticed there was no ring on her left hand. He was recently divorced and noticed all attractive women, considering dating in the future.

Laura did not register his dark good looks. She was wondering why he was at the conference.

"Good morning, Mr. Jacobs."

Laura turned to Benjii's teacher, Ms. Colson. She's very young and appears nervous, Laura thought.

"I was surprised to be called for a conference. I believe that Benjii has adjusted well to school. I believed she was doing well academically, socially, and behaviorally. Is there a problem I am not aware of?"

"There are certainly no academic or behavior problems. The problems are more social."

"I am surprised to hear that. She constantly talks about her friends here. I realize she needs more contact with other children outside of school, but as I explained earlier, we are new here, and I have not had the opportunity to meet the parents of her classmates."

Bob Jacob broke into the conversation, "We are not talking about those kinds of issues, Ms. McKenzie. We are concerned about the fact that Benjii does not seem to have any family ties. Extended family is very important to children this age. Children need to know about their heritage, grandparents, aunts, and uncles who love them, someone that they can trust to care for them if something should happen to their parents."

Laura was furious. She knew this was an inappropriate fishing expedition.

"Is this conference about Benjii's school performance, or is it an attempt to gain more information about our personal life? If there are no concerns about Benjii's school performance academically, socially, or behaviorally, this meeting is over, and I must excuse myself."

Laura could feel all four pairs of eyes follow her as she exited the room.

Why this fishing expedition? she wondered. Does someone at the school know or suspect her secret? What about the confusing comments made by Mrs. Cook and the team of teachers she works with. And what about the innuendos from Dodie Mcintire?

Surely, no one from either her or Benjii's school could have written the message that was on the chalkboard in her classroom the first day of school.

Oh lord, this is all I need, Laura thought as she spotted Dodie standing near her car. *How does he know where I am?*

"Hey, Ms. M. How you doing?"

"I am doing fine, Dodie. What are you doing here at the elementary school?"

"Just taking a shortcut home."

Laura did not know the area well enough to know if this was true, but she doubted it. She knew Dodie was stalking her, but she didn't know why. She was becoming very nervous about his attention.

I may need help, she thought. *Maybe Tim can advise me.*

She felt a warm glow when she thought of Tim.

I wish I could do something about him, she thought.

Chapter 40

Shortly after the conference day, Tim brought up the subject of the upcoming holidays. He was in the habit of walking Laura to her car as they left each afternoon. He broached the subject of Thanksgiving as they walked to the parking lot.

"Are you going away for Thanksgiving?" he asked.

"No, we are staying home."

"You are not going to visit family?"

"We have no family."

"No parents, grandparents, siblings?"

"My parents and sister all died a few years ago. I still can't talk about it."

"What about Benjii's dad's family?"

"There is no one. Look, Tim, I can't talk about the past. Can we drop the subject?"

"Yes, we can. I believe you must have a sad story to tell about your past. You must have a heavy burden to bear. Maybe someday you will trust me enough to tell me about it. I think I would like to build a serious relationship with you, but there has to be trust first."

"I would like that too. But I doubt I will ever be able to build a future with anyone."

"It is not good for you and especially Benjii to be so isolated from others. She needs to have friends her own age."

"I know how to take care of Benjii and myself. I have been doing it for over five years," Laura said testily.

"We'll talk about Thanksgiving later," Tim said as he walked to his car. He had a sense this was not a good time to talk about getting together for the holiday.

A few days later, again on the way to their cars after school, Tim broached the subject of Thanksgiving again.

"Why don't you and Benjii go out to dinner with Marcy and me for Thanksgiving," he said. "I know a little place that will serve turkey with all the fixings family style. The food is usually great, and I think I can still get reservations."

"I have a better idea. Why don't you and Marcy come to my house for Thanksgiving. I would rather do that than go out. Benjii would love to have you over, and so would I."

"Great idea. What can I bring?"

"Nothing, I guess. I bought a turkey when they were on sale a while back and have already baked pies and put them in the freezer."

"I should do something. I make a mean sweet potato casserole."

"That would be great."

"It seems I should do more."

"You will." Laura said with a smirk. "You can help clean up after dinner."

Tim smiled and scratched his head as Laura drove away. The thought of spending time with Laura and Benjii over the holidays brought him a great deal of pleasure. He knew Marcy would be pleased too. She really liked both of them.

As he walked to his car, he noticed Dodie Mcintire watching Laura's car as she drove away.

Something is going on there, he thought. *I better keep an eye on him.*

Chapter 41

At first Sue did not recognize the scruffy man who loomed in her doorway. He was dirty and smelled of perspiration. His T-shirt was stretched out and misshapen. His Levi's were torn at the knees, and his boots were covered with dirt and grime.

Sue had had to go to the office this Thanksgiving morning to check the holiday schedule. One of the officers scheduled to work in the morning had been injured the day before. She had to be sure the holiday shifts were covered while at the same time giving the men time to spend the holiday with their families. The wives of the officers were good about planning the big meal around their husband's shifts.

"What are you doing for dinner today, Alex?"

Sue knew Alex and his wife were having problems. His wife, Meg, was having difficulty dealing with the fact that Alex had to be away from home 24-7 when he was working undercover, leaving her to raise their three boys alone. This happened to a lot to cops. Sue knew Alex was the best undercover cop she had, and she needed him to work on the Max Bertolini case right now. She hoped it would be resolved before too much damage was done to Alex's marriage.

"Meg asked me over to dinner," he said, grinning. "I think she has decided having me home part of the time is better than no time at all."

"I hope it works out for you." Sue knew Alex was devastated by the possibility of a separation. "You better clean up and shower before you go home."

"Yea, if I do, Meg might let me stay the night. It's been along separation, but I have been faithful to her."

"My biggest problem is explaining my disappearance to the guys on the docks. I'm supposed to be homeless. Most of the guys on the dock will be at the mission for dinner. They will wonder where I am."

"Be careful. If they find out who you are, it could put both you and your family at risk."

"I know. That's one of Meg's hang-ups. She is afraid that my job puts the kids in danger. She was thinking of moving back to New England with her parents. Of course, I don't want her to go, and the kids don't want to go. They want to stay at their school and with their friends."

"They probably don't want to be separated from their dad either."

"Well, I've got to go and buy some clothes and a razor then find a place to shower and shave. I can't have Meg and the boys seeing me like this."

"You can go to my house," Sue offered. I'll give you my key and let my husband know you might be there in case he gets home before you leave."

"Gee, thanks. I appreciate you doing this for me."

"Why not? We're all working together toward the same goal. We all want to get Max Bertolini and the other drug lords. Only you are sacrificing a lot more that than the rest of us. I owe you."

"Yea, well, thanks, Sue. Maybe it'll all work out."

Alex arrived at his house around noon. When the boys saw him, six-year-old Terry and nine-year-old Rick went wild. They jumped into his arms and allowed him to smother them with kisses. Meg and thirteen-year-old Ryan were more reserved. Ryan considered himself to be too old for this behavior but still wanted to feel his father's arms around him. After a few minutes, Alex put Rick and Terry down and went to Ryan.

He crushed him to his chest in a big bear hug. Ryan did not pull away.

Meg had gone to the kitchen under the pretense of checking on dinner. She didn't want the boys to see the tears in her eyes. When Alex came into the kitchen, she allowed him to briefly hold her and kiss her, then she gently pulled away.

"Thanks for inviting me to dinner," Alex said.

"This is where you belong, Alex. I knew how happy it would make the boys to see you. But they will be terribly sad when you leave. I have explained to them that this separation has nothing to do with them, that it is your job, but they still miss you terribly, and I just don't know how long I can live this way."

"Do you miss me too?"

"I do, but I think I might leave this house and this town for a while. Having you gone so much is very difficult for all of us."

"It is just as difficult for me. I try to find a way to sneak home once in a while, but it seems to be impossible."

"I realize that, but the boys have to keep trying to explain to their friends why you are never home. We just can't continue to live this way."

"It's really none of their friends' business how we live our lives or where I am. Anyway if you leave, where will you go? Have you found someone else?"

"Of course not. Have you?"

"I will never love or want anyone but you, Meg."

"To answer your question, I may go to New England to be with my parents for a while. They have a large house and have enough room for us. The kids love them, and I think the change would be good for them."

Alex had to leave the house right after dinner. He went to the family room, where the boys were watching football.

"I have to go now," he told the boys. "But I will try to get back later tonight."

The look of distrust in their eyes as he made that promise nearly killed him.

He went to the kitchen and put his arms around Meg.

"I better go for a while so no one will miss me. Can I stay the night when I return?"

"We'll deal with that when you return, which I seriously doubt."

As it worked out, Meg's words would resound in his ears. When he arrived back at the docks, he was met with looks of suspicion and questions about where he had been.

Big Mac had the most questions. Mac was a dock worker who was 6' 1" and 200 pounds. He was not someone Alex wanted to tangle with.

"Hey, Lucky, where ya been? We didn't see you at the mission for dinner."

"Yea," said Jug, a smaller man but no less dangerous. "Didn't you want a turkey dinner? Don't you know it's Thanksgiving Day?"

"Sometimes we have appetites for something other than food."

"Yea, well, we know Rosie gave the girls the day off, so you weren't there."

"Sometimes," Alex said, "the doors are open for special customers."

Everyone knew that Jo, one of Rosie's girls, had an eye for Alex. They often met at the house for poker games with a guy or two occasionally absent from the table while pursuing other activities. No one questioned where those guys were.

So far Alex had been able to elude Jo's advances, saying he had another girl in town. He intended to stay faithful to Meg and certainly didn't want to take a chance getting something he could pass on to her when he returned home for good. Right now though, he hoped the dockhands would believe he had been with Jo.

They dropped the subject.

"There's a game down at Al's saloon tonight. You game?" Jug asked.

Alex groaned.

So much for getting back home tonight, he thought.

He knew he didn't dare disappear again.

Forgive me, Meg, boys, he thought.

"Sure, let's go. I can't wait to take your money."

Chapter 42

Johnny Cane had been a drug addict ever since he was in high school nearly ten years ago. He knew what kind of buzz he should have had after ingesting the drugs he bought from his supplier. He knew the supplier worked for Kim Lee. Kim Lee usually had good stuff he got from Max Bertolini, but this batch was shit. Max should know better than to try to stiff Johnny Cane.

"Hey, kid," he said the next time he met with his supplier, "you owe me $250. You can pay it in cash or merchandise, I don't care which."

"What the hell for?"

"I only got half a buzz from the stuff you sold me the other day. The stuff was shit. I'm only going to pay half this time."

"I can't let you do that. Kim Lee would take it out of my hide."

Johnny knew that was true. He didn't want the kid to get hurt. He was just a child already doped up at age thirteen.

"I know that kid. I'm gonna buy my stuff from somewhere else. Johnny walked away."

When Sammy met with Kim Lee to give him the money from his sales, he was petrified. He knew Kim Lee would not be happy with the take.

"This is not a very good take," he told Sammy. Sammy was one of his best suppliers. "What's going on?"

"I know, Mr. Lee." Sammy was shaking." The guys won't buy the stuff. They are saying it is no good. Johnny Cane wanted to pay only half the price today, so I wouldn't sell him anything. He said he was going to buy from someone else."

"You made the right decision, kid. If we start selling cheap, they will expect it all the time. Go home. I will try to get to the bottom of this. You still got the phone I gave you?"

"Yeah."

"I'll call you when I need you again."

Sammy left Kim's office relieved to still be alive and in one piece. Kim Lee picked up the phone.

Max paled when he saw the phone number on his cell phone. The number meant trouble. It was a number that would be used just one time and was used only in dire circumstances. When the call ended, the phone would be destroyed. Max couldn't imagine what was wrong.

He answered his phone.

"Hey, Kim, what's up?" Max tried to sound nonchalant. "We got a situation."

"What situation?"

"I been getting complaints about the stuff you been sending me."

"What kind of complaints? My stuff is first rate."

"Right now your stuff is shit. I think it's got sugar or something mixed in it. My clients are complaining. They want their money back, and they are threatening to buy from other dealers. My reputation is getting ruined. I'm gonna take it out of your hide."

"That's shit, Kim. I told you my stuff is top grade."

"You better check your stuff and then get back to me. You may live a few more days."

Max hung up and, with shaking hands, called Joe.

"We got a real problem. I just got a call from Kim Lee. He says his customers are complaining, saying our stuff is mixed with sugar or something."

"That can't be." Joe was glad that Max could not see the smile on his face.

"Someone's screwing us, Joe. It's probably someone in Bolivia, but we need to be sure. We need to check the stuff we got in right now."

Joe smiled. He knew that everything at the unit right now was pure. That might not be true later, but it was right now.

"I'll meet you there in an hour."

When Max and Joe got to the unit, two of Kim's thugs were already there. They couldn't imagine how they got there or how Kim Lee knew where the stuff was stored.

"What the hell are you doing here? This is a legitimate business. Having you around is going to give me a bad rep."

"Kim told us to stay on top of what you are doing. That's what we are going to do."

"Well, get inside where you won't be seen. We are taking inventory."

Max gave Joe a meaningful look warning him that none of the coffee cartons that held drugs would be checked at that time.

They went through the motions of checking the numbers on the cartons and recording just how many units of coffee, fruit, and nuts they had on hand. They labeled some cartons with the mailing addresses of the retail stores where they would be sent. Some cartons had fake addresses, but there was no way Kim's men would know that.

When their work was completed, they ordered the thugs out and returned to Max's office.

Max quickly jotted down a note and showed it to Joe.

"We may be bugged," the note said. "Our conversation needs to be about the legitimate cartons of coffee, fruit, and nuts that will be sent to legal specialty shops. We need to stay away from the unit for a couple of days. We better put the move on hold."

Thank you, Kim Lee, Joe thought.

Kim Lee was furious when his men returned to the office and told him that they had not discovered any useful information.

"What do you mean you couldn't find out anything? Why didn't you break open some of the cartons?

"You told us to follow Max and see what he was doing. That is just what we did."

"You idiots. Do you think Max and his right-hand man take their own inventory? They got help to do that. Why did you let them see you? What did you think they would do with you there?"

"Pete stayed to see what they would do after we left. Max thought he left with us. A mail truck pulled up to pick up the inventory they had checked. It was all shipped to legitimate specialty stores. No drugs left the premises."

They did not notice that one carton had a fake address. The post office would soon return it as undeliverable.

"Keep following Max and Joe Boccia. See what they are up to."

Max suspected he was being followed, so he went to his office each morning then went home and stayed there. When he felt safe again, he would visit Kim Lee with a proposal he hoped would save his life.

His problem was that a new shipment was on its way right now. He hadn't told either Joe or Lenny about it. He didn't know who he could trust.

Chapter 43

Max was scared. He couldn't trust anyone. Someone was screwing with his merchandise, putting him in a very dangerous position. He doesn't really think Joe has anything to do with it, but there was something in Joe's voice he didn't like the last time he spoke with him. Then there was the call from Carlos. He was surprised that Joe had contacted Carlos about selling drugs. Joe has drugs to sell; he is having trouble with the quality of his drugs. Max does not believe in coincidences. Max knows he has to team up with Kim Lee in order to find out what is going on. He doesn't have the resources for surveillance; Kim Lee does. Who does he have to have watched? Joe certainly. But who else? Probably Lenny Butler. But what about Jake Turner and Ruth Carter? Ruth Carter has access to his home but not to his business. How much does Jake Turner know? Max walked into the strip joint owned by Kim Lee. Kim Lee and two of his lieutenants were sitting at a table. Max began to sweat.

"Hey, Max, sit down, have a drink. To what do I owe this pleasure?"

Kim Lee was smiling. But his voice carried a threat.

"No thanks, no drink. We have to discuss our problem."

"You have a problem, I don't."

"Well, my problem is causing problems for you."

"Yeah, but one of my guys here can solve that problem for me right now. Chico, show him."

Chico reached over and chopped Max in the neck. Max felt dizzy and lightheaded. The pain was almost unbearable, but he tried to keep his composure.

"Do that shit, Kim, and you will never recoup your losses."

"How the hell am I going to recoup the money anyway?"

"I'm going to give you that money in return for a favor."

"What favor?"

"I want to borrow a couple of your guys."

"What for?"

"I think someone is stealing my good stuff and replacing it with the crap you got. It's the only explanation I can come up with for the complaints you have been getting. As far as I know, the stuff I am importing is top grade. I need to find out what is going on."

"How many people have access to your operation?"

"Two, maybe four."

"Why maybe?"

"Joe Boccia and Lenny Butler have access to the merchandise. Joe hired someone to do another job for me. He might have got some information, and my housekeeper may have overheard something, but I really doubt that. I am very careful about what I say from my home phone. She doesn't have any access to by business."

"My losses were high. Ten grand a week for two months. You got that kind of money?"

"I'll pay it. I'll have the money transferred from my offshore account into your account today."

"Do that. When the money clears, we'll talk about using some of my men."

Max left without another word.

"What do you think Max is trying to pull?" Chico asked.

"I don't know. I don't think Max really knows what is going on. He's confused and scared. That could make him very dangerous. I'll give him a couple of guys to keep track of his people, but you and Jimmy do the real surveillance. I want you to watch Max and Joe Boccia."

Chico decided to follow Max and have Jimmy watch Joe. A couple of days later, Jimmy reported seeing Joe move cartons of coffee from one unit to one next door. He had no way of knowing that Joe had made other transfers at night several days earlier. He would return later to be sure Joe did not make other transfers. If Joe was not the culprit, whoever was would get the message after he made arrangements with Chico.

Chico was a good explosives man.

Chapter 44

Joe had contacted Big Jake about applying more pressure on Laura McKenzie. He was hoping to create pressure on Max to give him time before Max made a plan to solve the problem he was having with Kim Lee. He was hoping Laura would crack and do something that would get the police involved again in searching for her and the child.

I know just what to do, Jake thought as he hung up from talking with Joe. He dialed the phone.

Dodie picked up the phone in his bedroom, hoping his mom did not hear it ring. She had just pulled into the driveway and had not come into the house yet.

I should help her bring in that bag of groceries, he thought. *But I need to answer this phone call. The note said to be at the phone at this time to get orders for a special job he wants me to do. If I get some extra money, I can get my mom a Christmas present. I won't be able to spend too much, she will want to know where I got the money. If I get a small gift, I can tell her I got it from tips I usually get at Christmas time from people on my paper route.*

"Hey, kid," said the voice on the phone, "there's gonna be a couple of extra bills in your box tomorrow. One is a Christmas bonus." He chuckled. "The other is for something I want you to do for me. In one envelope there will be a picture of a doll you can get from Targets. Use the money to buy the doll. They will wrap it for you and put a tag on it. Put the words 'Barbara Jean from Dad' on the tag. Take it to Laura McKenzie's house on Christmas day, put it on the doorstep, ring the bell, then get the hell out of there. You don't want her to see you. Can you handle that?"

"Of course, but who is Barbara Jean?"

"Information is on a need-to-know basis, and you don't need to know."

The phone disconnected.

Chapter 45

Laura had asked Tim if Marcy could stay with Benjii while she went Christmas shopping. She wanted to make Christmas day a special day for her. It would be their first Christmas out of the shelter, and she was looking forward to being alone with Benjii on Christmas morning when she came downstairs to see what Santa had brought. She knew she could afford more gifts this year for Benjii, but at the same time she wanted her to understand the real meaning of Christmas. Laura had taken her to the mall to purchase gifts for Toys for Tots. Benjii had purchased them herself and placed them in the bin provided by the toy store. Laura had read the Christmas story to her several times at bedtime, and they would attend Christmas Eve services at the church down the street. They had invited Tim and Marcy over for Christmas dinner, and Benjii had helped select the gifts they would give them.

She was excited about giving the gifts to them.

Now Laura needed time to shop for Benjii. Tim had offered to drop Marcy off at Laura's and take Laura to the mall. He would leave her there while he had his car serviced at Sears in the same shopping center. That would give Laura time to do her own shopping. Then Tim wanted her to help select gifts for Marcy. Tim had planned it this way. Laura wanted to shop after Benjii was asleep so Benjii wouldn't wonder what was going on. That would put her in the parking lot alone late at night, and he wanted to prevent that, especially on a Friday night.

They had to park a ways away from the mall entrance, so Tim walked her to the door. On impulse, he gave her a hug. He felt a twinge in his groin as he did this.

Boy, I gotta see to it that this doesn't happen, he thought.

Laura quickly hugged him back then quickly removed herself from his embrace.

Well, well, look at that, Dodie thought.

He was just leaving the mall after purchasing a gift for his mom. Tim saw him there.

I hope his being here is just a coincidence, he thought. *I think he might be stalking her, but I can't imagine why. I am going to have to monitor this situation.*

He did not tell Laura that he saw Dodie. He didn't want to spoil her fun.

Dodie was also giving the encounter some thought.

I think there is something going on between Mr. Atwood and Ms. McKenzie. I wonder if I should tell my benefactor. Maybe he will pay me extra.

Another pair of eyes was also watching this encounter. Tim and Laura had been followed from her apartment.

I don't like this, he thought. *This could cause problems.*

Tim and Laura had a wonderful time shopping for Benjii and Marcy. They bought several toys for Benjii, then carefully decided which ones Santa would bring and which ones would be from Laura.

"She will have gifts from Marcy and me too," Tim said. "Marcy and I had a lot of fun shopping for her the other night." Laura was glad that she and Benjii had selected gifts for Tim and Marcy when they shopped for Toys for Tots.

"What are you going to do for a tree? Tim asked as they were loading packages in his car.

"I haven't decided yet. I would like to get a real one, but I am not sure I can cope with buying it, getting it home, and putting it on a stand. I saw a pretty artificial one at Targets. I will probably buy that one. It should be pretty easy to put up."

"I have an idea. Why don't you buy a stand and some decorations tonight while we are here. Tomorrow the four of us can shop for a tree for both houses and set them up. We can decorate them together or alone at each house, whatever you prefer."

"We can let Marcy and Benjii decide that."

Laura did not know when she had felt so happy.

The next morning Tim and Marcy picked Laura and Benjii up at ten. As he drove to the apartment complex down the street, he saw Dodie again.

After the holidays, I need to discuss this with Laura, he thought *Right now I will just keep watch. I don't want to spoil Christmas for her.*

Tim had borrowed a truck with two sets of seats from a friend so there was room for the four of them to ride and room for the trees in the back. Dodie did not recognize them.

They drove to a local tree farm that was owned by a science teacher from their school. They wanted to support him in his efforts. When they got out of the truck and Laura, Benjii, and Marcy started down the path to look for a tree, Doug Stuart, the teacher/farm owner, put a hand on Tim's arm to hold him back.

"You got great taste in women, Tim," Doug said. "Laura's a looker and a sweet girl too."

"Don't get any ideas or spread any rumors, Doug. Laura and I are just friends and coworkers. There is nothing more between us. Also, Marcy babysits Benjii when Laura needs someone, which is really very seldom. I'm just helping her choose and set up a Christmas tree."

"Well, that's not the story your eyes tell when you look at each other," Doug said. "Lynn saw the two of you shopping at the mall last night. She said you looked like a couple of kids in love. She didn't want to disturb you, so she didn't speak to you. That's how cozy the two of you looked."

"Marcy stayed with Benjii while Laura did Christmas shopping for her. While she was at the mall, she helped me choose gifts for Marcy. If Lynn read more into our shopping than that, she is a hopeless romantic. If the two of you are interested in Laura' welfare, keep an eye on Dodie Mcintire around school. I think he is stalking her, and it makes me nervous."

"If he is stalking her, that would make me nervous too," said Doug. "But Dodie is harmless. He tries to put on a tough-guy image because he feels inferior to the more affluent guys at school. But

I don't think he would ever hurt anyone. Funny that you should mention him right now though. My son Denny works afternoons at the Sears store, and he mentioned that he has seen Dodie at the UPS store several times a month."

"What did he say he is doing there?"

"He doesn't know. He says he goes in with nothing in his hands and comes out again in a couple of minutes still with nothing in his hands."

"Hey, Dad, Marcy called, I think we found our trees."

That ended the conversation, leaving both men puzzled over what Dodie was doing.

The girls decided to decorate the trees together, first at Tim's house then at Laura's. After the tree was done at Tim's, Laura and Marcy made lunch at her apartment while Tim got that tree set up and the lights put on. Benjii was so excited she couldn't eat. When they were decorating the tree, they had all they could do to contain her enough so that they could keep her from dropping and breaking the decorations.

"Doing this two times is fun," she said. "But wouldn't it be easier if we all lived in the same house so we just needed to do it once?"

The other three knew Benjii did not understand the implications of her comment. And no one made a reply. Marcy noticed that Laura and her dad ignored the comment, so she did also.

"I think Benjii's comment about one house embarrassed you and dad," she said to Laura later. "But we do have a lot of fun together."

"Benjii is used to living with groups of people," Laura answered. "She doesn't understand the difference between the two situations."

Marcy dropped the subject.

Chapter 46

Benjii had gone to bed late after they returned home from the Christmas Eve Service. Tim and Marcy had not attended the service with them because Marcy had to be home to wait for the usual Christmas eve call from her mother. Still, Benjii was so excited on Christmas day that she was awake at five in the morning. Laura allowed her to have her stocking that Santa had stuffed and a doll that he had left under the tree then attempted to put her back to bed until a more decent hour. Benjii couldn't get back to sleep, so she and Laura had breakfast at six. After breakfast Laura allowed her to open the other gifts Santa had left. Other gifts would be opened later when Tim and Marcy arrived to have Christmas with them later in the day.

Laura was happy that Tim and Marcy had consented to come for dinner and spend the afternoon. Laura tried not to think about how this relationship between the four of them would eventually end. She was afraid they would all suffer some pain. She knew Tim wanted more from their relationship than she was able to give. Somehow, she had to stop this relationship from proceeding further. She could never tell anyone the truth about her and Benjii, and a serious relationship could not continue under a cloud of lies and falsehoods. Any steps she took would cause a lot of pain for the four of them. She knew she should never have allowed this closeness between the four of them to develop.

What was I thinking? she wondered.

Tim and Marcy arrived at Laura's house around one, and the four of had the delicious turkey dinner Laura had prepared. They decided to clean up from dinner then open gifts before dessert.

Benjii was so excited she could barely contain herself. Tim, Marcy, and Laura were all deeply amused by her antics.

I could get used to living like this, Tim thought.

They opened their gifts then had pie, coffee, and milk. Marcy had given Benjii the DVD *Rudolph, the Red-Nosed Reindeer*. And they decided to watch it together as a means of getting Benjii to settle down a little. Partway through the movie, the doorbell rang.

"I'll get it," Marcy said. "I've seen this movie several times, so I don't mind missing some of it."

"That's strange," she said when she returned. "There was no one at the door, but there was a package on the step. Someone must have dropped it off. There is no mail or UPS deliveries on Christmas day. It is probably for Benjii. It is a Target bag, so it may be a toy."

Laura was so happy and relaxed that she did not react quickly enough to worry about where the gift may have come from. Marcy helped Benjii open the box. Inside was a Raggedy Ann doll with a large note saying, "To Barbara Jean, From Dad."

I wonder what this as all about, Marcy questioned.

"Mama, isn't that the name that was written on our door the first day of school?" Benjii asked innocently.

Laura turned pale and felt dizzy and nauseous. She was shaking so hard that she had to sit back down. She was not able to speak. Tim ran to her and put her arm around her.

"Are you all right?"

"I'm fine."

She tried to sound calm as she spoke, but neither Tim nor Marcy had missed the severe reaction she had or the tremble in her voice.

"I think the store must have delivered this package to the wrong house," she told Benjii. "We will have to put it away and return it to the store so they can send it to the little girl it was intended for."

Benjii hesitated for a second but gave to doll to Laura without protest. Laura quickly put it on the top shelf of the hall closet.

"I don't think a store delivered this," Marcy said. "Department stores do not deliver packages, and if they did, someone would have stayed at the door instead of just leaving it."

"You are right," Tim said. "Stores do not deliver gifts to private homes."

He was thinking of seeing Dodie hanging around Laura so often. He couldn't help but wonder if there was a connection.

"Laura, what was Benjii talking about when she mentioned something written on your door?"

"Oh someone wrote the name Barbara Jean on our door. We saw it when we left the house the second day of school. I think someone had the wrong house, as they have today. Obviously someone has us mixed up with another family. Couldn't we forget about all of this please?"

"We can. But writing on a door and delivering a doll anonymously is not normal behavior. If there are more incidents, you should probably report it."

"Oh I will," Laura said, knowing that she never would.

It was obvious that Benjii was getting tired and that Laura was distracted, so Tim and Marcy decided to gather their gifts and leave for home earlier than planned. Laura did not protest. She refused to accept good-bye hugs from either Tim or Marcy.

"Dad," Marcy said as they were driving away from Laura's house, "something very strange is going on. Receiving that doll upset Laura more than she wanted us to realize. The incident turned her into a totally different person from what she had been earlier in the day. I think she knows who Barbara Jean is."

"I think so too."

"Do you think Benjii could be Barbara Jean?"

"I don't know, honey, but if she is, Laura has a lot of explaining to do."

Chapter 47

Tim and Laura's relationship was strained when they returned to school after the Christmas break. They kept their conversations to professional matters and did not discuss the events that occurred on Christmas day. The fact that Tim and Marcy has gone on a skiing trip during the vacation helped answer Benjii's questions about why they did not see them again during the holidays.

In mid-January it was time for grades to be issued and time for parent conferences. It was a busy time, and it helped Laura ignore Tim's coolness and the pain she was feeling.

Pat Cook again met with Laura and the team to discuss Tom's progress. When Laura entered the room for the meeting, she was surprised to discover that Pat had arrived and the conference had already started. Tim and Lynn Buckley, the foreign language teacher, walked in right after Laura.

"I am sorry if I am late," Laura said. "I hope I did not miss anything important."

"None of us are late," Tim said. "The meeting was called for ten fifteen. It is just ten after ten."

"You aren't late," Pat said evasively. "I arrived a little early. We are just chatting."

Laura caught a knowing look between the team of teachers. Pat seemed tense, and Laura suspected that she and the teachers had been doing more than just chatting but said nothing.

Pat then expressed her appreciation of Laura's work with Tom.

"His grades have improved from failing grades and Ds to Bs and a B-. I always knew he could get decent grades if he got his assignments completed. The time you give him, Laura, makes this possible. He thinks the world of you, and I greatly appreciate your efforts. How about going to high school with him next year?" she teased.

Laura was thrilled to see that Tim was flashing her a warm smile. *Maybe we can become friends again*, she thought.

The meeting was ending as Pat Cook left the room, so Laura walked out with her.

"I am pleased that Tom is doing so much better," she said. "I really appreciate your kind words during the meeting, but Tom is the one who deserves the praise. He has worked very hard."

As Pat exited the building, she turned around and said, "You are much nicer than I would have expected from what I have heard about you."

What on earth did she mean by that? Laura wondered.

The subject of Tom's progress came up again the next morning at the team's regular meeting.

"When did you say you met with Tom Cook?" Mrs. Hunt asked.

"He comes in and works on his assignments early in the morning and during my small group study during period 7."

"Why period 7? That is our free time."

"It is not free time, it is prep time. We are paid by taxpayers to work that period. I prefer to work with students. I can do my preparations after school and at home nights and weekends."

"You really do march to a different drummer, Laura," Mrs. Hunt replied. "I think someone in your position should be more careful."

"What do you mean my position? My position is no different than yours."

"Just give it some thought," she said as she left the room.

That afternoon, Tim resumed his habit of walking Laura to her car. Their conversation still remained strictly professional, but he hugged her briefly as he left her and walked quickly to his own car.

Dodie walked this exchange between Tim and Laura. He had not seen them together for a couple of weeks.

I guess he is going to start walking her to her car every day again, he thought. *That makes things tougher on me. I should have been bugging her lately, but I thought someone was watching when I left the doll. It was probably my imagination, but I need to be careful. I wonder if they have a thing going on or if she is afraid of me. She may have asked him to walk her to her car. I know she saw me hanging around yesterday, and this is the first time I have seen them together since school started up again. Maybe I'll have to go over to the kid's school. She is always alone when she goes there.*

Chapter 48

Alex was not able to get home again after his visit on Thanksgiving Day. Meg knew that her boys were devastated when he did not come home on Christmas Eve or Christmas day. They opened their gifts listlessly on Christmas morning. They wanted to wait until their dad arrived, but Meg knew that would not happen. She tried to make Christmas happy for them, but she could see the pain in their eyes.

"The tags on these gifts say from Mom and Dad," said thirteen-year-old Ryan. "But I don't think Dad even knows what is in the packages."

"Will Dad get any Christmas presents?" asked six-year-old Terry.

"We will keep them under the tree until he comes home," Meg answered.

"Yea, but they'll be pretty old by then," said Ryan.

The day after Christmas Meg called Sue and told her she was planning to move her family to her parents' house in New England in a couple of days.

"I don't know if you are in contact with Alex, but if you are, please let him know. I will leave my folks' phone number with you."

"Don't get discouraged, Meg," Sue said. "This may be over soon."

"I hope it is not too late by then," Meg said and hung up.

Meg did not know how long she would be in New England. She remembered how happy the boys had been when Alex was home for Thanksgiving. She didn't want to keep them from seeing their dad if the occasion arose. She knew the boys missed Alex terrible, and she did too, but none of them could take all the disappointments anymore. They were angry and upset when she told them that she had made the decision to enroll them in school in Mapleton.

"It doesn't mean that we can't go home if we want too, but I don't want you out of school for a long time."

Ryan was placed with Laura at the middle school. He did not have the learning or behavioral difficulties that her other students had, but he was sullen and refused to do his assignments. He wanted to go back home and be with his dad. He thought if he performed poorly at this new school, his mom would consider moving back to New Rochelle. He was a B+ student at his school there.

Whenever he mentioned New Rochelle, Laura was tempted to tell him she had lived there when she was young but was afraid to.

Rick and Terry were enrolled in the elementary school, and Terry was in the same classroom as Benjii. In her caring way, she took him under her wing, and they soon became good friends. Ms. Colson heard Terry tell Benjii that he had not seen his dad since Thanksgiving and that he missed him.

"I never had a dad," Benjii told him.

"How can that be? Everyone has a dad. Most kids see their dad every night. I used to, but I never see him now."

"I don't know why I don't have a dad. My mother never told me."

"Ask her," Terry said solemnly.

Ms. Colson wondered what she should do after hearing this exchange between Terry and Benjii. She didn't want to speak to Mrs. Ashton or Bob Jacobs. They might feel it was necessary to take steps that would create problems for Benjii and her mom. She didn't want to be responsible for anything that might happen.

I'll talk to Tammy Price, she thought. *We are becoming pretty good friends. Maybe she will be able to advise me.*

Chapter 49

Laura scheduled a meeting with Meg Hamilton and her team of teachers to discuss Ryan's transition to the school and to determine how to help him with transition issues.

"My husband is a policeman in New Rochelle Police Department," she explained. "For my safety and the safety of the children, he never discusses his assignments with me. Right now, however, I know he is working undercover. We do not hear from him for weeks at a time. He managed to spend a few hours with us on Thanksgiving Day, but we have not heard from him since he left that afternoon.

"The kids watch the door wistfully every time a car comes down the street and fight to see who will answer every time the phone rings in case it is their father. What they are going through right now is not good for them. For that reason, I have moved here to be with my parents for a while. They love the kids and spend a lot of quality time with them. Ryan wants to play basketball, and I think he is good enough to be on a team. I realize it is midseason, but I hope something can be worked out. I have a letter from his coach in New Rochelle explaining his skill level, which is very high. My father takes him to all the high school games, and we would all attend his games here if he were put on the team. His father would not be able to do that."

Laura was having all she could do to maintain her composure when she found out that Meg Hamilton's husband was a policeman in New Rochelle. She regained her composure enough to hear Tim answer Meg regarding her comments about basketball.

"I am the middle school basketball coach," he informed her. "I am sure he can be placed on the team. I have recognized that he is very talented when we play basketball in PE classes."

Laura felt a little tinge of jealousy when she saw the warm smile he gave Meg.

Meg is a very attractive woman, she thought.

"Ryan's father was a very good basketball player," Meg stated as she tried to hide the tears in her eyes.

Laura saw the tears.

I am going to put extra effort in helping Ryan, she thought. *Maybe I can help Meg in some way too.*

She felt another stab of jealousy when Tim covered Meg's hand warmly with his own and told her he would do all he could to help Ryan transition to his new situation.

"Maybe his grandfather and I together can help fill some of the void," he said.

Maybe Benjii and I will attend some of the basketball games, Laura thought.

At that point, Mrs. Hunt spoke up. "I don't mean to question what you are saying, but New Rochelle is not a large community, and I can't imagine crime there being so prevalent that it would require something as drastic as an undercover policeman."

"I believe there is someone in the community that imports drugs from South America and distributes them to other parts of the state," Meg replied. "As I said before, my husband does not discuss police business with me, but I overheard a conversation that led me to believe this. The person they suspect suffered a tragic loss several years ago, so the investigation was put on hold. I think they are renewing the investigation now."

Laura reached for her coffee mug, but her hand was shaking so badly that she could not pick it up. Only Tim seemed to notice. He watched her with questions in his eyes. He recalled her strong reaction when he told her he was originally from New Rochelle.

What the hell does she have to do with all of this? he wondered.

Mrs. Lewis, who often questioned parents' decisions about their children's education, showed her disapproval of Meg pulling up stakes and moving her children to a new community and school.

"I certainly hope you seriously considered the effect on your children before you made this move," she said.

"My children are not only my first but my only consideration when I make important decisions," Meg said coolly.

"I will do all I can for Ryan," Laura said. "I don't think he is lacking in any skills, but if I do recognize weaknesses, I will help him strengthen them."

"Laura thinks she can solve the problems of the world," Mrs. Denver said sarcastically.

I wish she could solve her own problems, whatever they may be, Tim thought.

Chapter 50

Joe was worried. He had expected events to slow down during the holidays, but they were over now, and still nothing was happening. There were too many things not going according to plan.

He had asked Jake to have his contact in Mapleton turn up the pressure on Laura McKenzie.

Jake told him about the Christmas doll delivery but said he had heard little from his contact since then. He had told Jake that one of the middle school teachers was watching him closely. He had to back off on his harassment of with Laura for a while.

Carlos had not committed to taking the merchandise. He wouldn't even accept a call from Joe.

Joe could offer the merchandise to another dealer, but that would take time, and it carried no guarantees. Joe didn't like keeping the stuff stored in his unit so close to Max's unit; it was too dangerous.

Max was also making things difficult. He was afraid of Kim Lee and wanted to move the stuff to a different location. He couldn't figure out why Max had insisted that both he and Joe be there when the last shipment of legitimate merchandise was sent to retailers. Joe was not sure if he would have access to the new shipments that came in. Max might keep the keys to the new facility to himself.

Right now, he doesn't trust anyone, Joe thought, *and for good reason.*

Lenny was at the unit the last time Joe went there to check the coffee cartons and got pretty nosy. He told Joe about the inspector who had been there several few weeks earlier.

Joe was surprised when the phone rang, and Max was on the other end of the call. He had not heard from him since they were met by Kim Lee's men the last time they were at the storage facility.

"We need to meet at the unit immediately."

"Why?"

"We couldn't do much last week with Kim Lee's men around. I need to open some of the packets to check the quality of the merchandise. I hate to, it will be a waste, but I gotta figure out what is going on. I can't believe what Kim Lee's telling me. I gotta check the shipments on a regular basis."

Joe could feel the sweat on his brow and under his arms.

I'm okay for today, he thought. *What's coming in next Friday is a different story. I'm gonna have to do something.*

An hour later, Joe met Max at the facility. They were not sure if they were being watched, so they carefully unpacked then prepared for shipping to retailer the nuts and fruit as well as the coffee. Max opened coffee cans at random and carefully tasted the powder in the moisture packets. All the samples were pure.

"Shit, I don't know what is going on," Max said. "I'll give these samples to Kim Lee to prove my stuff is good. I'll have to do this with every shipment that comes in. I think the next one is on Friday."

I can't let that happen, thought Joe. *Time to take drastic actions.*

Three men were unloading merchandise from the docks and storing it a few units down the complex from Max's unit. All three were watching carefully, not aware of the actions of the other two.

Chapter 51

Alex watched carefully as Joe and Max supervised the loading of the coffee shipment.

I wonder if Big Mac, Jug, and the others are suspicious, he thought. *It's unusual for guys in expensive suits to supervise the loading of a shipment of coffee, nuts, and fruit.*

I could try to drop one of the crates hard enough to break to see what is inside, but it would be just my luck to drop one of the decoys. I don't want to call attention to myself, so I better stay cool for a while.

I keep hearing them talk about something other than the shipment. I wish I could get closer and listen. All I've heard so far is the word cops, the woman, *and* the kid.

I wonder if that has anything to do with where the shipment will be sent. I also wonder why Boccia seems so tense.

"Hey, Lucky," Mac yelled, "stop dreaming and get to work. This stuff has to be loaded so the driver can get on the road."

Joe was also deep in thought.

Jesus, he thought, *I wish Max would get off the subject of the woman and the kid. Somebody might hear him. If he ever finds out what I've done, I'm done for.*

After the job was done, Alex dropped coins into the slot of the pay phone and dialed his in-laws house. He hoped Meg was home so he could talk with her. In this day of cell phones, and it was hard to find a pay phone, and it was getting harder and harder to get away from the guys on the docks.

The phone was picked up on the third ring.

"Hello, Mother Warner, is Meg home? It's Alex."

"She's helping the boys with their homework. I'll see if she wants to come to the phone."

Alex could hear the chill in his mother-in-law's voice.

"Hello, Alex." Meg's voice sounded formal. It was not the voice of a woman excited to hear from a husband she hadn't seen for several weeks.

"Hi, babe, I miss you. How are the boys?"

"They are fine. They have adjusted well to their new schools. Rick and Terry are doing well at the elementary school. Terry has developed a friendship with a little girl in kindergarten. She has taken him under her wing. It has helped him to adjust. She told him the other day that she never had a father, and he worries about that. I think it makes him miss you less. He knows he will see you again sometime. And he knows he has someone who loves him. Rick has also made new friends and seems happy."

"What about Ryan?"

"He is playing basketball at the middle school. His coach, Tim Atwood, is working hard with him to help him learn the plays so he can be an integral part of the team. Dad goes to all his practices then brings him home.

"Mr. Atwood is divorced and just has a sixteen-year-old daughter, so he seems to have extra time to work with Ryan."

"Divorced, huh? Just see to it that he doesn't try to spend extra time with Ryan's mother as well. Be sure he knows you are married."

"Don't be foolish, Alex. Dad is always there at practices, and the whole family goes to the games together."

"How's his schoolwork?"

"He's doing okay. He has a teacher named Laura McKenzie who makes sure he completes his assignments. By the way, just to ease your mind, if you saw the way Tim Atwood looks at Laura McKenzie, you would know you don't have anything to worry about."

"The boys seem to be doing okay. How about you?"

"I'm doing okay. I've got a part-time job at the town clerk's office, so I keep busy. It helps me be less lonely."

Alex was happy to hear she was lonely but made no comment.

"Well, babe, I'm out of change, so I have to ring off. I love you all and miss you very much."

"Why don't you call collect next time? Then the boys could talk to you too. They will be disappointed to miss you."

"I am not sure your parents would accept a collect call from me."

"I'll tell them to. The boys love you and miss you, Alex."

Well, thought Alex, *she didn't say just that she loves and misses me, but I am glad to hear as much as I did.*

"I think this job will over soon, and I'll be able to come home to stay."

"I hope so, Alex."

The phone clicked.

Where have I heard the name Laura McKenzie before? Alex wondered.

Chapter 52

Joe took steps to be sure his movements were not being detected. He took his car to the dealer to be serviced and took a cab home. It would appear that he was currently without transportation.

People will think I am not going out again tonight.

He had dinner delivered and watched TV until after the eleven o'clock news then went up to the master bedroom. He left the lights on for a few minutes then shut them off.

At one in the morning, he stumbled in the dark to a bedroom closet where he had hidden a woman's hooded coat, gloves, and shoes he had purchased months before at a yard sale. He knew he would need a disguise someday. After donning the outfit, he slipped out the patio door and walked up the street away from his house and toward an all-night bar and restaurant where he had left the car he had bought from the college kid several weeks back. There were always cars in the parking lot, and he hoped it had not been noticed and towed away. The license plates were stolen, and the car had never been registered, so there was no way it could be traced to him. Luckily, the car was right where he had left it. He got in the car and started his drive to Mapleton.

I'm glad I checked the town out earlier, he thought. *I know the best routes out if I have to leave in a hurry. I also know where I can park and get out of these woman's clothes. It sure is uncomfortable wearing them over my own clothes. I was smart to bring a plastic bag. I can put the clothes for the disguise into one of the bins I saw while in town before. They will never be able to be traced back to me.*

Later that afternoon, Joe watched outside the Edwards Elementary School. He knew there was no chance of snatching the kid from outside.

The teachers watch the kids too closely. I'll have to bluff my way inside. The ID I carry says my name is John McKenzie, a retired cop from Utica. I'll say I am the kid's grandfather and that the mother asked me to pick the child up because she has a meeting that will run late. It's a good plan. It should work.

After identifying himself and being buzzed into the school, Joe approached Tammy Price as she sat at her desk. He flashed his ID again and stated that he was there to pick up Benjii McKenzie.

"We don't allow children to be picked up by anyone but a parent without a note or a phone call," she advised him.

"My daughter said she would call. I guess she has not had time to do that yet. I'll just wait."

Joe knew he was taking a chance stating that.

"Our phones have been very busy," Tammy said. "Perhaps she hasn't been able to get through."

Joe decided it was time to get out of there.

"I'll skip across the street and see if I can find my daughter," he said. "Then I will be back with a note or have her call you."

Tammy thought about Laura's and Benjii's strange background.

Must be Laura and her father had a falling out and have since reconciled, she thought. *He has proper ID. I think it is okay for Benjii to go with him. She will be thrilled.*

Tammy thought about the things Amy Colson told her about Benjii and Terry Hamilton. It is so sad that Benjii tells everyone she has no dad or family. A grandparent is an approved person to pick up a child. He is probably not on the emergency form because he lives so far away. I'll double-check his ID.

"Please forgive me, but I would like to check your ID again."

"No problem. I am glad you are so careful. I feel that my grand-child is safe here."

Boy, am I good, Joe thought.

"By the way, would you like to see a picture of the three of us? It was taken at the playground here in town."

When Tammy was thinking about this later on, she knew she should have remembered that Laura stated that she and Benjii had no family. But she was completely taken in by Joe's polite demeanor.

Joe had had the foresight to take a picture of Laura and Benjii at the playground and was able to digitally superimpose his picture with the original. After scanning it through his printer and having it copied at the camera shop, it appeared to be genuine. On the back he had written "Dad and Benjii, 2008" in what appeared to be Laura's handwriting. He had taken some letters Laura had written to Lana and practiced copying her handwriting. He had carefully prepared for any difficulty that might arise when he made his plans to take Max's business.

Tammy looked at the picture and had no doubt that this gentleman was Benjii's grandfather.

"Mr. McKenzie, we don't have to bother your daughter if she is in a meeting. I'll call down to the after-school program and have someone bring Benjii to the office."

Terry had talked to Benjii often about his grandparents, how good they were to him and his brothers and how much he loved them. She wished she had grandparents. Terry did not believe her when she said he had no grandparents. "Everyone has a dad and has grandparents," he had told her.

"Maybe they live far away. Maybe you just have not met them yet." This seemed logical to two five-year-olds.

Therefore Benjii was thrilled when Mrs. Price called down and asked if someone could bring Benjii to the office. She was to be picked up by her grandfather.

"Told you so," said Terry.

The phone rang just as the teacher's aide brought Benjii to the office, so Tammy didn't pay attention to the exchange between Joe and Benjii. She waved to them absently as they left the office then the building.

Joe tried to be gentle with Benjii.

The last thing I need is to have this kid scream that she doesn't know me, he thought.

"Hello, Benjii," he said. "Your mom asked me to pick you up and bring you to her later. She has a meeting that is going to run very late today."

Benjii wondered why her mom had not told her about her grandfather and that she would be late today. She knew lots of times her mother did not want to answer questions about family, but she always told her if there was going to be a change in their schedule. Her grandpa seemed nice, and Mrs. Price said it was okay to go with him, so she did not question further. Terry had told her that grandparents were kind and loving, so she took Joe's hand and walked quietly to the car with him.

Joe was surprised the kid was so docile. She did not protest at all when she was told she would be leaving school with her grandfather. She even took is hand.

This kid is in for a surprise, he thought.

She did protest a little when he put her into the back of his car and started to buckle the seat belt.

"I can't ride in a car without a booster seat," she said. "It is not safe, and it is the law."

"I don't have a booster seat right now. We will get one later. You will be safe in the backseat, and I will drive very carefully."

Benjii was satisfied and was asleep before they had driven very long.

The booster seat is a minor detail, but I have to be more careful to pay attention to small details, or I will be in trouble, Joe thought.

Joe's part-time housekeeper had agreed to care for Benjii. She had no idea why he would have a small child to care for what he told her would be just a couple of days, but he offered her a substantial salary, and she needed the money to pay for medical bills that have accumulated since her husband has been so ill. She did not ask any questions. She also did not question why he rented an apartment for them instead of having them stay as his comfortable home.

The little girl seemed happy enough when Joe brought her into the tiny apartment but did look a little bewildered.

"Will my mom be picking me up here?" she asked.

He couldn't believe his eyes.

Boy, this guy's got balls, he thought. *He walked right into the school and took the kid. He noted the address of the apartment that Joe and Benjii went into. She won't be there long.*

Chapter 53

Tammy Price was surprised to see Laura walk through the door at three fifteen. It was only a few minutes later than usual.

"Hi, Laura," Tammy said. "I guess your meeting was not late after all."

"What made you think I had a meeting?"

"Benjii's grandfather told me that you had a late meeting, and that was why he was picking Benjii up from the after-school program."

"What are you talking about? Benjii does not have a grandfather. I have told you repeatedly that we do not have family. Just where is Benjii?" Laura asked, her voice shaking.

"Benjii's grandfather, John McKenzie from Utica, picked her up a few minutes ago. You just missed him. He said you called him and asked him get Benjii for you because you had a late meeting."

"Well, I did no such thing. I am going down to the after-school program and get her now."

"She is not down there. I told you she is with her grandfather."

Laura sank to her knees, shaking. She turned pale and felt dizzy, willing herself not to be sick.

"What are you telling me?" she screamed.

Lila Ashton came out of her office to see what all the commotion was about.

"What is going on?"

"Laura is upset because I allowed Benjii's grandfather to pick her up from the after-school program. He said Laura called him and asked him to get Benjii and bring her to her because she had a late meeting. I know this is the day for faculty meetings at the middle school, and he had ID, so I did not question his request. I let Benjii leave with him."

Laura willed herself to be calm enough to speak.

"How could you do that? You have all pried to my private life enough to know Benjii and I have no family. How could you possibly believe this man, whoever he may be, could be Benjii's grandfather?"

Laura hated to have anyone see her out of control, but when the enormity of what has just happened finally sunk in, she put her head in her hands, screamed, and sobbed uncontrollably.

"Tammy, we will discuss what you have done at a later time. Right now I want you to call Bob Cochoran and ask him to come to school immediately. No other child is to be picked up without my approval."

She spoke to Tammy quietly. She did not want Laura to be more upset than she already was. Also, she did not want to think that a child had been abducted from her school.

That stupid woman, she thought as she looked at Tammy. *I am going to have to fire her.*

Lila took Laura's arm and guided her into her office.

"Laura, come into my office. Maybe a cup of coffee will help," she said kindly.

Laura did not want coffee, she doubted it would stay down, but she was happy to be out of the limelight.

Teachers and other staff member had come into the hallway outside of the office when they heard her scream and cry.

Dodie had come to the parking lot outside of Benjii's school. He could not approach her at the middle school because Tim was always with her. His contact was putting him under pressure to continue his harassment of Laura. He had hoped to catch her before she went inside to get the kid. He didn't want to scare the kid. He was going to ask her if she was there to pick up her daughter and use his fingers to make imaginary quotes around the word *daughter*. He knew it would upset her. He did not know the truth, but he did not believe Benjii was really her daughter and neither did the man who called him to hassle her.

He was surprised to see Benjii leave school with a middle-aged man but was not concerned because Benjii was holding the man's hand and was smiling. He decided to hang around a while longer in case Laura still showed up. There were several parents in the parking lot, waiting to get their children, when he saw Laura enter the school, so he did not attempt to approach her.

I'll wait until she comes out, he thought. *She won't have the kid. She just left with the man.*

He was waiting near the entrance to the school when he heard a scream.

That sounds like Mrs. McKenzie, he thought.

He went into the school just far enough to look into the hallway outside the office. Laura was down on her knees, sobbing. There were several people around her. Then he froze in his tracks, suddenly realizing what must have happened.

I hope this doesn't have anything to do with the guy I'm working for. He said no one would get hurt. I hope he didn't take the kid. Dodie was feeling sick himself. She needs a friend. *I wish I could get in touch with Mr. Atwood. They seem pretty close.* Then self-preservation kicked in. *I gotta get out of here.*

Tammy had called Bob Cochoran at Lila's request, and he had arrived in minutes. He met with Laura, Tammy, and Lila in Lila's office away from the eyes and ears of the school staff gathered outside in the hallway.

"What is the problem?"

"I don't think there really is a problem," Tammy said, hoping against hope that she was right. "We have all sensed from the time Benjii was first enrolled in our school that Laura was estranged from her family. I think she overreacted when I told her that Benjii's grandfather picked her up from school today. He had proper ID, a picture of the three of them, and verbal permission to get Benjii."

"Mrs. Price," Lila said, using the formality to let Tammy and everyone else know how angry she was with her, "you know the rules. No one is allowed to pick up a child without written or verbal permission."

"He had verbal permission. Laura called him."

"We need to have that verbal permission, Mrs. Price, not the person coming in."

Laura was listening to the exchange as if it had nothing to do with her. Shock was settling in, and she could not speak.

"Mrs. McKenzie," Bob said kindly, "did you ever give your father permission to pick Benjii up from school?"

"My father died several years ago."

"Your father-in-law then?"

"I don't have a father-in-law. I never did."

"Why are you lying, Laura. Mr. McKenzie showed me a picture of the three of you in the park. You wrote a message on the back of the picture."

"That is impossible." Laura sobbed.

"Did Benjii go with him willingly?"

"I think so. The phone rang just as the aide brought Benjii in, so I didn't really pay attention when they left. That is how secure I felt. She certainly did not put up a fuss. When they left, I think she was holding his hand. He's a cop, for heaven's sake. He certainly is not a pedophile."

Everyone gasped at that term, and Laura began to sob violently again.

"We need to find out more about this John McKenzie from Utica. I will go out and call their police department from my car."

When he returned, his expression was very somber. The police department in Utica never had a cop named John McKenzie.

Laura fainted.

"Mrs. Price," Lila said, "you need to go home now and take a few days off. You have made a significant error that has put one of our students in grave danger. I will talk to the superintendent and school board about your future here."

"Just a minute, Lila. I have to speak with Tammy before she goes home. I need to get a description of the man and any other information about this incident that she may remember."

"Do it at the police station. I don't want people to see your car here any longer. Parents will get very anxious. I need to talk with the superintendent and devise a letter to go home to parents to explain what has happened."

Dodie was very worried about Laura. He decided to go to the high school to see if Tim Atwood's car was there. He knew Tim often went to the high school to pick up his daughter up if she had cheering practice or some other after-school activity. Once he saw Tim's car in the parking lot, he decided his next step. He went to a pay phone.

Jill Dixon was just putting her coat on, getting ready to leave, when the phone rang.

"Oh darn, I'll never get out of here," she said to herself as she went to answer the ring.

"Mapleton High School."

Dodie did his best to disguise his voice.

"Listen carefully," he said. "I am only going to say this once. I think Marcy Atwood's dad is with her in the gym. Find him and tell him to go to the elementary school at once."

The phone clicked.

Jill Dixon thought the phone call was a prank and was going to ignore it.

Oh well, she thought, *I have to go by the gym on the way to my car, so I might as well see if Tim is here and tell him about the strange call.*

Timing was perfect. Jill met Tim and Marcy in the corridor outside the gym.

"Hi, Tim and Marcy," she said. "You don't have a child at the elementary school, do you, Tim?"

"No, Marcy is my only child."

"That is what I thought, but a strange call just came in to the office for you. I think it was a prank, but as long as I saw you, I thought I should tell you about it."

She related what had happened.

"I am sorry to bother you with this, Tim. I am sure it was a prank. Well, good night."

She got in her car and drove off.

Tim and Marcy immediately thought of Benjii, but Tim did not want to say anything to Jill Dixon.

"We better get to the elementary school," he told Marcy.

When they arrived at the school, Bob and Tammy were just leaving the school.

"What are you doing here, Tim?"

"I got a call that I was needed here."

Tim decided not to relate the nature of the call to the chief.

"You got no business here, and I am ordering you to leave."

"I am not sure you can do that," Tim said evenly. "This is a public building, and friends of mine are in that building. I intend to go in and see them."

"I'm telling you to leave."

"Will you arrest me if I don't? Will you also arrest my daughter because she is going into the building with me?"

"I guess I could arrest you for disobeying an officer, Tim, but I don't want to do that."

"Then Marcy and I are going inside. We need to see Laura and Benjii McKenzie."

They walked past the chief and Tammy, taking care to be as polite as possible.

Bob made no move to stop them.

When they first entered the building, they wondered what they were doing there. The building seemed deserted, and of course, there was no one at Tammy's reception desk.

"Maybe we should leave, Dad," Marcy said.

"Before we do, look out the door to see if Laura's car is still there. I was so distracted by Bob that I didn't notice. By the way, Marcy, it is not usually a good idea to disobey a police officer."

"I know, Dad, but this is a special situation. I think we are both worried about Laura and Benjii."

"Something must be wrong somewhere or why the call?"

Marcy looked out the door and came back reporting that Laura's car was in fact still in the parking lot.

At that point, Lila Ashton and the nurse came out of Lila's office.

"Hello, Tim, can I help you?"

Tim decided not to be completely truthful.

"I received a call to come pick up Laura and—"

Tim did not have time to say Benjii's name.

"I'm glad you are here, Tim. We haven't been quite sure what to do. Laura must not go home alone right now. I'll get her."

Tim and Marcy exchanged puzzled looks but made no comment. They were shocked when they saw Laura come out of the office. She was pale and trembling, her eyes red and swollen from crying, her face mottled with purple splotches. As soon as she saw Tim, she rushed into his arms. She was still holding the cold washcloth the nurse had given her after she fainted.

How long have I waited to hold her like this, Tim thought. *But I didn't want it to be due to a difficult situation like this must be.*

Marcy watched with tears in her eyes.

"Laura, what is wrong? Let's get Benjii and get out of here. You can explain in the car."

"Benjii's gone," Laura whispered. "Someone took her."

Both Tim and Marcy gasped. Marcy started to cry then got herself under control.

I must not do this, she thought. *Laura needs Dad and I to be strong.*

But still, her heart was breaking. She had learned to love Benjii and had secret hopes that she would be her sister someday.

"Is that why Bob Cochoran was here?" he asked. "Is that why Tammy Price is with him?"

Laura nodded. "She released Benjii to a man who claimed to be her grandfather."

"Has anyone contacted her grandfather to see if he knows anything about this? Maybe he sent someone here to pick her up for him."

Laura shook her head.

"Benjii does not have a grandfather." She sobbed. "Bob said I must go home in case anyone calls. He will come over later. But why would they call? I have no money. Oh, Tim, we need to talk."

"Do you want Dad to drop me off at home first?" Marcy asked.

"No, the four of us have been like a family. You need to hear what I have to tell your father. You are old enough to understand what I have the say. It may be that neither of you will want to continue our relationship after our talk."

Chapter 54

When Laura, Tim, and Marcy arrived at Laura's house, Laura was too drained to think or to be sociable. She realized none of them had had dinner, but she knew she wouldn't be able to get anything down, much less keep it down. She was too tired to think about Tim and Marcy.

Marcy offered to make coffee and see what she could make to eat.

"I can make eggs or sandwiches while the coffee brews," she offered.

"Laura, I think you need something a little stronger than coffee," Tim said. "Do you have any wine or brandy?"

"There is some brandy in the top cupboard."

"I'll pour us some while Marcy rustles up something to eat."

"I will have the brandy, but I don't believe I can eat anything."

"You need to try. You will need your strength. This may be a long night."

Tim and Laura sipped on the brandy without speaking until Laura started to sob again.

"I keep thinking about Benjii. Is she safe? Is she scared? Will someone look after her, keep her warm, and feed her? Please, God, don't let that man hurt her!"

"I don't believe whoever has her will hurt her. Someone has an agenda. It is not a case of someone taking her for perverted reasons.

That type of person would not have entered the school and asked for a specific child. As far her being afraid goes, she probably believes this person is her grandfather and thinks this is a great adventure."

"I am not sure you are right, Tim. But it makes me feel a little better. Thanks."

"Okay, now we need to talk and see what we can figure out so we can get her back soon."

"I think I know who has her. But it is not the person who took her from school. I think she is with her father."

Marcy came in the room with a tray of milk, coffee, and sandwiches.

"But I thought—"

"Let me start from the beginning."

"My real name is not Laura McKenzie. It is Laura Mitchell. Benjii was christened Benjii Lynn McKenzie, and that is the name on her birth certificate, but that is not the name her parents gave her. The name they gave her was Barbara Jean, after my parents. My mother's name was Barbara, and my father's name was Gene. They died several years ago."

Tim and Marcy exchanged glances.

Laura continued with her entire story while Tim and Marcy listened carefully.

They all pretended to eat, but none of them could get food down.

When Laura finished her story, Tim sat quietly with no comment, but Marcy spoke decisively.

"Laura, this will not make any difference to us. Dad and I love you and Benjii a great deal. I love you, and my dad is in love with you."

"Marcy," said Tim, "this is not the time."

"Yes, it is. Laura needs to know how we feel and that she has our total support, doesn't she, Dad?"

"Of course, but we need to think how to handle this problem."

"In your eyes she did the right thing, and the only thing she could do to save Benjii. But in the eyes of the law, she is guilty of kidnapping and bank theft."

"I have more to tell you. I think someone knows or suspects the truth about Benjii and me. You already know about the writing on the door and the doll on Christmas day. One thing I never told you is that on the morning of the first day of school, I found the words 'Benjii is Barbara Jean' on the chalkboard in my classroom. I was so shocked I thought I would faint. I don't know how I got through the day."

Tim felt a new level of admiration for Laura.

"You did great," he said. "You were very professional and interested in all that was going on. As time as gone by, it is very obvious that you care a great deal about your students. You are professional and caring at the same time. That is one of the thing that has drawn me to you. You are very sweet as well as cute."

"I really have brown hair and am shorter than I look. I wear shoes that make me look taller, and I don't really need glasses."

"I like brown hair, short people, and people who do not wear glasses."

Laura began to sob again.

"None of this really makes a difference right now."

"Other things have gone on that makes me think someone knows about Benjii and me. Sometimes I think someone is watching us. Sometimes I think someone has been in the apartment."

Tim started. "What makes you think that?"

"Just little things. Sometimes I think someone has moved something in the house, things just that don't seem right. Nothing I can put my finger on."

That revelation obviously made Tim very uncomfortable.

"And there are things at school that I wonder about. I have always been very comfortable with you, but the other members of the team of teachers say things I don't understand. They say they I should be careful of what I do because of my position, and Mrs. Cook once said that she was surprised that I am as nice as I am because of what they know about me."

Laura burst into tears again.

"Can any of this have anything to do with Benjii's disappearance? Oh god, where is she? What is she going through right now?"

"I am afraid it probably does," Tim said, answering her first question. "I just don't know how. I am also concerned about Dodie Mcintire. It is not normal for students to hang around a teacher in the parking lot the way he does with you. I have also seen him in this neighborhood, and I don't like that. I think he is stalking you."

"He is constantly asking me about Benjii, how come I have a child when I'm not married, that sort of thing."

"We may need to have school officials look into the situation. There has to be a reason for his behavior. I don't know if it has any connection to Benjii's being gone, but every stone needs to be over-turned. Right now, we will do what Bob asked of us and wait here to see if someone tries to contact you."

Chapter 55

Tammy Price sat trembling in the chair in the chief s office at the police station.

"Bob, I don't want to be here. It looks like I am being arrested. It's embarrassing. I want to call my husband." Tammy began to cry.

"I have already had the dispatcher call your husband. He is on his way. Right now I need you to write down everything you can remember about what happened this afternoon. Don't leave anything out, no matter how insignificant it may seem. As you are writing, you may remember something you didn't recall before. I need a better description of the man who picked Benjii up from school."

"I don't know if I can give you a better description. I just didn't pay that much attention to him. I was satisfied once I saw the ID and the picture he showed me."

"Do the best you can. And write down everything you can recall about the picture. There is something strange about that situation. Where did the picture come from if Laura does not know the man?"

As Tammy was writing the things Bob asked her to, her husband, Cab, stormed in.

"What the hell is going on? What do you think you are doing, keeping my wife detained like a common criminal? Let her go at once. She has done nothing wrong."

Tammy ran into her husband's arms as soon as she saw him.

"A child was taken from our school this afternoon, and everyone is blaming me for it."

Cab glared at Bob. "Instead of picking on my wife, why don't you spend your time checking on the strange characters that have been hanging around town the last few months?"

"What do you mean 'strange characters'?"

"A big guy driving a semi was hanging around a day or two before school started. He went into the malt shop at the back of Carl's convenience and sat there for a long time. I thought it was someone the Mcintires knew because he left when Dodie left. I asked the kid about it the next time I saw him, but he didn't notice the guy and didn't know him. I just forgot about it. I have seen him around a few times since, but he minds his own business and seems harmless. And lately, I have seen a little Italian guy hanging around. Neither of these guys seem to be doing anything wrong. It is just unusual to see people like that is this town."

Bob handed Cab the paper Tammy had been writing on. He shook his head silently, warning her not to say anything.

"Here, read this," he said to Cab.

"Where did you get this? It describes the little Italian guy I told you I have seen hanging around lately."

"It is Tammy's description of the man who took Benjii McKenzie from school this afternoon."

"Christ," Cab said as he held Tammy closer.

"Thanks for your information, Cab," Bob said. "It could help Tammy. I have some phone calls to make. You two go home, but stay where I can reach you."

"I'll be either at the house or the store," Cab said.

"I guess I will just be at home since I lost my job."

Tammy cried. Cab put his arm around his wife, and they left the station.

Bob's first call was to Lila Ashton.

"Lila, we need to talk about the visit from Sue Patnode from the New Rochelle PD," Bob said over the phone.

Lila sighed. It had been a long and trying day, and she wanted to go home to her husband.

"What about the visit?"

"I don't think you were being completely honest with her when she showed you the picture of the woman and child she is searching for. I think you recognized that picture. I also think it may have had something to do with today's events. There is a little girl's life at stake, Lila. Don't put her in any more danger than she is already."

"Okay, the picture looked a little like Laura McKenzie, Bob. But the woman in the picture had long brown hair, did not wear glasses, and appeared to be shorter that Laura."

"Why didn't you tell Sue Patnode that?"

"Because I did not want to cause Laura any trouble. I don't believe for a minute that Laura kidnapped that little girl. They are very devoted to each other. I didn't want the child traumatized."

"Well, she may well be traumatized now."

Lila started to cry.

Bob then put a phone call into Sue Patnode at New Rochelle.

"Is this important?" Sue asked. "I am late picking up my kids at school. My husband has a coaches' meeting."

"It may or may not be," Bob admitted. "I am just wondering if an event that occurred this afternoon at the Edward Elementary School could be connected to the missing woman and child you came to see us about a few weeks ago."

"Let me make arrangements for my children to be picked up from school, and I will get right back to you."

Bob's phone rang ten minutes later.

"Okay, what have you got?"

"When you were at Edward's School a few weeks ago, asking about the missing woman and girl from your town six years ago, I didn't think Lila Ashton was being completely truthful with you. I didn't really have anything to go on except a hunch, so I let it go. This afternoon, someone saying he was her grandfather took one of our kindergarten students out of school. I'll fall short of calling it a kidnapping until I have more information, but the child's mother did not authorize anyone to pick the child up and is insistent that the child has no grandparents. Also, it appears that the man's identity was a fake."

"What does this have to do with my case?"

"Lila Ashton admitted to me that the woman in the picture you showed her resembled the mother of the little girl that was taken today."

"Oh my god. I wonder if it was her father who took her. If it was him, it is not a kidnapping. Why would he fake his ID?"

"I don't know. My guess is that it was not the father. The school secretary screwed up by letting the man come in and take the child. She should have checked with the mother first, but he was a smooth talker and convinced her he was legit. He did not claim to be the father. He said he was the grandfather."

"Grandfather? Both the maternal and paternal grandfathers are deceased if the child is who I think she is. What about the woman who claims to be the child's mother, is she a flight risk?"

"Flight risk?"

"If she is who I think she is, she took the child from the father. She is guilty of kidnapping, bank theft, and possibly other charges."

"Shit, I wouldn't want her to be arrested for anything. She is a good person, an excellent mother and teacher. She won't go anywhere without the child. She is very devoted to her."

"Well, just keep in mind she may be a felon. Keep your eye on her, and I will see what I can find out on this end."

Sue hung up without further comment.

Chapter 56

After speaking with Lila and Sue Patnode, Bob drove to Laura's house.

I hope she has calmed down, he thought. *I have a lot of questions, but I won't be able to get anything out of her if she is still out of it the way she was at the school. She couldn't even think straight.*

He was surprised when Marcy came to the door.

"What are you doing here? Ms. McKenzie needs some privacy. You need to leave."

"I am here with my father. He is with La…er…er…Ms. McKenzie."

"I need to see Ms. McKenzie."

He brushed past Marcy and followed the voices into the living room.

"Ms. McKenzie, we need to talk privately. You need to ask these people to leave."

"These people, as you call them, are my very close friends. In fact, they are the only friends and support system I have. They can hear anything you have to say."

Bob did not approve but did not argue. Ms. McKenzie we are in the process of putting out an AMBER alert for Benjii. We have her physical description from school, but would like you to tell us just what she was wearing in school today. We also need a description of her coat, hat, boots."

As soon as Laura gave Bob the information he asked for, he called the station to finalize the information to go out on the AMBER alert.

"I have a picture of Benjii in that outfit," Marcy said. "I gave it to her for Christmas and took her picture when she tried it on."

Bob felt a definite tension in the air when Christmas was mentioned but chose to ignore it.

Bob took the picture from Marcy then tried again to see Laura in private.

"I have a few more things to discuss with you. Perhaps we could move to another room for a few minutes."

"I told you that I have no secrets from these friends. I need them to help me get through whatever I will need to go through. What do you wish to discuss?"

"Have you had any recent contact with anyone who may not live in this town?"

"I do not know all of the people who live in Mapleton, just the people I connect with through my school or Benjii's school. If someone spoke to me, I would not know if they from here or somewhere else. However, I do know that I have not spoken with anyone except those connected to one of the schools. Why do you ask?"

"Mrs. Price stated that she was shown a picture of you, Benjii, and the man who picked her up."

"I have no idea how that could be. People can do almost anything with cameras these days."

Bob had to agree with her. "Mrs. Price gave us a description of the man who has Benjii. Her husband has seen a man who fits that description around town lately. Are you sure he has not tried to contact you?"

"As I told you a minute ago, I have had no contact with anyone except students, school personnel, and parents. All contact with parents have been at school with other staff members present if that is your next question."

"Cab Price also mentioned another man he has seen hanging around town lately. These two men probably have no connection with Benjii being missing. Cab tends to be overly concerned about things concerning the town."

Marcy gave Bob the picture of Benjii in the outfit she had been wearing in school. It would be used on the AMBER alert communication and on the posters the police department would be making up and posting. He excused himself and left the house.

I wonder what the hell is going on in there, he thought.

Chapter 57

Benjii did not like her grandparents. They were not at all like the ones Terry talked about, and she wanted to go home.

The place her grandfather took her to was not clean and comfortable like her home was, and her grandmother did not seem kind.

Wait until I see Terry, she thought. *Grandparents are not nice people. I don't think they like me. My grandmother did not hug me when she first met me. She just said hello and walked away.*

Her grandfather was okay at school, but since then he did not seem to want to have anything to do with her. She did not like the smoke in the room and did not like the smell of the stuff they were drinking.

"Can I go home now?" she asked her grandfather. "Is my mother coming to get me?"

"No, you will be staying here with us for a few days. We have missed being with you before this. We want to spend some time with you." Doris hoped she sounded convincing. "Hurry up and eat your Happy Meal. You can watch TV for a while before you go to bed."

"Mommy doesn't like me to watch TV. We play games and read stories after I have my bath."

"Well, we can skip the bath tonight, and we don't have any books or games. We can get some tomorrow."

"I have to have a bath so I can be clean for school tomorrow. Mommy always tells me that."

"You won't be going to school tomorrow."

"Why not?"

Benjii was close to tears. She knew if she went to school, her mother would be there to get her and bring her home.

"I have to go to school. It is my day for sharing. I'm going to bring the book Mommy is teaching me to read. I want to see my mommy," she added.

"You can do that another time, now don't cry."

Doris did not like playing grandmother to this little kid. She felt sorry for her. She was obviously scared and wanted to go home. She was doing this because she needed the money. Joe had promised that no harm would be done to the child. She would see to it that that was true. She was pretty frightened when Joe told he that the kid was Max Bertolini's daughter.

"I'm not fooling the kid a bit," she thought. But I will do my best to see that she is not too frightened."

Benjii was tired and went to bed with little argument. She asked to have a story read to her, and Doris promised they would read the next night. Benjii began to cry when she realized she would not be going home the next day. Doris sat with her and held her hand until she fell asleep.

Chapter 58

Marcy had spent the night with Laura. Tim had wanted her to stay with them, but she did not want to be away from home in case Benjii was returned or there was a phone call. Tim would not allow her to be alone. When Tim picked Marcy up for school, Laura told him she could not face going to school that day. "I think you do need some time off," he said. He couldn't imagine her trying to teach school that day. It was obvious that she had been crying, and he doubted she had slept at all.

After Tim and Marcy left, Laura called the school to tell them she would not be in for a few days. She had written contingency plans that would go for at least the rest of the week. Tim would take them to school for her. She did not know what would happen after that time. She fought tears when Donna, the school secretary, told her everyone was praying for her and asking what they could do for her. Mr. Knight, the principal, had told Donna to tell her she could take as much time as she needed. She had not missed a day of school so far. The team of teachers she worked with had not commented to Donna, but the other special education teachers and staff members at the school said that Laura was not to worry about her students. That they would see that they received the help they needed.

"There is an AMBER alert out," Laura told Donna. "The police department is making up posters with Benjii's picture as we speak. Perhaps some of the staff will help distribute them after school."

"I believe Tim Atwood is organizing a group of people to do just that. He seems pretty upset about all of this. You have become good friends, I believe."

"We have."

When Donna hung up, she turned to Mr. Knight.

"We are lucky to have a teacher like that at this school," she said. "With all she is going through, she actually sent in plans and a short profile of each student. I am sure she had the profiles written before all this took place but not the plans."

Carol Denver overheard this conversation but did not share it with anyone.

Laura did not let anyone know her plans for the day; no one would approve. She wasn't sure she did, but she had to find Benjii. She was sure Max had her or knew where she was. She just didn't know how he had found them or why he was doing this after six years. Did it have something to do with Meg Hamilton's husband's investigation?

The trip to New Rochelle would take five hours. She went to the bank and withdrew cash in case she needed to stay at a hotel. If she located Benjii and had her with her, she would not drive the long trip back home until morning. Or if she knew Benjii was safe at Max's house, she would not want to leave until she tried to get Max to let her take her back home with her. If she did not find Benjii, she would drive home. Tim would be looking for her.

Laura hardly remembered the five-hour trip. All she could think of was what she would find once she arrived at her destination. She couldn't imagine her feelings once she had answers. It would either be elation at finding her daughter or utter devastation if she did not find answers.

Ruth Carter was perplexed when she answered the door at Max's house. She wasn't sure who was standing there. The young woman resembled Laura Mitchell, but she did not want to make a mistake.

"Can I help you?"

Laura had to be careful not to disclose her true identity.

"My name is Laura McKenzie."

"What can I do for you? We don't respond to door to door solicitation. If you are requesting a donation to a charity, please do it through proper channels."

"I am not looking for a donation to a charity. I am looking for my daughter."

"Your daughter? How old is she?"

Ruth knew this woman was not old enough to be mother to any girl Max might bring home for the night.

"She is six years old and was taken from her elementary school yesterday afternoon. I believe she may be here at this house, and I want her back."

"What on earth makes you think she is here? There are nor have there ever been children here. There would be no reason to take a child and bring her to this house. It is owned and occupied by one middle-aged gentleman There is no woman who lives here to care for a child. I am just a housekeeper who works here through the day."

"You say there has never been a child here? I believe you are mistaken. I believe an infant lived here for a brief time over six years ago. I believe my daughter was mistaken for that infant, and that is why she was kidnapped from her school yesterday. I believe she was brought here."

"You are out of your mind."

"Is this the home of Max Bertolini?" Laura asked, knowing full well it was.

"It is."

"Then I want my daughter brought to me immediately." Laura felt herself go out of control and willed herself to stay calm.

Just then, Max came to the door.

"Young woman," he said, "I couldn't help but overhear your conversation with my housekeeper. You have her very upset, and your insinuations are crazy. You must leave now."

"Can I come in for a drink of water and a short rest? I have had a very long drive. Perhaps I could use your facilities."

Laura thought if she got inside the house and Benjii was there, they would somehow find each other.

"You may not. There are motels nearby that are for that purpose. You need to leave immediately."

Max gently pulled Mrs. Carter inside and firmly closed the door.

"Do you have any idea who that was?"

"She said her name was Laura McKenzie, that is all I know."

I believe I know who that was, she thought. *But I am not going to say anything to anyone right now.*

After Max closed the door, Laura had no alternative but to return to her car. She put her car into drive, trying to decide whether to check into a motel or start for home. She drove in the general direction of a motel she had spotted on the way to Max's house. She could stop there, or if she drove right by, she would soon be at the exit that would take her toward home. She did not have the opportunity to do either.

She suddenly became aware of blue lights flashing behind her. She pulled over to the right, expecting the police car to go by her. She was surprised when he stopped behind her and got out of his car. She rolled down her window a short way while at the same time checking that all her doors were locked.

"Is there a problem, Officer? I don't believe I was speeding."

"No, you were not. Could I see your license and registration please."

He took the papers to his car and apparently called in the information. When he returned to the car and handed her the license and registration, he asked her if the information on the documents was correct.

"Yes, it is."

"Please follow me."

"To where? I am headed home to New Hampshire, and I don't want to get a late start and drive at night. It is a five-hour drive."

"I am not sure you will be returning to New Hampshire tonight. Please follow me."

Laura followed the car but called Tim to tell him what was going on just in case this guy was not a legitimate policeman.

When Tim found out where Laura had been, she had to control his anger. He couldn't believe she would put herself in such danger.

"I don't want to discuss your trip with you at this moment. We will talk about it when you get home. Right now, we have to be sure you are safe. Stay on your phone until you have determined your destination. Do you have your doors locked?"

"Yes, and I believe we have reached our destination. We are at the New Rochelle Police Station. There are other people around, so

I believe I am safe. The officer who stopped me is waiting for me to park and get out of the car. I had better do that."

"Call me back when you know what's going on. And don't try to drive home tonight. It is supposed to rain, and the temperature is staying right around thirty-two degrees, so the roads may be icy later on."

"I won't. There is a motel nearby that has vacancy sign out and looks like a decent place. I'll stay there tonight. I'll call you when I am in a room."

She decided not to tell Tim the comment the police officer made about the choice being made for her.

"Is there any new news about Benjii?" she asked hopefully.

"No, you know I would call you if there was any news. The posters are out all over town, and the AMBER alert is being continued."

Laura got out of her car, locked the doors, and walked slowly toward the officer.

"I'm Officer La Bounty," he said. "I should have introduced myself earlier."

"I guess you know my name, but you have me at a disadvantage. I don't know why I am here. This is obviously a police station, but I can't imagine why you brought me here."

"All I know is that our chief of detectives, Sue Patnode, wants to talk to you. She asked me to direct you here."

"But you had no reason to stop me. I was not speeding, and all my lights are in working order. How did you choose me from all the other traffic?"

"I had a description of your car and your license plate number. I was just following orders."

"Let's go get this over with," Laura said.

Officer La Bounty held the door for Laura and then ushered her down a hallway toward Sue's office. The door was open, so he tapped lightly then stepped back to allow Laura to enter.

"Detective Patnode, this is Laura Mitchell. Ms. Mitchell, this is Detective Patnode."

"I think I can clear up this misunderstanding," Laura said immediately. "I am Laura McKenzie." She did not catch the look that passed between Sue and the officer.

"I believe Mitchell is correct, but let's leave that alone for a few minutes."

Laura was more than willing.

"Can you tell me why you are here in New Rochelle?"

"I came here to visit someone. I did not realize that was a crime in New Rochelle."

"Don't be smart. Who are you here to see?"

"I am here for personal reasons. I would prefer not to discuss those reasons with anyone at the present time. I can assure you I have not committed a crime and done nothing to warrant being arrested."

"You have not been arrested."

"Then I am free to leave? I am very tired and wish to check into a motel, get something to eat, then get some rest."

"You are free to leave, but could we talk for a moment first? Could I ask you a couple of questions?"

"You can ask. I may or may not answer."

"We knew you were in New Rochelle because Max Bertolini called and informed us. He wanted you picked up and questioned because he believes you kidnapped his infant daughter."

"That is ridiculous. You can see I have no child with me. I have no idea what you are talking about."

Sue was getting exasperated.

"Can we stop this cat-and-mouse game? You are Laura Mitchell, and you disappeared from Max Bertolini's house six years ago. His infant daughter disappeared at the same time. You took her. You are guilty of kidnapping and bank theft and are looking at serious jail time."

Laura tried to hide the fact that she was trembling. It took all she had in her to maintain her composure.

"Your officer checked my license and registration. I am also willing to show you my charge card and checks from my bank account. They all identify me as Laura McKenzie of Mapleton, New Hampshire."

"Yes, your IDs do say that is who you are. However, I believe they are bogus. Carrying false IDs could add to your jail time if some-one wanted to push the issue. However, at the present time, I cannot prove who you really are. You are free to go. Officer La Bounty will escort you to the motel of your choice."

"That is not necessary."

"Perhaps not, but it is going to happen."

Chapter 59

After resting at home for one day, Laura knew she had to return to New Rochelle. She was certain Benjii was at Max's house. If Joe Boccia took her, it must have been at Max's request. Joe would have to reason to keep her with him.

The visit the day before yesterday had been a disaster. She had learned nothing about Benjii's whereabouts, and now both Max and the police would be watching her. She didn't care. She had to get into Max's house somehow. She didn't tell anyone where she was going. She knew Tim would not approve.

When Laura arrived at Max's house, Ruth Carter answered the door again.

"What are you doing here?"

"I need to come inside."

"Well, you can't. After you left the other day, Max told me if you returned, I should call the police immediately. No way was I to allow you to enter the house."

"Then go inside and make that call."

When Ruth turned to go back into the house, Laura pushed her aside and went in herself. She had not been there for six years but remembered the layout of the house. She ran directly to the rooms that had been Lana's bedroom and the nursery. She believed that was where she would find her daughter. As she ran, she screamed Benjii's name. When she did not find Benjii in those rooms, she ran all through the house, calling the child's name. She went down to the basement and into the garage. She even looked into the windows of Max's cars. When she did not find Benjii, she fell to her knees on the lawn, sobbing.

While Laura was searching the house, Ruth had called the police. She was afraid to call Max. She was afraid of what he might do.

Just as Laura fell to the ground, Bill arrived. He put her in his car and drove her to the station.

An officer who had responded with him followed in Laura's car.

Sue brought the distraught woman into her office. She did not realize at that time that Laura had entered Max's house without permission from Ruth. Ruth's heart broke for Laura, and she did not want to cause her more problems than she already had. She simply told the police that she thought Laura needed medical attention. She had described Laura's actions to the police.

"What on earth were you thinking of running through that house, screaming like that?"

"I thought my daughter was there."

"Why?"

"Because for some reason Max Bertolini or one of his cronies has mistaken my daughter for Max's lost child. I know they have her somewhere. I need to find her. She must be terrified."

"There is something I am confused about. If you are not Laura Mitchell, how do you know so much about Max Bertolini and his business associates?"

Laura knew that question would come up sometime and had devised an answer.

"When Max's daughter disappeared, a friend of mine worked as a waitress at the country club he and his wife were members of. She used to tell me about Max and his beautiful young wife. When the wife passed away and the child disappeared, she sent me newspaper clippings of the story. She had also sent picture of a gala they had all attended. Joe Boccia was in one of the pictures. The man who took Benjii looks just like that man."

Sue wasn't sure she bought that story, but let it go for the time being.

Instead, she said, "Mrs. Carter has not contacted Max about your behaviors at the house, and she refuses to sign a complaint against you, so at this point I have no alternative but to let you go. However, I cannot let you get on the highways. I am going to have an officer drive you in your car to a motel. You need to stay there for the night. If you do attempt to drive, I will have you picked up. Have I made myself clear?"

Laura nodded. She knew she was too exhausted to drive the five hours home. When she was settled in her room at the motel, she called Tim. He had been frantically searching for her. She did not tell him everything that had happened that afternoon, just that she was in New Rochelle and would return the next morning. She hung up knowing that Tim was very upset about her return to New Rochelle. She would soon be very sorry that she had made the trip.

Chapter 60

Joe was surprised when Max called him and told him about Laura's second visit; he did not know about the first. He was as confused as Max as to why Laura thought he had Benjii. He was pretty sure no one would identify him as the kid's grandfather. No one really saw him except the airhead secretary. She going to be so upset about being blamed for a kidnapping on her watch that she won't be able to remember a thing.

He didn't know if Max thought he had taken the kid. He wondered why he had taken the kid in the first place. It was a stupid impulse designed to distract both Max and the NRPD from Max's business. They would be too involved trying to solve the kidnapping.

Well, maybe the cops, Joe thought, *but probably not Max. With all that was going on, Max would keep a tight rein on the events at the unit.*

The kid was asleep, so he told Doris he would return so she could go out and buy some clothes and books and games to keep the kid occupied. It wouldn't do to have him observed buying these things. Doris was upset when he called and told her he couldn't return after all. He told her he had some important things to tend to. The fact was he was afraid that Max was watching him and didn't dare leave his house.

"Joe, I need some time to shop. I promised the child I would get her some books and games. She needs a change of clothes. She does have a warm jacket that was in her backpack so she won't be cold, but all the clothes she has are the ones she had on yesterday. She is wearing an old T-shirt of mine to bed, but she will need a change of clothes when she wakes up."

"So put school clothes back on her. She'll be okay for a couple of days. Just make up some games to play with her."

"Then what?"

"I don't know yet."

They had no way of knowing that decisions were being made for them.

Chapter 61

It was easy enough to get the name of the man working for Max Bertolini at the storage unit. There are a lot of guys on the docks who are willing to give information for a twenty-dollar bill. He was surprised to learn that name and wondered if it meant anything to Joe Boccia.

Probably not, he concluded, *Joe would not have any way of knowing this man's history.* He followed the man home one day to get his address. A call to 411 provided the phone number. He knew he could get this guy to do what he wanted.

What luck, he thought.

Lenny Butler wasn't really a loser. He wasn't a winner either. He just drifted day by day, never accomplishing anything. He never married. He had all he could do to take care of himself. He didn't want to worry about a wife or, worse yet, kids.

He cringed at the thought of being a father. He never knew his but always felt his had somehow failed him and his mother. His mother always had a demeanor of being sad. As he grew older, he suspected it had something to do with his absent father. He never had brothers or sisters.

All the family he had at this point was a grandmother, and all he knew about her was that she lived in a home somewhere. He had a phone number for her but no address. He felt a little guilty about not visiting her but was afraid that if the facility she lived in knew she had a grandson, they would expect him to take some financial responsibility for her care, and that was impossible for him to do. So he ignored her. He just hoped she was well cared for and happy.

He liked his job with Max Bertolini. It paid pretty well, and he was never under any pressure.

Lately, Joe Boccia was doing a lot of his work. He was suspicious about Joe's motives, but it was really none of his business. It was okay with him. He worked fewer hours and still got paid the same.

Lenny had been surprised when his phone rang early one September morning. None of his friends were up this early on a Saturday. They were sleeping off the events of the night before.

"Hello."

"Lenny Butler?"

"Who wants to know?"

The caller ignored the question. "How would you like to earn ten grand?"

"Ten grand? Sorry, I'm not killing anybody."

"You don't have to. I just want to put you on retainer."

"On retainer? What the hell does that mean? What do I need to do?"

"I can't tell you yet. I don't really know myself. I have a situation I need to resolve. I may need help. I want someone I can call on at the last minute. Your job right now is simply to stay in the area, be available to answer the phone, and go to work at a moment's notice. Once you get the ten grand, you need to be that person."

"Get the money to me, then we can talk."

"No, it doesn't work that way. I'll send you five grand just to stay around and be available whenever I need you."

"How will I get the money?"

"I'll mail it. I have all the information I need to contact you. You just be sure you do your part. Don't think about taking the money and running off. If you do, I'll find you, and I know where to find you grandmother in that fancy facility."

"I'm not doing anything that might send me to jail."

Lenny ignored the threat against his grandmother. He knew he wasn't going anywhere.

"You don't have to worry about going to jail. Just stay around where I can reach you when I need to."

Lenny hung up. The man was smiling.

This is going to work out better than I thought, he said to himself.

Chapter 62

Lenny got the call he had been expecting early one morning.

"It's time for you to earn your ten grand."

"I thought I was already doing that."

"Well, this is the event I have been holding you for. You have to take a kid for me."

"Take a kid? I'm not kidnapping a kid. I may not be much, but I'm not the kind of guy that would hurt a kid. No way!"

"The kids already been kidnapped twice. You are not going to hurt her. You may be saving her. By the way, get a babysitter. You may need one for several days. You can't watch the kid because you need to live your life as usual so you won't be under suspicion."

"Why would anyone be suspicious of me? Besides, I have no way of getting a babysitter. I don't know anyone I can leave a kid with."

"Yes, you can. I know more about your background than you do. Go visit your grandmother before you get the kid. You'll get your answer."

Lenny felt guilty contacting his grandmother. He hadn't contacted her in several years. He didn't even remember to send birthday or Christmas cards. He couldn't fathom why the mysterious caller told him to see her. He decided to try to get this mystery cleared up.

His grandmother's voice was cold when he identified himself and said he wanted to visit her.

"What a surprise," she said sarcastically. She did, however, give him directions to the home she was living in.

Lenny was shocked when he arrived at his destination. All he ever had for his grandmother was a phone number and address. He had expected to find her in a county home. The complex she was living in was beautiful. It provided both private rooms and apartments for its residents. It had a library, pool, gym, hair salon, and dining room, everything a person could want. The receptionist directed Lenny to the gym, where his grandmother was taking part in a yoga class. She told him to wait in the library until she was ready to see him. When her class was over, she met Lenny in the library and took him to her apartment. It was a beautiful apartment.

"You are probably surprised to see me living in this beautiful facility," she said. "I am sure you believed I did not have money."

She held up her hand when he started to protest.

"You are my only grandchild, so I keep track of you. I know the kind of place you live in. It leaves a lot to be desired. You will never be hungry or homeless, but neither will you ever share any of my money, unless, of course, you prove yourself worthy. So far you have been lazy and shiftless. Your grandfather forbade me to give you or your mother any money until you proved yourself worthy. Your mother never did, and so far you haven't.

"Your grandfather and I were never wealthy, but we worked hard and saved. We paid insurance premiums every month so we would have money for our retirement and final expenses. Your grandfather always believed he would be the first to go because of the differences in our ages, and he was. He made sure I would have the money I needed to live comfortably after he was gone. There was enough money to allow me to live in this beautiful place. I miss your grandfather and mother terribly, but otherwise I am happy. I miss seeing you, but as I said before, I have always known you were okay even though I wish you had made better choices for yourself. Why are you here today after all these years?"

"I have a job to do for someone that I think is going to be hard. The person I am working for told me I need to understand my past and that if I did, it would help me do the job he has assigned to me. I have no idea what he is talking about. That is why I am here. What is there in my past that I need to know about?"

"I don't know who you are working for or what he knows, but there are some things you need to know. Your mother never wanted you to know about your parentage, so she always told you your father died. That is not true. Let me explain."

"Your grandfather was always a wonderful father to your mother but was furious when she had an affair with a married man."

She heard Lenny gasp at this revelation but went on.

"Outwardly, he refused to help your mother financially, but covertly he arranged to pay a large junk of her rent so the two of you would have a decent place to live. I am surprised that she never wondered how she could lease such a nice apartment for the small amount of rent she paid. She may have suspected her father was helping, but the subject was never discussed.

"She loved you very much and did her best to make a decent life for you, but she never got over her affair with this man. Your grandfather always suspected your mother continued to see this man. I knew that was not true, but your grandfather would not listen to reason. Her depression caused her to drink too much, eventually causing the kidney problems that finally took her life. I guess it is time you knew the name of your father. It is Joe Boccia."

"No, Grandmother, that cannot be. I work with a man named Joe Boccia. He is not old enough to be my father. He is close to my age."

"Is this man from New Rochelle?"

"Yeah."

"I always wondered what happened to the kid after he grew up. The man you know is your half brother. His father is the man who hurt your mother so terribly. He was despicable. Soon after he learned you were on your way, he took off. Not only did he leave you and your mother, he also left his wife and three young children, one a newborn girl. The little boy was three years old. The older girl was about thirteen months old. The poor woman was forced to put her two little girls up for adoption. She raised the little boy. I know he graduated from New Rochelle High School but don't know what happened to him after that. His mother died shortly after he graduated."

After hearing this story, Lenny left his grandmother, promising he would return to see her soon. They both knew he would not. He needed to know if he was really related to Joe Boccia.

Time to visit Jim Fallon.

Lenny rang the door of the apartment that Joe had just left. He had his .38 but didn't expect to have to use it.

Doris came to the door.

"Where's the kid?"

"Getting ready for bed."

"Well, get her dressed. She's going with me."

"Joe didn't tell me she was being moved."

"Well, he's got a lot on his mind. He probably forgot."

"Can I go with her? She'll probably be scared."

"No, you can't. Just give her this. It will make her sleep. I can't have a screaming kid on my hands."

"I had better stay with her so she won't be scared."

"I won't give her anything that will hurt her."

"It won't hurt her, it will just put her to sleep."

Doris made some hot cocoa and put the powder Lenny gave her into it then went to get Benjii.

"Benjii, I am going to have you put your clothes back on," Doris said.

"Why? Aren't I going to bed?"

Benjii didn't especially like Grandma Mitchell, but she was no longer afraid of her. She had taken good care of her, but she wished she could go home to her mother and back to school. However, she did what she was asked to do and got dressed again.

"A maintenance man came to the door and said they had to turn off the heat for a while. If you have your clothes on, I won't have to worry about you getting too cold. And drink this warm cocoa. It will keep you warm inside."

"I am not hungry or cold."

"No, but you may be later on. Please do as I ask. I will tell you a story."

While dressing, Benjii drank the cocoa then climbed back on the bed. Doris did not have books to read to her, but she told her stories as well as she could remember that her mother had read to her when she was little.

Benjii always liked these stories. She soon fell asleep. Lenny wrapped her in a blanket and put her in his car.

Doris had mixed feelings about seeing her go. She was glad to be relieved of her responsibility but feared for the child's safety.

Lenny knew the child would probably sleep through the night. It would give him time to arrange for her care. He laid her on a cot, covered her with a blanket, and went to the phone.

"Mr. Bertolini's residence."

"Ruth Carter?"

"Yes."

"I need a babysitter."

"I don't hire out as a babysitter. I have a job."

"You will this time."

"I don't think so."

"How will Max like it if he finds out you eavesdrop on his phone calls? He gets rid of people who know too much about his business."

"Your threats do not bother me at all. I am not afraid of you, whoever you are, or of Mr. Bertolini."

"Well, how about your sister and her kids. They are being watched right now."

"I don't have a sister." Ruth hoped he did not know about her family and was bluffing.

"Really? You make frequent calls to Pat Cook. She has a son in middle school, one in high school and a girl in college. I would hate to hurt them. I don't want my guys to hurt that little coed. A word from me and anything can happen."

Lenny knew this was all a lie, he wasn't into hurting women and kids, but Ruth didn't know that.

"What do you want me to do?"

"I'll give you an address. Get here as soon as you can. A little kid's safety is dependent upon you. Be prepared to stay for a while and be prepared for shock. I have a long story to tell you."

Ruth was glad Max was not home and not expected to return for several hours. It gave her time to put as many of her belongings into her car as possible. She did not know if she would ever return to Max's house. She had no idea what she was getting into. She was scared to death.

When Ruth arrived at the address given her, Ruth realized she was near a decrepit apartment building. She was met in the parking lot by a man she didn't know. She walked up to her car and indicated that she should roll down her window. She did just about an inch.

"This is not your final destination," he said.

Like Joe, Lenny was not keeping Benjii at his own apartment. He had been given an address by the man who hired him. Actually, the place where was Benjii was being kept was better than his own place.

"You need to park your car at the Dunkin' Donuts across the street and come with me."

"I am not going anywhere with you."

"Okay, I guess I don't blame you. I will not hurt you. I just don't want you to know where you are going. You can call me Lenny. Drive over to the Dunkin' Donuts, we can go in and have coffee, and I will explain everything to you. We must hurry, I left the child alone. I don't want her to be scared and let out a howl if she wakes up."

"How old is the child? How could you do such a thing?"

"She is about six years old. I had no choice."

Ruth could not think of a young child being left alone.

"Skip the coffee. I will follow you to wherever we are going."

"No, you must park your car and ride with me. I will blindfold you. I need to be sure you do not tell anyone where the child is until I am sure everything is okay."

"What about my car?"

"You need to give me the keys. I will bring it to where you will be staying, but I will keep the keys for a while. I will also need your cell phone if you have one."

Against her better judgement, Ruth parked her own car and got into Lenny's. She allowed him to blindfold her and gave him her cell phone. She felt she had no other choice. After about twenty minutes, Ruth felt the car stop. She knew they had driven around many streets because they kept stopping as if at a red light or stop sign. She believed they were not far from the Dunkin' Donuts but had no idea where they were. It seemed she was at a small house at the end of a long street.

"You will be comfortable here," Lenny said. "I will see to it that you and the child have everything you need. I hope you will not be here very long, but while you are here, you cannot communicate with anyone but me. There is no phone here, and you will not be able to use your car. I have the keys, and it will also be disabled."

"Why are you doing this?"

"I am being well paid. I am following the orders of an employer. I don't think he has any intentions of hurting you or the child. You do not need to be afraid."

"How did you find me? Why did you choose me for this task?"

"When I called you I told you to be prepared for a shock. Sit down. I have a long story to tell you. What do you remember about your early childhood?"

"I remember from the time I was about three and a half. Pat was thirteen months younger than me. We were adopted by Marion and Arthur Forbes. They told us our birth mother was a lovely lady who loved us very much but was not able to care for us. She wanted us to live in a loving home with parents that could provide for us, and we did."

"What did they tell you about your brothers?"

"We have no brothers."

"Yes, you do. You have two."

Ruth paled. "That is impossible. Our birth mother was not well enough to have more children. I believe she died fairly young. My adoptive mother could not have children of her own. That is why she adopted me and Pat."

"Hold on to your hat, Ruth. I have a lot to tell you. A couple of months ago I got a strange phone call. The caller told me I had better watch out for Joe Boccia, that he's got it in for me."

"Joe Boccia—" Ruth started to say.

Lenny held up his hand to silence her so he could continue to speak.

"I asked the caller why Joe Boccia would have it in for me. We work for the same guy but, other than that, have little or no contact. He knows I am no threat to his job. The guy told me to check my family history. I thought this was some kind of a prank, so I ignored it. I think the guy who called me then is the same one I am working for now. The voice sounds the same on the phone. He has made no attempt to disguise it any time he has called. When he told me to take the child, I told him I had no one to care for her. Again he said to check my family history, then I would know who to call. I thought I had better do it this time.

"I never knew who my father was, and my mother is dead, but I have a grandmother. I decided to pay her a visit. I felt guilty visiting her to get information. She has lived in the facility for about ten years, and I never once went to visit her, but I needed to get things cleared up."

Lenny related the story he had heard from his grandmother. He spoke slowly, giving Ruth time to process all he had to say. He could see that she was becoming more and more upset as he told her about her past family. She was soon trembling as if she were bitter cold.

When he was done speaking, she said haughtily, "You are crazy. You have no proof that any of this is true. And why should I believe you even have a grandmother who told you these lies?"

"I needed proof that this was true too. How do you think I found you? I have a friend who can hack into town and city documents. He found your birth records and your adoption papers. He also found my birth certificate as well as Joe's. You all had the same last names until you and Pat were adopted. I was given my mother's maiden name as my last name, but a Joe Boccia was listed as the father on my birth certificate. Do you have any idea how sick that made me?"

"About as sick as I am right now, I suspect. But how did you find me after all these years?"

"It was a simple matter to find marriage certificates. I know you married a man named Carl Carter and that you are a widow. I know your sister married a no-good bum named Roy Cook. He and Pat had three children, then he left for parts unknown, and Pat has been raising the three kids alone. I know their names, that one is in middle school, one in high school, and the girl is working her way through college."

"If you ever hurt one hair on their head, you will pay!"

"Relax, I never had any intention of hurting any of them. I just needed to scare you so you would meet me. Now here is more that you need to know. The kid I took was first taken by Joe Boccia."

Ruth gasped. She just could not believe all she was hearing.

"Why would Joe Boccia kidnap a kid? It is a dangerous thing to do. He has plenty of money, why would he take a chance?"

"I think the kid might be Max Bertolini's kid."

Ruth recalled the visit from the young woman who thought Max had her child.

I know why she seemed so familiar, Ruth thought. *It was Laura Mitchell. Could this child be Barbara Jean?*

She decided not to tell Lenny of this.

Lenny continued, "I have no way of really knowing who this kid is, but if she is Max's kid, she and her aunt may be in grave danger. I am asking you to help with the care of the child, but I don't want you to tell anyone about her right now, not even your sister. That is why I am not allowing you to have a phone and not allowing you to leave the house."

Ruth was sick over what she had just heard and was numb with fear but meekly nodded her consent. She had no intention of telling Lenny about her argument with Pat about Tom's teacher.

The following morning, Benjii woke up in a different bed and a different room.

She felt groggy and wondered where Grandma Mitchell was. She began to cry and called for her.

A different grandma came in.

"Hush, don't cry," she said. "There is no heat at Grandma Mitchell's house. So you need to stay here." Lenny had told her about taking Benjii. "You can call me Auntie."

"If I can't stay at Grandma Mitchell's house, why can't I go home?"

"Your mom can't take care of you right now. You need to stay here."

"Is she sick?"

"No, she is fine. She just has some business to tend to."

"When can I go home?"

"Soon, honey, I hope."

Chapter 63

The morning after Lenny took Benjii, Doris woke up feeling very groggy. She had been worried about Benjii and couldn't sleep. Partway through the night, she had taken a sleeping pill and was having a hard time getting rid of the effects of the medication. The sun was shining brightly, so she knew she had slept past 8:00 a.m. She made coffee and sat at the table thinking while she waited for it to brew.

I have got to do something to help that child, she thought. *I can't let anyone hurt her.*

She decided to make a phone call. After the call, she would thoroughly clean the place, being sure neither she nor Benjii left any fingerprints that could be discovered if there was an investigation.

Benjii was a very sharp little girl and knew the name of her school. A call to 411 did the rest.

"Mapleton Elementary School. How can I direct your call?" the temp who was filling in for Tammy Price answered the phone very formally. She was probably hoping the temporary job would turn into a permanent one.

"I would like to speak with the school principal." Doris had decided not to call the police. She knew the call could be traced if she was on the phone too long.

"May I ask what this is in reference to?"

"Tell her it is about Benjii McKenzie."

Lila Ashton came to the phone immediately. "How may I help you?"

"I called to tell you that Benjii McKenzie was taken from her school by a man named Joe Boccia. I have no idea why. I know Joe works for Max Bertolini, and Joe told me that Max is the child's biological father. Max never came to see the child, and I don't believe he knew Joe had her."

Lila realized that the caller was speaking in the past tense.

"All the time she was with me, Doris went on to say, she was safe. I kept her warm and fed, told her stories that I could remember from my childhood, and played games with her. She was scared and missed her mother but otherwise was okay.

"Last night, after Joe left, someone came to get her. I don't know who the person is or why he took the child. I wanted to go with her so she wouldn't be scared, but he would not let me. I fear for her safety."

"Where do you think the child is?"

"I don't know, but I believe she may still be in New Rochelle. You need to call the police."

"You should do that."

"No, I don't want to go the jail. All I did was accept pay to care for the child. I did the best I could, but she was not happy. She just wanted to go home to her mother and go to school. I can't imagine what she is going through now. You need to call the police. I need to get out of here."

Lila called the Mapleton Police Department.

"I need to speak to you Chief Cochoran immediately."

"May I ask who is calling?

"Tammy, is that you?"

"Yes, Bob's dispatcher is out for a few days. His wife is expecting a baby. I volunteered to sit in for him for a couple of days. It keeps me busy."

"I am glad, Tammy. Now let me speak with Bob."

Lila told Bob about the anonymous call she had just received.

"Do I have your permission to check with the phone company to get a record of this call?"

"You do."

"Some paperwork will have to be completed later to make this all legal, but right now time is of the essence, and we will have the recording of this phone call."

"I will notify my superintendent of what is happening, but I am sure there will be no problem."

After getting the phone number where the call originated and an address, Bob called Sue in New Rochelle.

Sue and Bill went immediately to the residence in question. They were met there by the landlord, who was visibly shaken by the police presence.

"The apartment was rented by a man from New Jersey. He wanted a six months lease. He said he would move his family into the apartment while they looked for a home to purchase. He paid three months in advance. He sounded very pleasant and professional over the phone. I had no reason to be suspicious of him."

"We understand that. You have no reason to worry, but I would like to have you hand over the keys to me and wait outside while we go in."

After opening the door, Bill and Sue went in carefully with guns drawn. They were surprised at what they found. There was nothing there except the furniture the landlord had told them would be there. The apartment was spotless. There were no clothes, no books or toys. There was nothing in the medicine cabinet and no food in the refrigerator. They called the landlord in to assess the furniture.

"This is crazy," he said. "I have had some good tenants that left the place clean when they left, but this place is sterile. I could rent it again without doing a thing. What does all this mean?"

"It means," she said, "that someone did not want us to find even a fingerprint to indicate that someone had been living here. I will send someone over to look for further evidence, but I can bet they won't find anything. I will let you know when you can rent it again. It should be soon."

Sue and Bill returned to the office, and she immediately called Bob Cochoran. After receiving the call from Sue, Bob went to Tim's house to talk to Laura.

When she saw him drive up, she immediately asked Tim and Marcy to come to the door with her. Tim was the one who opened the door.

"Laura here?'

"Yes, Bob, please come in."

They all gathered in the living room. Laura was shaking.

"I have some good news about Benjii," Bob started. "But there are also some complications regarding the information."

He went on to explain about the phone call and that it seemed that Benjii had been well cared for a few days.

"But where is she now?" Laura's voice quivered as she spoke.

"That's the part that is complicated."

Bob told Laura, Tim, and Marcy about Sue's visit to the apartment.

"We know she was in a clean, warm home with a woman who took excellent care of her. What we don't know is where she is right now."

Bob opted not to tell Laura that Benjii was removed from the apartment by a man and that the caller was worried about her safety.

Better to give her some peace of mind until we find out more, he thought.

After Bob left, Tim and Marcy tried to be positive about the information they had just received.

"You can be sure," Tim said, "that Benjii is not in the hands of anyone who will hurt her. Someone has her for different reasons."

"You are probably right," Laura tried to smile. *I need to get back to New Rochelle,* she thought.

Chapter 64

"Laura, I don't want you to drive to New Rochelle again. It is too long a trip and will do no good. You have been there two times with no results. I wish I could take you there, but I have coaching now as well as teaching. I can't be away from school right now."

"I am sorry, Tim. I know how much you worry about me, but it is different this time. We know Joe Boccia had Benjii. I want to meet Max face-to-face and get Joe's address from him. I want to talk with Joe even though he may no longer have Benjii. I am sure he knows where she is."

"Okay, call me when you arrive in New Rochelle and keep me informed about what you are doing. If you are tired, don't drive back home until tomorrow."

Tim left to go to school.

Around noon the next day, Laura drove into New Rochelle. She had burst into tears when she saw posters with Benjii's picture on nearly every telephone post and storefront when she left Mapleton. She knew the town was doing everything it could to help find Benjii.

However, she believed the only way to accomplish this goal was for her to meet face-to-face with Joe Boccia.

I needed to make this trip as much as I dreaded it, she thought.

When she got back to New Rochelle, she was exhausted from worrying about Benjii all night then five hours of driving. She knew she wouldn't be able to make the trip a second time that day, so she checked into another motel. Once she regrouped, she decided to contact Max again to get Joe's address.

She decided to drive to his office instead of calling.

He will probably hang up once he realizes it is me that is calling, she thought.

Laura noted how plush Max's office was when she walked in.

The drug business must be good, she thought.

When Laura approached the receptionist, she asked formally to speak with Mr. Bertolini. She hoped the receptionist would think she was a business associate.

"Do you have an appointment? Mr. Bertolini only sees people by appointment."

"No, but I am sure he will see me. Just tell him Laura is here to see him."

The receptionist was surprised when Max told her to send Laura in.

"What are you doing here?"

"I came to get Joe Boccia's address."

"Well, you are not going to get it here."

Just then a burly security guard walked in to Max's office.

"Take this lady downstairs," he told the guard. "The police are waiting for you there."

Laura was shocked at this event.

"What are you doing?" she asked. "I just came here to get an address."

Max turned his back and did not answer. The security guard took her by the elbow and walked her out. The receptionist looked on in surprise.

Bill met them at the front door of the office building and directed Laura to drive to the police station.

"Well, here you are again, harassing Mr. Bertolini. I am getting a little tired of this. You are to get in your car and return home this minute. I don't want any more trouble from you."

"I can't drive home this afternoon," Laura said. "I am too tired. I have driven for five hours."

Sue recognized that Laura should not be driving on the highways.

"What are your plans?" she asked.

"I have checked into a motel. I had planned to get Joe Boccia's address from Max and go there to look for my daughter."

"What you are going to do," Sue said, "is go the motel and stay there until you are fit to drive again. Detective McDermott will follow you there. You are not to leave the motel without my permission. We will make periodic checks this afternoon and evening to be sure your car is still there. You are to let me know when you leave for Mapleton. Do you understand? Allow the police to do their job and find your daughter. You are just making our job more difficult."

Laura nodded and left Sue's office. When she got to the motel, she had a sandwich and dropped down on the bed. She was surprised when she woke up next and it was early morning.

Laura called Sue Patnode to tell her she was heading back to Mapleton. She was surprised when Sue asked for her home phone and address. She was sure Sue had access to that information but gave it to her anyway. She called Tim to let him know she was on her way. She could tell he was still upset that she had made the trip to New Rochelle but did not show anger.

"School will be out about then," he said. "I'll have my assistant start basketball practice and should be at your house when you arrive. You can decide if you want to stay at my house or if you want Marcy to stay with you. I love you."

Laura smiled. No one except Benjii had said those words to her since her parents died.

"I love you too, and I need you. I could never have dealt with Benjii's disappearance without you and Marcy. But she doesn't have to stay with me. She needs to get on with her own life. I will be okay alone."

"No, you won't. You can stay in the guest room at my house again. See you in a few hours. Remember, Benjii will be found safe and sound soon. I am sure of it."

"I think so too. If I didn't believe that, I wouldn't be able to function, even with the support I am getting from you and Marcy."

After completing the call, Laura began to cry and continued to all the way home.

She did not realize she would not be sleeping in either house that night.

It was not Tim who was waiting for Laura when she arrived home. Bob Cochoran and one of his deputies were there waiting for her.

"Hello, Chief Cochoran. Do you have news of Benjii?" Laura asked hopefully.

"Laura, this is Deputy Mary Kenyon."

"Hello, Deputy, what can I do for you?"

"Laura, we are here on business. I have a warrant for your arrest. I also have a warrant that allows Deputy Kenyon and myself to search your home and car."

Laura was deeply shocked but tried not to show it.

"Please let me see the warrants. I am sure there must be some mistake. I have committed no crimes in Mapleton or anywhere else. I can't imagine what the charges might be. I have never had even so much as a speeding ticket."

"I am arresting you for kidnapping, Laura. It is a felony offense. You could get a long jail term for an offense this serious. I suggest you cooperate with us to the fullest."

"Of course I will cooperate, but who am I supposed to have kidnapped, my own child?" Laura immediately recognized her mistake but went on. "What child except my own is missing? I really wish you would put some time and effort into finding my baby. You're wasting your time here."

Laura dissolved into tears again. She was surprised she had any tears left. She began to feel faint. Mary Kenyon, who had been standing silently, watching this exchange, rushed to her side and put her arms around her. Mary did not like this job she was forced to do. She had heard that Laura was a dedicated teacher, and she liked her immediately. But she was the only female deputy on the force and had to be there to search Laura when she was arrested. She would do so as gently as she could and try not to embarrass Laura.

At that moment, Tim drove up.

"Hi, Bob, what are you doing here?"

"I have a warrant for Laura's arrest and one to search her home and car."

"Really, and just what is the charge?"

"Laura has visited a man in New Rochelle named Max Bertolini several times since Benjii disappeared. She has accused him and his associate of taking Benjii. He is now certain that the child Laura claims to be hers is actually his infant that disappeared over six years ago.

"He filed a complaint at the NRPD accusing Laura of kidnapping that child. Sue Patnode took the complaint to a judge who issued the two warrants. Sue faxed the warrants to me. I have no choice but to honor them."

Tim was as shaken as Laura and was upset to hear she had visited Max Bertolini.

"You had better do what he asks, Laura. I'll do everything I can to help you."

Laura watched as Mary and Bob searched her car then her apartment. She could tell they were trying to be considerate. They put things back neatly after searching through them.

This is not like the movies, she thought.

She was upset when they took Benjii's clothes, books, and toys. They also took her comb and toothbrush.

"Do you need to take those? Benjii will be upset that all her possessions are gone. I have to have things as normal as possible when she comes home. She will have suffered too much trauma as it is."

"Laura," Bob said gently, "you must face the fact that Barbara Jean will probably never return here. You may not either for a long time."

When Laura heard Bob refer to Benjii as Barbara Jean, she suddenly realized what was happening. Her child would be lost to her. She cried out and fell to the ground in anguish.

Both Tim and Mary ran to help her. Mary suddenly recognized the true relationship between Tim and Laura and stepped back so Tim could hold Laura in his arms. She had tears in her eyes.

After they got Laura calmed down and finished searching the house and car, Bob had one more task before leading Laura away.

"I need to get a DNA sample, Laura. Would you rather do it here than at the police station?"

Laura nodded her head. She felt numb. She was losing everything that mattered to her. Benjii was gone. She knew her short teaching career that she loved so much was over. No one would hire a felon to teach the children in their schools.

She was hardly aware of Bob placing the cotton swab in her cheek and then placing it in a plastic bag.

"We need to go now," Bob said. "I need to book you at the police station. You may have to spend one night in jail. I'll try to get your case before a judge tomorrow. Will you be able to post bail?"

Laura thought of the money left to her and Lana by their parents but knew there was no way she could access it without incriminating herself. She still needed to have people think of her as Laura McKenzie, not Laura Mitchell.

"Not if it is more than a couple of thousands of dollars."

Tim lifted her up and held her close.

"I'll get the bail money somehow. I won't allow you to remain in jail."

Chapter 65

As soon as Laura was taken away, Tim began to plan how to get bail money. Bob guessed that bail would be about $100,000. Tim needed to talk with Marcy because his plan could threaten her college fund.

He told Marcy about the events of the afternoon. When he finished, she started to cry softly. Tim felt a tinge of guilt. He had been so concerned about the welfare of Laura and Benjii that he had not given Marcy's feelings enough consideration. He knew how much she had grown to love Laura and Benjii. He verbalized his feeling of guilt to her.

"That's okay, Dad. We need to talk about what we can do to help them."

"I don't want Laura to have to stay in jail. I need to borrow money to post her bail. I can use the house and your college fund as collateral, but that is putting your future in jeopardy, and I need your mother's permission to use your college fund."

"I'll talk to her, Dad. She will listen to me."

"No, I'll call her. This is my problem."

Sonja Atwood was irritated when the phone rang. She had had a writer's block, and the ideas were just beginning to flow again.

"Sonja Atwood."

"Hello, Sonja. It's Tim."

"Well, what a pleasure, it has been months. How has Marcy been behaving?"

"Don't be sarcastic, Sonja. Marcy is fine. She'll get on the line to talk with you in a few minutes. First I have some business to discuss with you."

After listening to Tim's explanation, Sonja felt a tinge of jealousy. She had chosen her career over her marriage and family but was not sure she wanted another woman in Tim's and Marcy's lives. That had not been a problem until now.

"Is this little friend also a lover?"

"No, Sonja, she is not."

Tim did not tell her he hoped it would come to that someday soon.

"Well, as you say, this is business. There has to be something in it for me."

"I can't imagine how that could be."

"I do. It sounds like quite a story. I want exclusive rights to it."

"I can't promise that. It is Laura's story, not mine."

"Just promise me that you will discuss it with her. She'll owe both of us. I'm betting she will give me the rights."

"I'll talk to her."

"Okay, I'll call the bank and okay the deal. But I want more than that."

"What?"

"Some time with you."

"I'll talk to Marcy. Maybe we can arrange a visit. She is pretty busy right now with school activities."

"Darling, you wouldn't want Marcy around for what I have in mind." Sonja laughed huskily as she hung up.

Tim hoped she was joking.

Chapter 66

The next morning, Laura was led into court. She hardly remembered the humiliating experience of being booked, searched, photographed, and put into an orange jumpsuit. She could not eat the sandwich and coffee Mary Kenyon had brought her. She slept little on the hard cot provided to her. At least she was placed in a solitary cell.

Before her court appearance, she met briefly with a lawyer Tim had hired to represent her.

Brenda Simpson exhibited a no-nonsense air.

"Laura, we know who you are and that the child you call Benjii is not your biological child. We will have to discuss that fact later."

"You won't know that until the DNA tests are completed."

Laura was hoping that being the twin of the child's mother would provide positive DNA results.

"Oh give me a break, Laura. But as I just said, we will discuss that matter at a later time. Right now our task is to convince the judge that you are a good girl and not a flight risk. I'll try to get you released on your own recognizance, but I am sure the judge will set bail."

"I don't have money for bail."

"I believe Tim Atwood has that covered."

"I can't accept money from Tim."

"You had better, or you may sit in jail for months. It takes a long time to get a new case on the docket."

Laura was allowed to wear her own clothes to her arraignment. She tried to hold her head high as she walked into the courtroom surrounded by deputies. Mary Kenyon had removed her handcuffs outside the courtroom to give her some dignity. She was surprised to see Pat Cook watching the proceedings. Also in attendance was Mr. Winter, the superintendent of schools. Of course, Tim was there.

The actual proceedings took less than ten minutes. The prosecutor outlined the charges, presenting Laura as a kidnapper, a common felon, and asked for the maximum bail allowed by law.

The defending lawyer presented her as a model citizen, an outstanding educator, and a grieving mother whose child had disappeared nearly a week prior to these proceedings, being careful not to use the term *kidnapped*. She asked that Laura be released on her own recognizance.

The judge set bail at $100,000 and told Laura she was not to leave the area without the permission of Chief Cochoran.

Laura and Tim met with the county clerk to pay the bail. John Winter, the superintendent of schools, approached them.

"Laura," he said, "I regret to inform you that you have been placed on unpaid leave until further notice. I am sure you understand why."

Before Laura could respond, Tim spoke up.

"Why unpaid? Last year the business manager was suspended for embezzlement, and he was paid full salary until the matter was settled."

"The decision is irrevocable, Mr. Atwood. Don't get yourself into trouble by supporting a felon."

"That would be impossible for me to do. I don't know any felons."

Tim and Laura walked away.

Chapter 67

Alex knew it was time to check the merchandise at Max's storage unit.

Something is going down, he thought. *Why are Max and Joe doing their own grunt work? Who are the thugs that appeared when Max and Joe were working there?*

He dressed in blue jeans, a dark sweatshirt, and sneakers and walked from his motel to the facility. Dock workers did not have cars. He had an escape route planned if it became necessary. As he approached the unit, he looked around and assured himself that there were no vehicles and no other people around.

Opening the locks that secured the door into the unit was no problem with the tools he brought with him. Once inside, he was sure he knew what to look for. He had heard Max and Joe talk about separating the cartons by number and designate where each was to be sent. He needed to take one coffee can with each number and secure them in the knapsack he had slung over his shoulder. Later, the powder he believed he would find hidden in each can would be analyzed at the police lab. If he found what he thought he would find, his job would be over, and he could go home to his family. *If I have a family to go home to*, he thought. He carefully selected a carton, loosened the tape, opened the carton, removed one can, then rearranged the bubble wrap so the empty space left when he took the can would not be easily noticeable. He was carefully replacing the tape on the fourth carton when he felt the cold barrel of a .38 pressed against his temple.

"Put up your hands and turn around slowly."

Alex followed orders.

"Christ, Lucky, what are you doing here?" asked Big Mac.

"I guess I could ask you the same thing."

"I don't need to explain, you do. To be honest, I am surprised to see you here. I never took you to be a crook. I thought you were a good guy, just down on your luck."

"What would you know about being a good guy. You're nothing but a low-level crook. Now move that damn .38 from my head."

"Sorry, Lucky, can't do that. I'm afraid you are going to jail for a long time. I guess my cover is blown, so I will introduce myself after I cuff you. Then I will put the gun away if it makes you nervous. Get your hand behind your back. What is that stuffed in your waistband? I'll take it if you don't mind."

Alex was surprised when he saw the handcuffs Big Mac had.

"What the hell is a lowlife like you doing with those handcuffs? They are government issue," he asked as he felt them being snapped around his wrists and his gun being snatched from his waist band.

"As I said, I will introduce myself," Big Mac told him as he produced a badge.

"Christ, FBI. I don't carry my ID. It is too dangerous. My real name is Alex Hamilton. If you will take me to the New Rochelle Police Department, they will identify me as an undercover cop. By the way, what about your buddy Jug? Is he FBI too?"

"I can't talk to you about Jug."

"Then he must be an informant. Boy, did I have you two guys pegged wrong. Can we go to the PD now. I want to get these damn cuffs off."

"We aren't going anywhere right now. I have work to do."

"How can I help?"

"You can't. As far as I am concerned, you are Lucky, a dock worker and probably a drug dealer. I'm locking you up in the next unit. No matter what you hear, keep your mouth shut."

Trapped in the next unit, Alex had never felt so helpless in is life. His wrists were raw from trying to release them from the handcuffs. He knew it was almost an impossible task, but he tried anyway.

He could hear voices coming from the next unit. He thought he could hear heavy movement and assumed the cartons of coffee with the drugs were being moved. He could also hear what he thought were heavy trucks. It seemed like he had been in there for hours, though he realized it was only for a short while when suddenly the door swung open. He felt a blast then lost consciousness.

Mac had somehow survived the blast. He was working way in the back of the unit, and the explosion was designed to blow the front door away, so he didn't get the brunt of the blast. He was stunned and slightly burned but managed to stumble out of the unit before emergency vehicles arrived. Before he passed out, he was able to toss a ring of keys to a nearby policeman.

"There's a man in the unit next door," he whispered.

They found Alex inside.

"I doubt this one will make it," one EMT stated.

Chapter 68

Sue was just getting ready to leave the office when she received the disturbing call.

"This is Peggy Newman from at New Rochelle General Hospital. We just had a patient brought in to the emergency room that we think may be a member of your police department. He was injured in an explosion at the storage units on Commercial Street. Someone called 911 and waited for emergency personnel to arrive. He spoke to an EMT telling him to call the NRPD, then he disappeared while the patient was being treated. We need to have this man identified."

"Oh no," Sue said, immediately thinking of Alex. "Bill, we need to go to the hospital immediately. I think Alex has been hurt."

They arrived at the hospital about ten minutes later. It was twenty minutes after that before the doctor came out of the treatment area to speak with them. He requested ID before giving them information about his patient.

Both Bill and Sue showed their ID. They were exasperated by the delay. They wanted to know if the patient was Alex, and if so, they wanted to know his condition. However, they knew they had to appease the doctor before he would give them information. After checking their IDs carefully, he asked them to enter the cubicle where Alex was to see if they could identify them.

They gave the doctor his name then asked about his condition.

"He has suffered a severe head injury. We need to wait to see if there is any swelling in the brain before we can decide on treatment. If we are lucky, the injury will just be a severe concussion. We need permission from next of kin in order to treat him. Is he married?"

"Yes, but his wife is out of town, visiting her family."

Sue did not want the doctor to know that Meg and Alex were estranged. She was sure this was only temporary and wanted Meg to be able to make the decisions about Alex's care.

"I will return to the office and contact Mrs. Hamilton immediately. I have her parents' phone number on file there. I am sure she will call you right away. Bill, please stay with Alex. I will be back soon."

"I wouldn't want to be anywhere else right now. After you contact Meg, please call my wife and tell her I won't be home for a while."

Chapter 69

Becky Watson answered the phone on the first ring. She was sure it was Meg checking on Terry. He was not feeling well when he came home from school. So she decided to stay home from the basketball game so he could get to bed early.

"Hello."

"Could I speak with Meg Hamilton please?"

"She is not available at the moment. Can I ask who is calling?"

"This is Sue Patnode from the New Rochelle Police Department."

"Oh my god, is it Alex?"

"With whom am I speaking?"

"This is Betsy Watson, Meg Hamilton's mother."

"Mrs. Watson, I don't want to alarm you. Right now Alex is okay, but he has been seriously injured. I need to get in touch with Meg. She needs to contact the hospital in New Rochelle as soon as possible. I will give you the number."

"My husband and Meg are at her son Ryan's basketball game. They both have cell phones. I will contact them immediately."

"Do you want me to call them instead?"

"No, I will contact my husband and have him give the news to Meg."

Doug Watson was irritated when his cell phone rang.

I should have shut the thing off, he thought.

He hadn't done that because Becky and Terry were home alone, and Terry was not feeling well. He had told Becky to call him if they needed anything. He recognized his home phone number on the screen.

This had better be important, Becky, he thought. Mapleton is down 71–70, and Ryan is about to attempt a 1-1 foul shot. If he hits them both, they will win the game.

Doug listened carefully to what Betsy had to tell him. He put his arm around Meg as he listened. Rick, who was sitting next to his mother, tensed, suspecting something was wrong.

"Everything seems to be okay right now," he told Meg. "But a police detective from the New Rochelle Police Department just called your mother. Alex has been hurt. You need to call the hospital, I have the number. Then we need to get the boys home, and I need to get you to New Rochelle. Alex's condition is critical."

Laura had been sitting next to Meg at the game. Tim would not allow her to stay home alone while he coached the game. Marcy was at a club meeting. Laura knew people in the stands were watching her. She did not realize their hearts were breaking for her. She was pale and looking at the game without seeing it.

"I doubt she even knows what the score is," one parent said to another.

She perked up a little when she heard Doug speak to Rick.

"I need to get Ryan off the court and get you two boys home immediately. Your mother and I have to get on the road to New Rochelle as soon as possible."

Laura had reacted when she heard Sue Patnode's name. She knew that the call had to have something to do with Meg's husband. She listened as Mr. Watson explained to Rick that his father had been hurt. He tried to relay the information gently so Rick would not be overly frightened. Laura put her arms around Rick.

"Mr. Watson, why don't you and Meg get on the road right now. Rick can stay here with me. I promise to take good care of him. I will go down to the floor before the team goes to the locker room and let Mr. Atwood know what has happened. He can tell Ryan. We will drive the boys home and check with Mrs. Watson to see if she needs anything. Meg, call me once you get to the hospital and let me know if you need me to bring anything to you tomorrow."

"Thanks for taking care of the boys now. I can't let you come to New Rochelle for me. It is way too long a drive."

How well I know, Laura thought.

"I also need to tell you that I pray for Benjii every night. I believe she is safe and will soon be home for you."

"And I will pray for your husband. Now get going. I know it is a long drive, but I won't mind driving there tomorrow. It will give me something to do besides sit around and worry about Benjii."

After the game, Laura went to search for Tim. She spoke to the assistant coach.

"Please let him know I must speak with him immediately."

The assistant coach was not pleased. The team was wildly celebrating their win, and he believed Tim needed to be a part of it. However, he could hear the urgency in Laura's voice and was worried that she had heard something about Benjii. He spoke to Tim immediately. Tim came right out of the locker room also thinking there was news about Benjii.

"I am glad you sent Meg and her dad on their way," Tim said when he heard what had happened. "Why don't you and Rick wait by the door that leads to the lot where we are parked. I'll speak to Ryan, and we will meet you there. My assistant coach can stay with the team until they are picked up by their parents."

Laura put her arm around Rick as they left the gym. He was trying to be brave, but Laura could feel his shoulders shake.

"Your dad will be okay. I am sure he will. Your mom and grandpa will call as soon as they arrive at the hospital. I bet the news will be good."

Laura wished she felt as confident as she tried to sound.

Soon Ryan and Tim came to meet Laura and Rick as planned. Ryan went immediately to his kid brother and hugged him. He kept his arm around him as they headed to the car.

What a close family, Laura thought. *I hope their dad will be okay.*

Doug had called his wife to explain the arrangements to bring the boys home, so she was waiting at the door to meet them when they arrived at the house. She ran to hug the boys but made no comment.

"Is Terry okay?" Ryan asked.

"He was asleep when the call came in. We will talk to him in the morning."

"Mrs. Watson, I will come over in the morning and get things for Meg and take them to her. She will probably be in New Rochelle for a while. She will need changes of clothing, toiletries."

"Thanks, Laura."

Tim scowled but did not say anything until they returned home.

"Laura, I don't like the idea of you driving alone to New Rochelle again. You are exhausted. You could fall asleep at the wheel."

"I will take one of the sleeping pills the doctor gave me so I can get a good night's sleep tonight. I am not on any schedule, so I can sleep as late in the morning as I want. I'll take coffee with me."

"Laura, I'll go with you," Marcy said. She had just come into the room and heard the conversation. "Dad can write me an absence excuse. I don' mind missing one day of school."

"No, you need to be in school. I don't mind going alone." Laura did not want anyone with her on this trip."

"Okay, Laura, do it your way if you insist. Call me when you arrive at the hospital, and be sure to leave early enough to get home before dark."

"I will. I promise."

Laura knew she would not be keeping that promise.

Tim walked her to her bedroom door and gently kissed her good night.

I hope I have her in my bed someday, he thought then felt ashamed of the thought because of the current circumstances.

Chapter 70

He was shocked when the explosion occurred at Max's unit. He woke up early the next morning to get a newspaper at the newsstand. He could have purchased one at the hotel, but he didn't want anyone who knew he was staying at the hotel to be able to tell the cops he has purchased a paper.

When he returned to his room, he quickly scanned the paper, hoping to see an article about a drug bust or about drugs being found at a storage unit after an explosion and fire. He hoped to read that drugs were found in a unit leased by a well-known importer and exporter named Max Bertolini, but he knew Max was probably smart enough not to put his name on a lease for a storage unit that contained something illegal.

He was surprised when at first he could not find the article he was looking for. He searched the paper again.

Shit, that can't be right, he thought.

He read the article again. It told about a blast that seriously injured an undercover cop. The cop was listed as critical, but the article stated that his condition could possibly be upgraded to serious later in the day.

How the hell did that happen? He was there. He knew the blast occurred in the unit Max owned. He had never seen anyone there at night except Max and the people who worked for him. The article went on to state that another person at the unit narrowly missed being seriously injured in the explosion. He had called 911, told the EMT that someone was in the next unit, then disappeared without waiting for treatment.

The name of the undercover policeman was not being released.

I wonder who it is, he thought.

Chapter 71

After leaving Ruth with Benjii at the secret apartment, Lenny went home to his own apartment to call his benefactor.

"I have the child and a sitter put safely away. The sitter does not know her location. She does not have any means of communication and no transportation. She does have plenty of food, water, and heat. She will have to stay put for a while.

"Good. Were you able to get a hair sample and a bit of blood?"

"Yeah, I got a brush someone was using to brush her hair. The kid was so out of it that she never knew I pricked her finger to get blood. I even washed it off, so hopefully neither she nor the sitter will notice the prick."

"Okay, now you have to go to the unit to get a product sample."

"That may be a little tricky. Joe has not let me work at the unit much lately. I think he is up to something."

"Of course he is."

"I am not sure I can get the right packet."

"Just do it. No excuses."

As he hung up, he decided that having Lenny take the kid was a good idea. Joe must be going crazy wondering what happened to her. He himself kept thinking about the kid and her mother. He watched them enough to see their devotion to each other. They must both be going crazy. He hoped things would work out so he could get the kid back to the woman he knew must be Laura Mitchell.

He also felt sorry for Joe; he had a rough beginning and a rough life. But at the same time, he was stupid. He never should have gone to work for Max. Now Joe's stupid move of taking the child gave him the opportunity he needed to implicate Joe as a route to get to Max.

He settled down to wait to hear how Lenny made out at the unit.

Lenny drove to the unit but had no idea what he would do once he got there. As he neared the complex, he heard a rumble. He watched in horror as part of the unit crumbled in flames. He never stopped; he drove away as fast as possible.

This can't bode well for Joe, he thought. *Maybe I can accomplish what I need to do to earn my money without a sample of the drugs.*

He drove around Joe's neighborhood several times to be sure the coast was clear. When he was certain no one was around, he approached Joe's house. He knew there was an alarm system in the front hall, so he approached the house through the back. Using his picks, he was able to open the door, praying there was no alarm. Too late, he saw lights blink in the house.

He hesitated long enough to realize no alarm was sounding. Taking a deep breath, he walked in.

Joe, he thought, *you had better learn to check your alarm batteries. Come to think of it, it may not make any difference to you at this point.*

He gave some thought to what he would do next. He had to be sure that the evidence he planted did not look like an obvious plant. He put the hair from the brush down into the drain then pocketed the brush. He smeared the blood from the prick on Benjii's finger on the floor. He was lucky he was able to keep the blood damp with a bag of ice. After making the smear, he left the house quietly and used his disposable phone to make a call.

Chapter 72

After leaving Joe's, Lenny made two anonymous phone calls from a disposable cell phone. He called Max's house first but received no answer. He decided to leave a message similar to the one he would leave at the police station. He couldn't wait to get an answer at Max's house or office. He would have to get rid of the phone as soon as he hung up from calling the police department.

The dispatcher answered at the NRPD.

"I think you are looking for a kid missing from Mapleton, New Hampshire. A guy named Joe Boccia has her. You better find her fast before she gets hurt."

"Who is this?" Russ asked.

The caller had already hung up.

Maybe this is the break Sue has been hoping for, he thought as he dialed her home phone number.

After seeing and hearing the blast, Joe decided to head for home. He had no idea what was going on, but he knew he didn't want to be any part of it. When he approached his house, he did not notice a car parked down the street. He didn't react when he heard the car door slam and noticed two people walking toward him.

Sue had called a judge after Russ contacted her. She had been able to get a warrant to search Joe's house after she related the phone call and other evidence that pointed to him.

"Hey, Joe, do you mind if we come in for a minute two?"

"Sorry, I have a date, and I am running late. I need to change and get out of here."

"Is your date with a six-year-old?"

"What the hell does that mean?"

"We have a tip that you have Laura McKenzie's daughter. Actually, you don't have to invite us in. You don't even have to be here. We have a warrant to search your house and car."

"Well, be my guest. You won't find anything."

Joe was confident. Benjii had never been in either his house or his car.

Bill and Sue searched the car first and found nothing of interest. Next, they searched the garage and basement. Again, the search was not productive.

Next they went to the main part of the house.

"A pretty fancy house for one guy," Bill commented.

"I entertain a lot."

"Six-year-olds?"

"Shut up. Do what you need to do and get out."

Bill walked into the kitchen.

"Hey, Sue, come look at this," Bill called from the kitchen. Bill was using a sharp knife to carefully lift a red spot from the floor. He showed it to Sue before carefully placing it in an evidentiary bag. "What does it look like to you?"

Sue looked at the specimen carefully. "How did you get blood on your floor, Joe?"

Joe blanched but was still confidant. The kid had never been in his house.

"Maybe from the steak I took out of the fridge last night."

"We will soon find out."

After completing the search of the house without further success, the detectives left to take the suspicious stain to the lab. They neglected to check the drains in the sinks.

Joe poured a double scotch as soon as they left.

Chapter 73

Alex slowly opened his eyes. He could hardly move. He had tubes everywhere including places he would prefer not to have tubes.

Meg was sitting by his hospital bed, looking pale and drawn. He tried to reach over to pat her hand to let he know he was awake but couldn't manage it.

"Hello, sweetheart," he whispered.

Meg jumped up, and tears rolled down her cheeks. She quickly pushed the button to call the nurse then bent over to kiss him.

"Does this mean we are okay?" Alex asked.

"Meg ignored that question but said, "I have been so worried about you."

She did not have the opportunity to say more because the nurse rushed in at that moment.

"Welcome back, Sunshine," she said, smiling.

"Where the hell am I?"

"You are in the ICU at the hospital."

"How long have I been here?"

"About thirty-six hours. You suffered a concussion and injured your shoulder. The shoulder injury is not bad, but you have a serious concussion, and you have been unconscious as a result of that concussion for nearly thirty-six hours."

"Where was the explosion? What happened?"

Alex was not awake enough yet to remember being at the storage unit and the events that occurred there.

"I don't know all the details, but I understand you were injured in some kind of explosion. The police want to talk to you about this when you are well enough to be questioned. However, we are not going to rush about calling them. You need to rest and spend some time with your wife. She needs to rest too. She hasn't left your side for nearly thirty hours. She wouldn't even have eaten if we hadn't brought sandwiches and coffee to her. You are lucky to have such a fine woman love you so much."

Meg smiled at that comment and shrugged.

Maybe this marriage will survive after all, Alex thought hopefully.

"How did you know I was here? How did you get here?"

"Detective Patnode called my parents' house, then my dad brought me here. I got here just a few hours after you were brought in. Dad has gone back home to help Mom with the boys. Tim Atwood and Laura McKenzie helped out too. They brought the boys home from the basketball game so Dad and I could leave immediately to be here with you. Laura is bringing me some things I will need so I can stay here with you."

"Atwood is the basketball coach, right? Who is this Laura McKenzie?"

"She is a teacher at the middle school that Ryan attends. She has helped him with some adjustment issues when he started school there, though she has missed a lot of school lately. Her daughter was kidnapped about two weeks ago. She is pretty much out of it now. She can hardly function. She looks like she will collapse at any minute, but somehow she keeps going. I don't know how she survives."

As Meg was talking, a memory of something flashed in Alex's mind, but he soon lost it.

Chapter 74

Laura called Chief Cochoran to let him know she was going to New Rochelle. As a condition of her bail, she had to let him know if she was going to leave Mapleton.

"Do you think that is a wise move?" he asked.

"I am going to bring some things to Meg Hamilton. Her husband has been critically injured, and she left hurriedly last night to go to him. She did not take time to pack clothes. I will deliver things to her, get a cup of coffee, and head back home. I will call you when I return."

Bob approved the trip then immediately called Sue Patnode.

"Please check to be sure she really goes to the hospital as soon as she arrives in town then leaves for home."

Sue promised she would have someone take care of that detail. What strange twists and turns, she thought. Alex is hurt trying to stop the drug business run by Max Bertolini, who may be the father of the child Laura McKenzie is searching for. She is helping Alex's family. What other strange things are going to happen?

After speaking with Bob, Laura went to the Watson's to get the items she had requested. Meg had called her mother, and Becky had the things ready for Laura when she arrived at the house.

"Are you sure you are up to making this trip by yourself?" Like everyone else, she was very worried about Laura. "Maybe someone should go with you."

"I will be fine," Laura said.

"Well, be sure to leave in time to get home before dark."

"I will," Laura lied.

Laura spent the five hours driving thinking about what she would do after she visited Meg at the hospital. By the time she arrived at the hospital, she had a plan. She rode the elevator to the fourth floor that housed the intensive care unit. She saw the nurses' desk as soon as she exited the elevator.

She spoke to the nurse on duty, telling her that she was there to deliver clothes to Meg Hamilton.

"Oh yes, Ms. McKenzie, Mrs. Hamilton asked to be informed as soon as you arrived. There are no phones in the patient's rooms. I will send an aide to let Mrs. Hamilton know you are here. It will take just a minute or two."

When Meg came out to meet Laura, she seemed more upbeat than Laura had expected her to be.

"Alex is doing much better, she explained. "He has regained consciousness, has been upgraded from critical to fair."

Laura was glad the news was good and told Meg that. When she handed the suitcase to her, Meg asked her if she would like to have a cup of coffee before heading back to Mapleton.

"I have decided to stay the night," Laura answered. "I am tired and would rather wait and drive back in the morning. I called Tim to let him know my plan. I will leave my cell phone number with you. If you need anything, don't hesitate to call."

Meg was a little perplexed when Laura told her this. It was still early in the day, but she decided not to ask questions.

As Laura left the hospital, she felt she had covered all her bases.

No one asked for my motel number. They are comfortable they can reach me on my cell phone. I will be able to answer that no matter where I am.

Laura checked into a different motel from the one she stayed in her last visit to New Rochelle. This motel also had a side door she could exit and enter from using her room key if she did not want to be seen leaving or returning to her room. She then visited the public library to get a map of the city.

She read the city tax report, hoping it would provide her with an address for Joe Boccia She was disappointed to find he was not listed as a property owner and was not listed in the phone book.

When she returned to her motel room from the library, she used the side door. She did not want the desk clerk to be able report her movements if asked. He was probably curious about her because she paid in cash. She did not expect anyone else to be curious about her movements, but better be safe than sorry.

What a waste of time the trip to the library was, she thought as she removed her jacket and lay on the bed in her motel room.

I am going to have to visit Max. I had better call Tim. I will tell him I need to charge my phone and will call him later. That will give me a couple of hours of freedom.

When Laura arrived at Max's house, she was surprised to find it dark.

It is not surprising that Max is out, but I wonder where Mrs. Carter is. She seldom went out in the evening. She did not like to drive after dark, Laura remembered.

Laura decided to drive down the street a little ways and wait.

No one will be suspicious of my car if I don't wait too long. I wish I had brought some coffee and a snack.

She suddenly remembered that she had not eaten since she left Tim's house in the morning.

I will have to get something at a convenience store on my way back to the motel. I can get something for breakfast too. Thank goodness there is a coffeemaker in the room. I don't want to eat in a restaurant. A woman eating alone is too conspicuous.

After about a half hour wait, Laura saw Max pull into his driveway. Laura drove in behind him.

"What the hell are you doing here? You ought to be in jail. I called the cops the last time you were here."

"I'm not in jail because I have not done anything wrong. I came to get Joe Boccia's address from you. He is not listed in the city directory or the phone book. I know he has Benjii, and I want her back. She has been gone for over a week. I can't imagine what she is going through. She must be very frightened."

"Barbara Jean is not at Joe's house. Come in and I will explain."

"I am talking about my daughter, not Barbara Jean. Where is Mrs. Carter?"

"I don't know. She left a couple of days ago. No one has heard from her since that time."

"I don't want to come into the house, Max. We can talk out here."

"Afraid I'll jump you?" Max sneered. "Okay, I'll drive down to the Dunkin' Donuts on the corner of the street. We can talk there."

Someone up there likes me, Laura thought. *I get to have coffee and a sandwich and can buy a muffin for morning. I hope Max will give me the information I need. I just have to find Benjii.*

Max and Laura ordered then found a table at the back of the room where their conversation could not be overheard.

"Explain to me why you think Benjii is not at Joe's."

Max told her about Sue and Bill searching of Joe's house.

"The cops went over the place with a fine-tooth comb," he said.

He did not know about the bloodstain that was found. Joe had called him about the search so Max would not be suspicious of him.

"She simply is not there. I also have reason to believe that they have Joe under surveillance. If he has her stashed somewhere, which I doubt, he is smart enough not to lead the cops to her. If the cops can't find her, you can't."

Tears came to Laura's eyes.

"Max, I was so sure Joe had her. What do I do next? She is only six years old. I can't have her going through whatever she is going through any longer."

"Why don't you go to the cops?"

"You know why. You made it impossible when you had me arrested. Why did you do that?"

"All that crap about a lost kid was getting me a lot of attention from the cops I didn't want. I needed to divert their attention away from me to something else. You were the perfect scapegoat."

"Don't you care about what is happening to Benjii?"

"Why should I care about *your* kid?" Max sneered.

Laura knew she was going to lose control. She walked out of Dunkin' Donuts without another word.

Chapter 75

As soon as Laura pulled out of the Dunkin' Donut's parking lot, Bill McDermott pulled her over.

Laura stopped and opened her windows a few inches, keeping her doors locked.

"Ms. Mitchell?"

"My name is Laura McKenzie," she said, handing over her license and registration.

"Okay, I guess that is the name you are going by now."

"I go by that name because it is my name."

"Okay, let's not quibble about your name. Detective Patnode asked me to check to see when you will be returning to Mapleton, New Hampshire. You were supposed to head back as soon as you left Meg Hamilton's things at the hospital. If you don't adhere to your to your bail agreement, you face prison time."

"I realize that. Believe me, I will do nothing to jeopardize my freedom. I hated the night I spent in jail. I called Chief Cochoran and received his permission to stay overnight so I could see Meg in the morning in case she needs something more."

"Why were you at this Dunkin' Donuts? It is nowhere near the hospital or the hotel where you are staying."

Laura tried not to show surprise that Bill knew where she was staying.

"I remembered it from the time I lived in New Rochelle as a child. It seemed to be an appropriate place for a woman eating alone."

Boy, she thought, *I have never had to lie so much. I wish I didn't find it so easy.*

"Really?" Bill said. "I didn't realize the Dunkin' Donuts was built back then."

He decided to let the topic drop because he wasn't sure of his grounds. He would check later to see when the facility was built, if he deemed it necessary.

"Are you headed for your hotel now? I will follow you there to be sure you arrive safely."

Neither Laura nor Bill noticed the car that was following behind them.

When she arrived at her hotel, Laura was forced to park in the front parking lot. Bill tooted and waved as she entered the front entrance. She felt the curious eyes of the desk clerk follow her as she entered the elevator.

She was happy to be back in her room. *Damn*, she thought when she realized she had forgotten to buy something to have with her coffee in the morning. There was a convenience store across the highway, but she wasn't sure she was brave enough to cross four lanes of highway to get to it. She decided it would be just coffee in the morning.

She called Tim and Chief Cochoran. Her conversation with Bob was quick. She just needed to check in. She spoke longer with Tim. He wanted her to start for home first thing in the morning. He told her he loved and missed her and was worried about her. He also told her that Chief Cochoran was reluctant to talk to him about the search for Benjii without Laura present. There was some activity in New Rochelle, but the chief would not tell what it was.

"I doubt the NRPD will give you any information," Tim stated.

Laura could not tell Tim anything she had heard from Max. He would be angry about her meeting with him. She had no idea what Chief Cochoran would do if he knew she had met with a suspected drug dealer.

Chapter 76

The DNA analysis of the bloodstain found at Joe's was given top priority but still took three days to come back from the lab. It was determined to be type O positive human blood. A check with Benjii's school records confirmed that that was Benjii's blood type.

"We need to contact Bob Cochoran and have him let Laura know what has transpired. We need to compare it with Laura's blood type also," Sue told Bill.

After hearing about the bloodstain found at Joe's house, Bob decided to contact Tim before talking to Laura. He had accepted their relationship and knew Laura depended on Tim.

"I sense that the two of you are very close. I thought you might like to be with her when I give her some news. We can meet after school."

"Bad news?"

"Disturbing news."

When Laura saw that Bob was with Tim when he arrived home from school, she knew that what he had to tell her would not be good.

"Let's go in and sit down, Laura. Bob has several things to tell you."

"Some confusing events have been occurring in New Rochelle that have to do with Benjii's disappearance. As you know, a man resembling Joe Boccia, Max Bertolini's right-hand man, took Benjii from school.

"You know about the woman calling to say Joe had Benjii. You also can be assured that she was being well cared for during that time. We also know Benjii was taken from her and moved to another place. Where that place is, we still don't know.

"Several days ago, Sue received another call saying that Benjii was at Joe Boccia's."

"Was she there? Where is she now? Is she okay?"

"Relax, Laura. Let me finish my story. All that information was enough to convince a judge to sign a warrant for Sue and her partner to search Joe's house and car. They did not find Benjii. I don't want you to be upset about what I have to tell you next. It does not prove anything about Benjii's whereabouts or her welfare. At Joe's house, the detectives found one very small bloodstain."

Laura began to shake. Tim put his arms around her.

Bob went on, "The bloodstain is a human bloodstain and matches Benjii's blood type. However, the blood type, O positive, is a very common blood type. Therefore, it may not have anything to do with Benjii. There was no evidence that she had been in that house. I sent Sue a sample of your DNA; she will have it analyzed to see if it is a match to Benjii's. That may clear up some questions we all have."

Sure, Laura thought, *you want to prove that Benjii is not my child*.

"You hang in there. Things are beginning to move. We know Benjii was safe and well cared for just a few days ago. There is no reason to believe that she is not okay now."

Bob patted her hand and let himself out.

Chapter 77

Ruth knew she had to do something to help herself and the child. The little girl did not appear to be frightened but was bewildered and sad. She continually asked when she could go home to her mother.

She had been wearing the same clothes for nearly two weeks now. Ruth wished she could wash them at night, but she had no way to dry them for the next morning. Benjii had told her that she wore a T-shirt that belonged to Grandma Mitchell when she went to bed at night. Ruth had a loose-fitting blouse Benjii could wear if they were still at the house another night. She hoped that they wouldn't be.

Ruth had no idea where they were. They were in a small but comfortable house trailer, but there were no other homes or buildings around.

I think it is okay to go out, Ruth thought. *Benjii has a jacket, ski pants, mittens, and boots. I'll bring an extra one of my sweaters she can wear if we are out for a long time and she gets cold. Her mother had her well prepared for school outdoor activities.*

Ruth knew Benjii was too small to walk a long distance but hoped to find a gas station or something with a pay phone before they went very far. Ruth had a small amount of change with her—just enough to call 911.

She had no way of knowing what direction to go in when they got outside. She had become completely disorientated when they drove there last night.

242

She decided to turn right. They walked for about a half a mile. The child did not complain, but Ruth knew she was getting tired.

"Just a little ways more, then we will turn back," she told her.

Ruth heard a car approaching and flagged it down when it came into view. The driver stopped and rolled his window down.

"Thank God you found us," she told the driver. "Do you have a cell phone? Can you call 911 for me? I need help."

"I don't think so, Ruthy, the driver said," showing a gun. "If you want to live, you better get into the car."

"No, I won't," Ruth gasped

"Look, I don't want to hurt you or the kid, but I will if you don't do what I ask. I will shoot you right here and leave the kid alone to deal with it."

I hope she complies, he thought. *I wouldn't do any such thing*.

Ruth did not want Benjii to be frightened.

"Come on, Benjii," she said. "This nice man is going to give us a ride back to the house. He knows you are getting tired."

"I can't ride with strangers," Benjii said solemnly.

"He is not a stranger. He is an acquaintance of mine."

Benjii allowed Ruth to buckle her into the backseat. She did not ask for a booster seat; she knew it would be useless."

Ruth was afraid to get into the car. She did not know this man and did not know how he knew her name, but it did not seem that she had an alternative. They arrived back at the house and went inside.

"Now, Ruth," the man said.

"How do you know my name? I do not know you," she said that softly so Benjii would not hear.

"That is not important right now. Just listen to me. I don't want to lock you in. You would not be able to get out if there was an emergency. You need to promise to stay put for a couple of days. You should be able to leave soon."

"What about the child?"

"I hope to return her to her mother when the two of you are released from here."

Chapter 78

Benjii likes Aunt Ruth a lot more than she had liked Grandma and Grandpa Mitchell. Aunt Ruth didn't smoke those smelly cigarettes and didn't drink the stuff Benjii didn't like the smell of. She even made her some new clothes. Benjii was tired of wearing the same dirty clothes every day.

"I like to sew, it relaxes me," Aunt Ruth had told her. "I always bring cloth and things to sew with when I leave my house. I will use some of the cloth I have and some of my own clothes to make new things for you, then I can wash the clothes you have been wearing."

"Won't you need your clothes?" Benjii had asked her.

"I can get along fine without them," Aunt Ruth had told her. "Right now you need them more than I do."

Aunt Ruth even made her a rag doll to take to bed with her at night, and she played with her. She took some paper plates and made cards from them so they could play fish. They watched TV together, but Aunt Ruth made sure they were watching educational shows. She allowed her to watch one cartoon a day for a treat. But Aunt Ruth never told her why they were at that house where no one else was near. She decided to ask Aunt Ruth questions.

"Aunt Ruth, why are we here? How long will we have to stay? When will I see my mommy again? Why doesn't she come to get me?"

Ruth decided to answer her questions as honestly as she could.

"Your mommy has not come to get you because she doesn't know where you are. She came to the house I was living in, looking for you, but no one at the house, including me, knew where you were at that time. The man who took you from school is not you grandfather. The lady there was not your grandmother either. I do not know why he took you. Then another man took you from those people. He asked me to take care of you. I am glad I said yes. You are a very brave, sweet little girl. I will take care of you until someone finds us. I am sure your mommy is working very hard to find you."

"Why can't we just leave?"

"We tried, remember? But we don't have a car, and the walk to where other people are is too far. The man who picked us up and brought us back here said we must stay here. Right now, I am sure we are safe. I think it is best that we stay here for a little while longer."

Ruth saw tears in Benjii's eyes. She held her tightly in her arms.

"Everything will be all right," she told her.

She certainly hoped that was true.

Chapter 79

Pat knew she would make Ruth angry, but she couldn't help it. She had to figure out a way to help Laura McKenzie. She was the first teacher to take an interest in Tom; she had really helped him. Now it seems she is the one who needs help.

Ruth may need help too, she thought. *I am very worried about both of them.*

Pat had become more confused and scared every time she hung up the phone. She had been calling Ruth two or three times a day for the last few days. Ruth always answered the phone right off when Pat called her at the Bertolini residence. If she was going to be away from the Bertolini residence, which was very seldom, she always let Pat know ahead of time.

Last night, when she called, Max Bertolini answered the phone. When she asked to speak with Ruth, he was very rude, said he had no idea where she was, then slammed down the phone. Pat couldn't imagine why Ruth would leave without letting her employer know where she was going and how long she would be gone.

She decided to call Chief Cochoran. She was immediately put through to him when she mentioned that she wanted to talk about Laura McKenzie.

"Chief Cochoran, my name is Pat Cook. I am the mother of a student at the middle school. He sees Ms. McKenzie in the morning and during the school day for extra help completing his assignments.

I know Ms. McKenzie and may have some information about her lost daughter."

"Mrs. Cook, can you come into the police station? I want to hear what you have to say, but not over the phone. Also, if I have your permission, I would want to record what you have to say."

"I can be there in an hour."

Bob was surprised when he met Pat. She looked older than her forty-seven years. He had checked on her right after he hung up from the phone conversation earlier. He wanted to be sure he could trust her. There was nothing in her background that would suggest there would be any problems with what she had to say. He had learned that she was a single mother of three. Her husband had disappeared several years ago. There was an outstanding warrant for his arrest for nonpayment of court-ordered child support. Pat had to work two jobs to support her family.

No wonder she looks older than her years, he thought.

Bob made her as comfortable as possible under the circumstances.

"Mrs. Cook, I want this interview to be informal but would like to record our conversation if I have your permission."

Pat nodded her permission. Bob spoke into the tape recorder, giving the date, time, people present, and the subject of the interview. He had Pat verbally give permission for the conversation to be recorded.

God, he thought, *I really sound like a big-city cop. Maybe I can really find this little girl.*

"What can you tell me about yourself? he asked.

"I have lived in Mapleton all my life. I currently live on Fairview Street. I have three children. Tom is my youngest and, as I told you before, attends the middle school. His brother Jim is in high school, and my daughter, Carrie, attends college. She only goes part time because she has to work. I work two jobs. I work at the insurance company during the day and at Targets at night and on weekends."

"What about your husband? Does he help support your family?"

"He left when Tom was a baby. I have not heard from him for years. He was court ordered to pay child support but never has."

Bob knew that everything Pat said was true.

"Chief Cochoran, I am not here to discuss my personal life. Why all these questions about my personal life? The reason I am here has nothing to do with any of that except for the fact that Ms. McKenzie is Tom's teacher."

"Mrs. Cook, when we discuss serious police business with potential witnesses, we need to ascertain that they are reliable."

Pat had to concede that point either she did not think of herself as a witness.

"Now let's get to the reason you are here. Tell me about the information you have concerning Benjii McKenzie's kidnapping."

"I don't know if anything I say will be helpful, but I wanted to give you some information. My sister, Ruth Carter, lives and works in New Rochelle, New York. She is the housekeeper for a man named Max Bertolini. She believes he runs some sort of illicit business but does not really know. He has always been good to her, but she is still a little afraid of him. She does not like some of his business associates that come to the house, and she knows he has a cruel streak if someone crosses him. She stays because the money is good, and the work not to taxing.

"He was married about seven years ago to a beautiful woman about twenty-five years his junior. Her name was Lana Mitchell. At first, their relationship seemed to be ideal, but Lana was a party girl and a flirt. He was jealous and soon became possessive and domineering. Ruth thinks Max hit her sometimes when they argued.

"A few months after they were together, Lana, became pregnant. Max was furious. He was nearly fifty years old and did not want to start a family. However, he did the right thing and married her.

"The baby was born early in September of 2002. Sadly, Lana died several days after the birth. Everyone believed her death was due to her drug and alcohol abuse, but Ruth thinks he may have hit her in a fit of rage. She was totally devoted to the baby and had moved from Max's bed into the nursery. She had resisted Max's sexual advances."

"Did she report this to anyone?"

"No, this young woman believed she was beyond help, and she was worried about her baby's security."

"Did Mr. Bertolini raise the child after his wife's death?"

Bob thought he knew the answer to that question.

"No, Lana's sister was at the house for the funeral. The day after the services, she and the infant disappeared. Many people think Max did away with them, but Ruth doesn't believe that. She believes Laura, that is the sister's first name, ran away with the infant to protect her from being placed for adoption and that they are still in hiding."

"That is what brings me here. She believes that Laura McKenzie and Benjii are that missing sister-in law and child, but I don't believe that for a minute."

"Why not?"

"Ms. McKenzie cannot be a kidnapper and felon. She is too professional and caring."

"If you don't believe that, why are you here, telling me this story?"

"To protect people I love and admire."

"How so?"

"My sister has a bad habit of listening into her employer's phone conversations. She overheard one of Max's associates claim he found Laura and the baby. Ruth believes he was talking about Ms. McKenzie."

"How would she make that connection?"

Pat's eyes started to mist.

"I told her about the wonderful teacher Tom had. I wish I hadn't, but it is too late now. She put all that information together and came up with an incorrect conclusion.

"After Ruth heard about the child's disappearance, she came to the conclusion that an associate of Max's has the child. He is not a nice man and would not hesitate to harm a child if it was in his best interest."

"I really don't believe there is any connection between this man and Benjii's disappearance, but I don't want any child hurt. Both Benjii and this other child must be found before they are hurt.

"Mrs. Cook, you did the right thing coming here with your story. I don't know if these children are one and the same. But I will contact the New Rochelle Police Department immediately. You can be assured we will do all we can to find these children."

"I have another reason for being here," Pat confessed.

"And what is it?"

Pat told Bob about her concern for Ruth. Bob told Pat he would call Sue Patnode immediately and get back to her as soon as he had anything to report.

"Bob," Sue said after hearing his request, "I am a little concerned about Ruth Carter myself. I spoke with Max Bertolini last night. He is furious with Mrs. Carter. Apparently about three nights ago she packed up some of her belongings and drove away somewhere in her car. It seems that no one has heard from her since. This is not normal behavior for her. We will look into the situation and try to determine what has happened to her."

Chapter 80

After accepting the first payment for substituting the new moisture packets placed in the coffee cans before they were sealed, Jose Santiago became increasingly worried about what kind of situation he was getting himself into. The words "You already are" when he told the caller he did not want to do anything illegal kept echoing in his mind.

His wife, Carla, was always up when he got home from his night shift. After kissing her good morning, he usually went up to their bedroom and tried to get a couple hours of sleep before helping her take care of the children and do household chores. They would both sleep again in the afternoon when the little ones took their naps. This morning, however, he kissed his wife then poured a cup of coffee and sat down at the table beside her. He knew he was too wired to sleep, and he had decided to talk to Carla about the situation he found himself in.

"Jose, no coffee," she said. "You will not be able to sleep."

"I won't be able to sleep this morning," he told her.

Carla could read her husband like a book and immediately knew something was wrong.

"Okay, what is it, Jose?"

He reached into his pocket and pulled out a small brown manila envelope.

"Look inside."

When she did, she gasped. She had never seen so much money at one time in her life.

"Where did you get this?"

"At work."

"They don't pay like this at work."

Jose told her about the packets placed in the coffee cans during the night shift and the phone call he received to substitute the packets with different ones.

"The caller paid me this money for doing the substitution. He will send me more and pay me again."

"Jose, why did you say you would do this? You must have known something was not right about it. Not for this kind of money."

Jose did not want her to know about the threats. If he got scared, he would send his family to stay with her brother. He would see to it that no harm came to her or the kids.

"We need the money for the baby and to see that there are no more."

"Well, there will be no more if you are in jail, and how would I take care of all of us alone? You need to report this."

"I'll go and see the foreman when the kids take their nap this afternoon."

"No, it won't work to see the foreman. He may be involved and may not be able to be trusted. You need to go to the top man."

"You're kidding. I couldn't get in to see him. He wouldn't give me the time of day."

Carla loved her husband but recognized that sometimes he was weak, never dared to take a chance.

"You need to get some sleep then take a shower and put on your suit you wear when you go to a wedding or funeral. Then drive to the office and demand to see Mr. Roy. Take that packet and the money with you."

"What about you and the kids?"

"I'll be okay. I'll let the kids watch TV this morning. It will be a treat for them. They will be quiet so I can get chores done."

"You need to rest."

"I will. Now get some sleep then get ready to go see Mr. Roy."

Jose was overwhelmed by the opulence of the office building.

People work in places like this and live in mansions because people like me work and sweat for them. Then they fuss when we ask for a nickel raise.

The company Jose worked for was owned by an American.

I would never do this if the company was owned by a Latino, he thought. *The Latino owners are too afraid of the drug lords.*

He had heard that Mr. Roy was a decent man.

It must be true, he thought. He pays us a decent wage and sees to it that working conditions are good and are safe.

He followed directions to the corporate office and took the elevator to the fourth floor. He opened the door that had the name Adrian Roy painted on the glass. The office was bright and airy and well furnished.

One of these chairs probably cost more than my whole house, he thought.

He went to speak to the girl behind the glass window. She had noticed him when he came in and noted his shabby suit. She decided to ignore him. She couldn't imagine why someone who looked like him would even be in this office. She had a lot of work to catch up on and didn't have time for unimportant things. She continued working on her computer and pretended not to see him. Jose waited three or four minutes then cleared his throat to get the girl's attention.

When she continued to ignore him, he said, "Miss, I would like to see Mr. Roy."

"Do you have an appointment?"

"No, ma'am."

"Mr. Roy doesn't see anyone without an appointment. He is a very busy man. I might be able to get you in to see him later this month." She had no intention of doing that.

No, ma'am, that isn't going to work. I need to see him right now. There is something going on at work I need to tell him about before my shift tonight."

"Do you work at the factory?"

"Yes, the third shift."

"I can't possibly get you in to see Mr. Roy today."

"Well, I guess all I can do is sit in one of these comfortable chairs and wait until he comes out of the office. He's got to come out sometime."

Donna White did not want this man sitting around the office suite all afternoon.

"Mr.," she said then realized she did not even know this man's name, "whoever you are, I can't have you sitting around here all afternoon."

"Mr. Santiago."

"Mr. Santiago, I can call security and have you escorted out."

"Yes, ma'am, you probably could. But I am sorry to hear that. You will be too because I have to report that something strange is going on at the factory, something that could hurt his business. When he finds out you stopped him from finding this out, it will not go well for you."

"Okay, I will listen. Just tell me what is going on, and I will relay this information to Mr. Roy."

"That won't work. I need to talk with him face-to-face. And I have something important to show him."

"Then I will have Mr. Bradley, the vice president, come out and speak with you."

Jose thought about what he and Carla had talked about, about not knowing who could be trusted.

Carla had told him to stand his ground and be strong, and that is just what he intended to do.

"I'll wait," he said.

The door opened, and Adrian Roy came out of his office. Jose immediately stood up.

"Mr. Roy, I need to speak with you for a moment. It is important."

Roy looked confused.

Donna White spoke up, saying, "I told this gentleman that you were too busy to see him today, but he refused to leave the office."

"Mr. Roy, I am putting my family's life at risk by being here. If anyone finds out I am reporting what I know to you, I may have to send my wife and kids away. My wife is expecting a baby in two months, and my other two children are three and five. They are my whole world. I think you should take five or ten minutes to hear what I have to say."

Roy was shocked at Jose's passionate plea. "What is your name?"

"Jose Santiago."

"Do you work at the factory?"

"Third shift."

"That is just a skeleton shift. Why don't you work first or second shift?"

"My wife is suffering a difficult pregnancy. I need to be home to help her during the day. I asked the foreman to change me to the third shift so I could be home to help with the two little ones. He agreed to the change."

"Do you get paid the same?"

"No, sir. That part was hard, but right now I need to be home. If there is an opening, maybe I can change to another shift in a few months."

"Ms. White, please notify the business that I want third shift people to be paid the same scale as other shifts. Have that pay increase start immediately."

"Won't that request have to go through the proper channels?"

"Ms. White, I own this company."

"Now, Mr. Santiago, let's go into my office, I need to hear what you have to say."

Adrian Roy sat at his desk and indicated that Jose was to sit in the chair opposite him.

"Okay, Mr. Santiago, what is this all about?"

"It's about the money that is in this envelope and the moisture packets that are placed in the coffee cans before they are sealed."

"Moisture packets? There are no moisture packets placed in any of the coffee cans."

"Yes, there are, sir. It is my job, and has been ever since I changed shifts, to see that these packets are placed in the cans before they are sealed. I got a phone call about a month ago about these packets, and that is why I am here. That phone call and the money in that envelope are bothering me."

Jose went on to tell Adrian Roy about the phone call from Joe and about his threat to his family.

"So you can see I was tempted. I have been substituting the old packet with the new for about three weeks now. I found this money in my locker today. I don't want the money, and I don't want to keep substituting the packets. I talked to my wife about it this morning, and we agreed that I needed to come to you with this problem. Someone at the factory knows about these packets. I don't trust anyone there."

Jose took the packet from his pocket and placed it on top of the envelope with the money.

"I'll have Ms. White give you a receipt for the money. I need to keep that and the packet for a while."

"No thank you, Mr. Roy. No one except you and my wife and I know about that money. I want to keep it that way."

"Okay, I'll just keep it in my desk for now. I want you to keep substituting the packets for now so you won't arouse any suspicions. You and your family will be safer that way. I will call the police and have the powder in this packet analyzed."

"No cops please. I don't want to go to jail. I need to be home to take care of my family."

"Mr. Santiago, I promise you will not get into any kind of trouble. The police may want to talk to you depending on what is in the packet, but that is all. Now I need to get to my meeting. I am already fifteen minutes late. Just act natural at work and don't change what you have been doing. I will get back to you after I hear from the police department."

Jose left the office with his head held high. He smiled pleasantly at Ms. White as he walked out the door.

Chapter 81

He needed a distraction. He knew exactly what to do.

It may be tough on the kid for a while, he thought. B*ut it will give me the time I need to finish my work.*

Sue put her coat on wearily. She was anxious to get home to her husband and kids. She knew how fortunate she was to have her husband on the same schedule as her kids. She seldom had to worry about day care, but when it got to be this time of day, all she wanted was to be home with them.

When her phone rang, she ignored it and let Russ take the call.

"Sue, you had better take this call," Russ said.

"I'm headed home, Russ."

"You better take this one."

"Hello," Sue said tiredly.

"I know where you can find the McKenzie kid," a voice said. "She's really Max Bertolini's kid. She is in an apartment in Mapleton, New Hampshire. You had better hurry, she is going to be moved again."

An address was given, then the call was disconnected.

Sue called the Mapleton Police Department. When the dispatcher answered, Sue asked to speak to the chief.

"He has gone home for the day. He cannot be disturbed."

"Really? He better be disturbed. This call is of utmost importance. Call him now and have him call this number immediately."

Within ten minutes, Chief Cochoran returned Sue's call.

"I just received an anonymous call giving me an address where the McKenzie child can be found. The caller said that was of the essence because the child is going to be moved again soon."

Sue gave the chief the address.

"My god," he said, "I know the family that lives there. I'm on it right now."

He hung up and went to get his jacket.

Chapter 82

Sending the Mapleton cops to that kid's house will confuse things enough to give me the time I need to set things up. First the New Rochelle cops, then Max.

"Police Department."

"I need to talk to Detective Patnode."

"May I ask who is calling?"

"Just tell her it's about the McKenzie kid."

"This is Detective Patnode."

"Joe Boccia had the kid."

"I don't think so. We have been to his house. There is no evidence that a child has been there."

"Yea, well, I know better. I know you found some evidence."

How could this caller know anything? Sue wondered. *We have kept our investigation close to the vest.*

"Anyway," the caller went on, "you are right about the kid being at his house. He kept her in another location."

"If you know something, you need to report it. Otherwise you could be found to be an accessory to kidnapping. That could mean years in jail."

"You don't know who I am, and you will never find me. I will tell you one thing. I think you know the kid has been moved. I know where the kid is, and she is being well cared for. She's back in

Mapleton. Call the chief there and ask him if he knows a kid named Dodie Mcintire. He's got the kid."

"I believe the child is still in New Rochelle. There is no evidence that suggests she has been transported out of state."

"Hey, I told you what I know. Do what you want with the information."

So much for this phone. Into the river it goes. Next phone. Next call.

He dials the phone.

"Max Bertolini."

"Joe Boccia knows what is wrong with the drugs. You might want to call Kim Lee."

Chapter 83

Lenny's apartment was shabby as his grandmother had suggested. The only furnishings were a bed that doubled as a sofa, a table with two chairs, and a TV. There were no closets. The bathroom off the part of the room that served as a bedroom / living room yielded just a toilet and a shower. There was seldom any hot water. He couldn't even have a woman over. He was too ashamed.

He didn't mind. He was on the move. He didn't know who his benefactor was, but all he had had to do so far was feed him information. He had only received five grand, but he was sure more was coming.

He knew Joe was planning on making a move to take over Max's business. Joe would never suspect that someone was watching him.

He also knew Joe had had a meeting with Big Jake. He wanted to find out why, so he had followed Big Jake for several days. Jake often went to a small town in New Hampshire named Mapleton. All Jake ever did was visit a mail drop in town. He hadn't got that one figured out yet. But he would soon, he thought.

He hoped to get some of his answers today. He had been watching Big Jake when he traveled to New Hampshire a couple of times each week. He usually went on a Tuesday, so he would be watching today. If Big Jake went there today, he would follow him again to see what he was up to.

He would be glad when this ride was over. He was starved, and he had to pee.

Maybe Jake was in the same boat and would make a pit stop somewhere. He wouldn't be suspicious if another car stopped at a gas station and went into a restaurant. People did that all the time.

Big Jake did not stop but drove straight to Mapleton and went to a mail drop where there were boxes to rent.

Why would he drive five hours to go to a mailbox business? All he had in his hand was a large brown mailing envelope. All he had to do was mail the large envelope he took into the store from the post office at home. Was it because he didn't want it to be traced back to him?

Do I stay here to see what's up, or do I follow Jake? It looks like he is headed back home.

Is it possible that someone will pick the envelope up? I guess I had better hang around to see.

It was not long before Lenny saw a teenage boy come out of the mail pickup.

He had a brown envelope in his hands. Lenny couldn't tell if it was the one Big Jake had brought in.

He got out of the car and approached the boy.

"Hey, been in there long? he asked.

There was something about the man that made Dodie nervous. "No, why?"

"I was supposed to meet someone here. I was wondering if you saw him. He's a big guy with tattoos. You couldn't miss him. Maybe I got my signals crossed and got here late."

"I've only been here a couple of minutes. I didn't see anyone."

Dodie got on his bike and left. He did not notice that a car was following him until he went into his yard. He realized the guy in the car was the guy at the post office. He hurried into the house without acknowledging that someone was there. He locked the door.

His mother watched as he checked the back door and locked that one too.

"Dodie, what's wrong? Why are you locking all the doors?"

"It's probably nothing, Mom. I thought someone was following me from school."

He did not want his mom to know that he had stopped at the mail drop on the way home.

Jane Mcintire looked out the window just in time to see Lenny drive away. She caught the last three numbers of his number plate and knew it was a New York plate.

"I am going to call the police. I don't know why someone would follow you, but it would not be for a good reason. I got part of the license plate number, and I saw the car. They may be able to find out who it is and what they want."

"No, Mom, I don't want you to call the police. I am sure it is nothing."

"It won't do any harm to speak with Bob Cochoran. He would want to know about an incident like this."

"Mom, I am telling you not to call Chief Cochoran," Dodie yelled. "If you do, I will deny everything and say it was all your imagination."

"Why? What is wrong? What are you involved in? Besides, who do you think he will believe, a concerned mother or a kid with questionable behavior?"

"I'm telling you, Mom. If you call, there is going to be trouble for a lot of people, not just me. Just give me some time and I will explain everything. I might be in trouble, but not for anything you might think. It's not anything like drugs or theft or anything. I don't think I will be in trouble with the police or anything, but I could have trouble at school. I could even be expelled."

"Okay, Dodie, sit down and tell me everything."

Chapter 84

At that moment, Jane and Dodie heard someone bang on their door. Jane looked out the window.

"Oh, Dodie, what trouble have you gotten yourself into? It is the police."

"I told you, Mom, I haven't done anything the police would want me for. I may be in trouble at school, that's all."

"Before I open the door, give me a clue. What have you done?"

"Sort of stalking and harassing Ms. McKenzie at school, that's all."

"What on earth for?"

"Money. I got paid to do it."

"I had better let Chief Cochoran in. You can tell both of us at the same time what you have been up to."

Jane was nervous that it was the chief at her door. He had a reputation for sitting at home or in his office, letting his officers do most of the police work in the community.

"Good afternoon, Chief. What can I do for you?"

"We would like to come in and look around for a bit."

"Sure, but can I ask you why?"

"I'll ask the questions. Does Dodie do any babysitting to earn extra money?"

"No, he works some afternoons and weekends bagging groceries at the supermarket. Once in a while he helps Tom Cook with his paper route, but not very often. Why?"

"We just received a report from another police department that a little girl was being held here. She has been missing for a couple of weeks. We need to investigate all leads. Can we look around?"

"My god, do you think we would be involved with something like that? You have known us for years. Who is the little girl?"

When Jane heard the child was Benjii, she turned pale and started to shake.

"We need to talk," she said.

Dodie confessed all. He told his mother and Chief Cochoran about the phone call he received the day before school, about writing on her board, harassing her in the parking lot at school, and about the Christmas doll. He also told them about being at the elementary school and seeing Benjii leave with someone. He didn't give it a thought because they walked out of the school, so he knew school personnel knew she was leaving with the man. He told them about Laura arriving at the school and about contacting Tim when he realized that something was terribly wrong.

"I think they have a thing going," he said. "I figured she would need him."

Jane cried softly. "Why, Dodie, why?"

"We needed the money, Mom."

Chief Cochoran broke in, "Why would someone call NRPD and say you had the little girl?"

"I don't know. I don't know how someone from there would know me or know where I live."

"Someone followed Dodie home from school this afternoon," Jane said. "They really scared him."

"It was not exactly home from school."

"What do you mean?"

"It was from the mail drop where I pick up my money from the caller."

"This sheds a different light on everything," Bob said. "Did you pick something up from the drop?"

"Yea, an envelope with money in it."

"You need to hand it over to me. There may be prints on it that will help us with our search for Benjii McKenzie. There has to be a connection between your situation and the missing child. I don't believe in coincidences. I need to call the NRPD to get more information about why someone would want to implicate you."

Dodie retrieved the envelope from its hiding place in his room and handed it over to the chief.

"Dodie, I can't let this go. You stalked Ms. McKenzie. You harassed her, threatened her, and scared her. I will need to talk with the school officials and the DA. You may be in serious trouble, but I will see what I can do for you. You are basically a good kid, just misguided. Stay away from Ms. McKenzie and keep your nose clean from now on. Otherwise, I will let you hang for what you have done."

Bob let himself out.

Chapter 85

Sue had gone home after her call to Chief Cochoran. She had instructed Russ to call her at home if there were any further developments.

He called to tell her that the chief had called, and related the events as the chief had outlined them to him.

"It looks like this call was a hoax," he told Sue.

The chief found no evidence that the child had been in that home. He did tell her what the chief had revealed to him about Dodie Mcintire's involvement with Laura.

When Sue told Rick about these events, he said, "Okay, let's look at the reasons why this happened."

"I think the person who called knows who has Benjii," Sue said. My guess is that someone has an agenda and that the child is safe, at least for now."

"Have you called the mother to let her know what happened this afternoon?"

"No," Sue said, "I probably should. I just don't want to upset her further."

"She should be informed."

Sue called the latest number Laura had given her. It was at Tim's house, but Laura was the one who answered the phone.

Sue told Laura about the events of the day without mentioning any names.

"We believe this was a diversion so someone could move her to a new location. This suggests that she is safe."

"Thank God. I am so worried about what she is going through. She must be so scared. Is she warm? Is she being fed?"

Laura lost control and began to sob uncontrollably. For the first time it occurred to Sue that this child could really be Laura's child.

"Listen to me," she said. "We are doing all we can to get Benjii back to her family, whether it be you or Max Bertolini. We believe this second kidnapper has a reason for taking Benjii and that she is safe and being well cared for."

"Thank you." Laura sobbed. "I hope you are right."

"I have just one question Do you know Jane and Roger Mcintire?"

Laura was shocked to hear that question.

"I had a boy in my classes named Roger Mcintire. He likes to be called Dodie. He lives with his mother whose name is Jane. Why do you ask?"

"They are the people the caller named as having Benjii. Of course, that is not true."

"But there must be something about this. Dodie has been stalking me all year. Ask Chief Cochoran to go back and search again."

"Dodie confessed to stalking you. He was paid to do it."

"Paid by who? Max?"

"We don't know."

Sue told Laura about the contacts, money drops.

"Anyway, why would Max do this? Why didn't he just come and claim his daughter?"

"Maybe it is because it is not his daughter."

Chapter 86

The results of the analysis matching Laura's DNA to that of the bloodstain were inconclusive.

There were some similarities to the DNA in the bloodstain but not enough to determine a match. Everyone realized that the true mother of this child could possibly be Laura's twin sister.

That could really complicate things, Sue thought.

"We need to go see Max Bertolini," Sue told Bill. "We need a DNA sample from him. It may help with the investigation, and it will most definitely prove the little girl's parentage."

Max answered the door. He was still irritated that Ruth Carter had left with no warning. He did not like having to fend for himself.

"What the hell do you want now?"

"Can we come in? Where is Mrs. Carter? She usually answers the door."

"That's what I'd like to know. I haven't seen her for a couple of days. This place is a mess."

"Are you worried about her?"

"No, I'm pissed. She could have at least told me she was taking a few days off."

Sue decided that she would try to locate Mrs. Carter as soon as she returned to the office.

"Can we come in?"

"Yeah, if you have to. But what do you want?"

"A DNA sample."

"What the hell for?"

"We got a tip that Joe Boccia had Laura McKenzie's daughter. When we searched Joe's house, we found a small bloodstain on his kitchen floor. The blood type matches the little girl's blood type. We matched the DNA from that sample to Laura McKenzie's DNA. The results were close but inconclusive. We want to match that DNA to yours. It might help us find her, and it will determine once and for all if she is your daughter."

Reluctantly, Max swabbed his cheek and placed the sample in the evidence bag.

"If Joe has that little girl and has hurt her, I will kill him."

"Max, stay out of this investigation. Let us do our job. It could be that he had her but did not hurt her."

She told Max about the call to Lila Ashton.

"The call was anonymous. We have no idea who the woman is. We do know the child was safe while she was with this woman. We don't know who the person is that took her from there. The caller said she was assured that the child would not be hurt and that there was someone waiting to care for her. By the way, if this child is your daughter, why would Joe take her?"

"He has been doing some strange things lately. I think he has some grandiose idea about taking over my business. He could never do it. I don't know why he thinks that taking the kid would help him."

"Maybe he was going to do away with her and blame you for it".

Max was furious when he heard from Sue several days later that his DNA matched that of the bloodstain found on Joe's kitchen floor. *I'll kill that slime*, he thought.

The more he considered that idea that Joe might be trying to take over his business, the more he thought it was true. He decided to pay Joe a visit.

Joe was not happy when he saw Max at his door. He had been laying low since the explosion and the visit from the police. He still had no idea what happened at the unit. He had not heard a word from Max, Lenny, or the cops. He sure as heck was not going to contact any of them. He didn't dare try to find that big mouth Doris

Abbott. He knew she was the one who had tipped the cops about the kid. No one else knew anything about it. There was no way the school secretary could have fingered him. Boy, this was the longest two weeks of his life. Everything had gone wrong.

Joe tried to act nonchalant when he opened the door.

"Max, come in. what brings you here? I'll mix us a scotch."

"Haven't seen much of you lately, Joe."

"I thought you would want all of us to lay low after the explosion at the unit. What happened anyway?"

"I don't know. You tell me. You have a lot of explaining to do. You weren't home that night like you said. I came here to the house, and it was dark. You didn't answer the door."

"I had probably left for the delivery at the unit."

"You couldn't have. The timing was not right. What happened at the unit anyway?"

"How would I know?" I just felt the explosion, saw the fireball, and got the hell out of there."

"The cops told me there was some kind of explosive device placed there. It was set off remotely probably by a cell phone. Is that how you did it, Joe?"

"Max, for Christ's sake, why do you think I would do such a thing?"

"Same reason you took my kid."

"Are you crazy? Why all these accusations?"

"Laura Mitchell came to my house the other night. She said someone matching your description took the kid away from her school. She thought I had the kid. What did you do with her? You hadn't better have hurt her."

"Feeling fatherly all of a sudden? How do I know you don't have her." Joe smirked. "He was beginning to feel brave."

"This is what I am feeling, Joe. I am feeling betrayed. I think you are trying to take over my business. I think you tried to set me up at the unit. I think you killed my kid and you are going to try to frame me for it."

"That's crazy. I told you I don't have your kid."

"You may not now, but you did have her here."

"That's bullshit. She was never in this house."

At least that much is true, Joe thought.

"The cops found her blood on your kitchen floor. The got a DNA sample from me, and it matched with the bloodstain. My kid was here."

"Like hell."

"You had better start talking, or hell is where you are going."

Before Max could say more, the doorbell rang.

Chapter 87

Sue requested and was granted a second warrant to search Joe's house after the judge saw the new DNA evidence. When Sue and Bill approached the house, they were surprised to see the BMW parked in front.

"It looks like Joe has company, Sue," Bill commented.

"It doesn't really matter. We have the warrant, and the crime-scene people are on their way, so we can go in."

They rang the bell but received no answer. Bill went to the garage and looked through the window.

"Joe is home," he said. "His car is in the garage, the other car is outside, and the houselights are on."

Bill rang the bell, and Joe opened the door.

"What the hell are you doing here? Can't you see I have guests?"

Sue questioned whether Joe had many guests. There was only one car parked outside, and she thought she knew who it belonged to. The house was too quiet. If Joe had several guests, one would expect to hear people talking.

"Joe, we have a warrant to search your house again. The stain we found on your floor matched Benjii McKenzie's blood type. The DNA match with Laura McKenzie's DNA was inconclusive but still leaves many questions. However, it matches Max Bertolini's DNA perfectly. We know the child taken from Laura McKenzie is probably Max's child. We believe Laura McKenzie is Laura Mitchell. She was arrested for the kidnapping in 2001 but is currently out on bail. We believe you now have or did have that child. You need to let us in."

Joe stepped away from the door. Max could see and hear this exchange. He decided to hang around and see what would happen.

I have nothing to worry about, Joe thought. *The kid has never been in this house. But how the hell did the bloodstain get here?*

Joe and Max sat down to finish their drinks while the police did their job.

Russ had taken forensic classes before he was injured and was helping the crime scene unit at Joe's house. He knew what kinds of things to look for and went into the bathroom.

After a few minutes, he called to Sue and the other members of the crime unit.

"Well, look at what we have here," he said. He showed Sue what he had found. "This hair is light and pretty soft. Looks like it came from a child. Any explanations, Joe?"

"I have no idea what you are looking at. There has never been a kid in this house since I have lived here."

"I think we are done here for the time being. We will be back, Joe, after this strand has had DNA testing. Again, don't leave town without informing my department. Max, I think you had better leave with us."

Both Joe and Max were confused.

Chapter 88

Joe was relieved that Max did not call again that night. He needed to think and develop a plan.

The next morning he called Max.

"Joe, why are you so fired up about moving the stuff before Friday?" Max asked after listening to what Joe proposed.

"A couple of reasons. One is the visit from the cops yesterday. I think someone is setting me up and maybe trying to set you up too."

"I think so too. I was suspicious when the cops found the hair in the sink. You ain't the kind of guy to give a kid a shampoo in the sink. I think the cops think so too. That is probably why they left right away."

Neither Max nor Joe mentioned the events before the arrival of Sue and Bill.

"I got a bad feeling about Kim Lee and his goons," Joe continued. "I think at least one of those guys was on the docks when we were at the unit the last time was Kim's guy. The new shipment isn't due until Monday. I think we need to contact all the drivers and have them drive steady and get the stuff here by Friday."

"Well, that would mean contacting the first driver and set up a chain of calls from one driver to the other. I don't like that much communication between the men."

"It's the same as when they meet and exchange vans."

"Yea, but this would be by phone. I don't want them to know each other's number. They could find out names and addresses if they have that information."

"We can't call because we don't want them to have information that would point to us. How about Lenny Butler making the phone calls? He's expendable."

"Okay, we can give him a list. He can call at each exchange point. As soon as one switch is made, he can call ahead to the next guy and tell him to be prepared to be at the switch point several hours earlier than originally planned. That way we can have to shipment here by Friday. That will give us time to change the delivery addresses. Get on it right now."

After trying to call Lenny about the calls to the drivers, Joe decided to go to the apartment to check on Doris and Benjii. He couldn't believe what he found when he unlocked the door and entered the apartment. All evidence that anyone had lived there recently was gone. Joe decided to get out of there.

I've been wondering why I took the kid, he thought. *I don't know what the hell to do with her. Maybe my problem has been solved. I wonder what Doris did. She would never hurt the kid, and she won't do anything to implicate me. She knows I will see to it that she goes to jail for aiding and abetting a kidnapping if she does. She needs to care for her husband.*

Now that I have convinced Max to make the move I wanted I can get things moving. Max won't have to worry about Kim Lee unless he's in the same jail. Once I am done, neither one will be free again for a long time. I'll have the business to myself. I won't even need Carlos.

Chapter 89

The blue panel truck rolled quickly to the customs building at the New York–Canadian border at Niagara Falls. Two agents started toward the truck.

"I'll get this one," one of the agents said. "You get the cars in back so things won't get backed up."

"We need to keep this traffic moving."

The driver of the truck, following specific orders, had planned this stop during a busy time. He was getting weary. He was the last of a relay of drivers and still had several hours left to drive before reaching his destination.

Traffic was backing up on both the north and the south lanes. He hoped the truck would get little attention. He handed the agent the required license and registration along with an envelope that the driver suspected was full of bills.

The truck started out as an electrician's van down in Mexico. It had been driven up the California coast to Oregon, Washington, then across the border into Canada. The van had changed in appearance, and the driver had been changed several times during the trip. It was an expensive trip, but the cargo inside would pay these costs and still make someone very wealthy. It was supposed to be the last trip. The employer was planning on retiring.

Yea, right, thought the driver. *You can't just walk away from the drug business. Too many people will want the business to continue. Too much money is at stake. Jesus, what am I thinking? Why am I thinking drugs? I don't really know what I am carrying. I don't want to know. I can't get into trouble. I got a couple of kids to worry about.*

He was planning on staying in Niagara Fall for a few hours. He needs food, sleep, and maybe a drink. Just as he was crossing the border, his cell phone rang.

"Hello."

"Where are you?"

"I just got through the border in Niagara Falls. I'm stopping here to get some food and rest."

"No, you are not. The boss says to get to New Rochelle stat!"

"Why? I've been driving for hours. I'm beat."

"Pull over at a rest stop and grab a half hour or so sleep then get back on the road. If you don't get here in time, you can kiss your share of the profits good-bye."

I don't recognize that voice. Who the hell is this guy giving me orders? Ben wondered. *He's getting pretty bossy for someone who's probably way down in the chain of command. How come I'm not getting orders from my regular contact? I don't know who he is, but I would recognize his voice. Well, they told me that the load I am carrying is worth six figures. That is probably why they need to get it fast. I better cooperate. I can't afford to lose my pay. I need it for my kids.*

"I'll get there as soon as I can."

Ben hung up.

After talking to Ben, Lenny began to panic.

What the hell am I doing? he thought. *Can I pull this off? What about my contact? Will he help me? I don't even know how to get in touch with him.*

Maybe things will work.

Ben had a lot of thinking to do during his five-hour drive. He figured whatever he was doing was illegal. He also knew he would never be hired to do this job again. He was told when he was hired that the person he was working for was paranoid. He didn't want anyone to do the route more than one time. As it was, the route was done in relays. Ben didn't know where or when the route started. He only knew where he picked it up and where it would end. He rationalized that one time was not bad. If he didn't do the job, someone else would. Just driving a van wasn't illegal. He didn't know for sure what the cargo was; he just guessed because of the secrecy and the money involved. He was paid a lump sum up front and promised 2 percent of the profit, whatever that was. Hell, the five grand up front would have been enough. He needed the money to hire a lawyer to get his kids back.

It was just that he was feeling so guilty. That cop from the NRPD that he met outside the school grounds was so damn good to him.

Now, I may be doing something that is probably illegal and may just be hurting the department that was good to me.

He kept looking at the card Bill had given him.

He's a detective. Maybe he could get a raise or promotion if I tell him what is going on. I won't have to identify myself. I can't. I'd probably get jail time if I am transporting what I think I am. Then I would lose my kids altogether. I can't let that happen. I don't trust the little prick their mother is living with now.

I guess I need to make a phone call. I can't use a pay phone. It could be traced to this area, and I would have to disguise my voice. Well, I've got five hours to think about it. No, I haven't. I need to call from as far away as possible.

Ben pulled into a parking lot for a family restaurant and a CVS pharmacy. He purchased a disposable cell phone from the pharmacy, paying with cash. He went into the restaurant to eat because a family of five was just leaving the restaurant just as he was returning to his truck. He didn't want to be connected with the truck. If he went into the restaurant, they wouldn't give him a thought. He would call when he got back into the truck.

Russ, the dispatcher at the NRPD picked up the phone as soon as it rang. Every time he answered, he hoped it would be good news about the missing girl. This case was weighing heavily on the whole department.

"I need to talk to a cop."

"You are."

"I mean a detective, not someone on the desk."

Russ had all he could do to maintain his cool. He hated this desk job but reminded himself again that was lucky to have a job at all after the injury he suffered in the line of duty a few years back. He knew he couldn't respond in a way that would jeopardize his job.

"Do you have a particular officer in mind?" he asked politely. "I might be able to steer you to the correct person if I know what your issue is. Do you need to talk to an officer or a detective?"

Ben did not want to specify that he wanted to talk to Bill McDermott because he didn't want the call traced back to him. Bill would remember their conversation at the school and put two and two together.

He looked at Bill's card and said, "I guess I need to speak to an investigating officer."

"Well, that would be Bill McDermott. Hang on, I will see if he is available."

Ben couldn't believe his good luck.

"This is Detective McDermott. How can I help you?"

Maybe I am helping you, Ben thought. He did his best to disguise his voice.

"You can help yourself if you listen carefully. In about five hours, a secret shipment is being delivered to the New Rochelle Mini Storage Unit 9 in New Rochelle, New York. It may be drugs."

Ben hung up, pulled to the side of the bridge, and threw the phone into the Niagara River. He had no knowledge of the drama being played out at that same time.

"Are you sure the call is legitimate?" Sue asked Bill when he reported to her.

"I have no way of knowing. Why would the caller specify the kind of officer he wanted to speak with? Why didn't he call the FBI and ask to speak to a narc? I can't imagine how I would know this guy, but something about the voice seemed familiar."

"Well, we can't descend on the unit now. It would blow Alex's cover."

"I don't have a good feeling about tonight. I hope all is well there."

After talking to Bill, Ben kept driving and thinking. He had orders to alternate from the interstate to secondary state roads in case he was being watched. Anyone tailing him would have to stay two or three vehicles behind to avoid detection. If Ben took sudden turns, he would be able to lose the tail. However, Ben had been watching carefully and was sure he wasn't being followed.

If I follow the interstate all the way, I can be in New Rochelle in four hours. Then what? Cops or unit? I'm in deep shit either way. I never should have listened when I was offered this gig. I knew five thousand and a cut was questionable. I was told I was being offered the money to speed things up. But I wasn't born yesterday. I knew it was a bribe. Boy, I've got a lot of thinking to do.

The more Ben drove and the more he thought, the more Ben panicked about what he was doing.

He looked again at the card the policeman had given him when they were outside the school. Should he call him directly? Would it mean the he would end up in jail? He couldn't lose the time he spent with his kids. He decided to make another call.

"New Rochelle Police Department."

"Can I please speak with Bill McDermott?"

"May I ask who is calling."

"Tell him it is Ben Johnson."

"Hi, Ben, this is Bill, what can I do for you?"

"I told you I was a truck driver, right?"

"You did."

"Well, I am on a run from Canada right now, and I am afraid I might be hauling something illegal."

"Why do you think that?"

"I am driving a van instead of a big rig for a lot of money. That is pretty unusual."

"How much money?"

"Five grand."

"For how long a haul?"

"About ten hours all told. This was a relay job. Drivers were changed every six or eight hours. I was told the frequent change was a safety issue so no one gets too tired. My gig is supposedly longer because it is the final lap. I think there is more to it than just safety."

"Why?"

"There is a lot of secrecy to this job. I don't know the name of the driver I took over for, and he doesn't know my name."

"How did you hook up?"

"At a rest area in Ontario. I was given a license number to look for and a description of this van. I was given new plates and told to change them before moving on. I was told to do it at the rest area after the other driver left."

"That should have been a red flag. How did you get to the rest area?"

"I was given a rental car. The other driver was to return it. Yes, it was a red flag, but I was there and had no other means of transportation. I decided to drive the van to Niagara Falls, rest a while, then decide whether to proceed.

"However, I received a phone call from a guy named Lenny saying there was a rush on the delivery. I was not to stop to rest or eat. Of course, that is against CLD rules, so he finally gave in and said I could make a very brief stop. I was to grab coffee and a quick rest, but that was all. I won't know the delivery address until I get to New Rochelle. I have no idea what my cargo is. I was told to just drive and not check the van in any way. I was told I was being watched, but I don't believe that is true.

"Bill, I wish I had never taken this gig. I'm afraid of getting into trouble. I can't lose my kids."

"You are in a tricky situation, but I will do all I can to help you. When you get the delivery address, call me. By the way, how did you get the job?"

"Sometimes I work for a company called Taylor Transportation. I got it through them."

"Have all your other jobs through them been on the up and up?"

"As far as I know."

"Do you know who called you?"

"The regular operator, a girl called Staci. She is not the one who called to put a rush on the delivery. I told that person I needed a name in order to comply with the order. He said it was Lenny and that is all I needed to know. None of that sounded right. That is why I am worried and why I decided to call you."

"Did you call a while ago?"

"Yeah, at first I wanted to remain anonymous, then I changed my mind."

"Where are you calling from?"

"Now from my cell. The first call I used a disposable cell. I ditched it in the Niagara River."

"Give me your cell number. I may need to contact you."

"There's one other thing before I hang up, though it may not be important. When I got my orders to keep moving, I was just driving out of customs and didn't shut my phone down right away. As this guy named Lenny hung up, I thought I heard him say something about picking up some kid. As I said, it probably doesn't mean anything."

On the other hand, it may mean a lot, Bill thought.

Chapter 90

Joe knew he had to do more to protect himself from Max and Kim Lee. The only way to do that was to be sure they had to guard from each other. He needed to make another change in the plans. Joe called Lenny and had him start the calls to the first drivers but could not get him for the final change.

He had called Lenny's cell phone several times but got no answer. All he got was the message that no one was available to accept the call.

I'll have to make the call myself, he thought.

"Hello," Ben said.

He was getting very nervous about all these last-minute changes. He was glad he had been in contact with Bill.

"Change of plans."

"I just got the changes. Someone called a little while ago, about a half hour ago, I think."

"This is a new plan."

"Why another change?"

"It's not your job to ask questions. Just follow orders if you want to get paid."

The poor chump probably won't get paid, Joe thought. *He'll be lucky if he doesn't land in jail.*

After receiving the new directions, Ben closed his phone and pulled back on to the highway and continued driving. When he was within a half hour of his destination, he called Bill again.

"Ben," Bill said, "that fits with an anonymous phone call we got telling us to be at the back entrance of a lumberyard that is owned by a man named Kim Lee. He is a suspected drug dealer. I am not sure what is going down, but I don't want you involved."

"Why not? Maybe I can be of help."

"You've already helped more than you know. You have probably helped us get a lot of drugs off the street. I talked to my partner, and we want to give you a chance to redeem yourself. You probably made an error in judgement, taking a job that you were suspicious of, but you made it right by calling us. Drive the van to the Target parking lot on Center Street. I'll be there to meet you."

Chapter 91

Pete Needham was feeling pretty lucky. He had been after Kim Lee and his associates for years. He knew Kim and Chico had been responsible for the deaths of competitors and for fires that had been set at the competitor's businesses. In one of those fires, two homeless men had died of smoke inhalation. Kim Lee and Chico would have been charged with manslaughter if they had been charged with that fire. *They would have been put away for a long time*, he thought as he brushed his fingers through the brown hair that was slowly growing gray. He was fifty-five years old, but his medium build showed none of the telling fat that was evident in some men his age. Discipline and exercise have kept him trim.

Sue Patnode met Pete at the site of the fire. She was impressed with the professionalism of the five-man team that was sifting through the debris.

"How is your agent that was hurt in the explosion?" Sue asked Pete.

"He is going to be okay, I believe. He suffered a minor concussion, and his hands were badly burned. He will soon be able to be released from the hospital and will go home with his wife. She will wait on him hand and foot. He's sick over the way he treated your undercover officer. He knows he was badly hurt."

"Tell him not to feel guilty. He needs to remember that he alerted the first responders about Alex and, in that way, probably saved his life. It is a credit to Alex's skills that he could go undercover and even fool an FBI agent. He still has a long recovery but eventually will be good as new. There is a plus to this story. Alex's wife had found it difficult to raise their three sons by herself and had moved her family to her parents' home in New England. Alex was afraid she wanted a separation because of his undercover status. His wife is home for good now and is planning to have her parents bring the boys home as soon as Alex is well enough to leave the hospital. It will be the first time the family will be together for several months. They are all very happy about that. The boys call Alex every day at the hospital. They can't wait to be home."

Just then Sue's phone rang. She listened intently as Bill told her about his calls from Ben and his meeting up with him.

"I left him at the mall. I borrowed his jacket and cap. I hope I can fool whoever is waiting for the shipment."

"Bill, be careful. I can't imagine Max accepting a shipment after what has just happened at his place of business."

"The address I have is not the address of Max's business."

"Then give me that address of your destination. I'll call for backup then meet you there."

"You can't do that. If Max gets suspicious, it will blow our chances of arresting him when he accepts the shipment of drugs."

"I'll have people in unmarked cars. They will only move in if they think you are in danger."

Sue repeated the address as Bill gave it to her. Pete's ears perked up.

"What are you doing with that address?"

Sue did not want to tell Pete what was going on.

"Oh just some minor police business."

"Minor, huh. That is one of the addresses we have as a possible drop site for Kim Lee's drug shipments. We need to head for that address."

He gave instructions to his men, then he and Sue left for the site.

Bill was not surprised when Sue pulled up behind his truck at the address he had given her, but he was surprised to see that she was accompanied by a man wearing a jacket with the FBI logo on it.

"What gives, Sue?"

Sue introduced the two men.

"Did your driver know who was to retrieve the shipment?" Pete asked.

"No, he has no idea. He received his orders from a phone that did not register on his caller ID."

"That ought to help Ben's situation," Sue stated.

"I think he would recognize the voice if he heard it again. We could have him meet us at the office then call Max and Joe Boccia on some pretext. He might recognize someone's voice."

"Where is he now?"

"Hanging around Targets, at the mall. The poor guy doesn't have a jacket or transportation."

"Call the office and have an officer pick him up. Tell them to get him something to eat and have him wait for us at the office."

"Okay, I'll call him too so he won't think he is getting arrested."

"Oh I just remembered. He told me that when he was hanging up after one call, he thought he heard the word *unit*. It may not be important."

"But it could be," offered Pete.

After waiting for about a half an hour, Sue, Pete, and Bill realized that neither Kim Lee nor any of his associates were going to arrive at the lumberyard to accept what they believed was a drug shipment.

"We will wait ten minutes more then shove off," Sue decided.

"What about the van and the merchandise?"

"We will park the van at the station.

"I will take charge of the merchandise in the van," Pete offered.

"No, you won't. This is my jurisdiction. If it is drugs in the van, I will have it unloaded and locked up in our evidence room."

Pete thought he could pull rank and reverse that decision but decided not to. He waved to Bill and Sue and returned to the crime scene at the unit.

Bill and Sue returned to the station to meet with Ben. As soon as Ben saw Bill, he stood up and thanked him for the ride to the station and the food.

"Actually, it was my partner's idea," Bill told him.

He introduced the two then went on to tell Ben that they wanted him to listen to some voices on the phone.

"You may be able to help us in an investigation," he said without elaborating.

Ben listened first to Max's voice but said he did not recognize it as any voice he had heard before.

He did recognize Joe's voice.

"He was the last caller, the one who made the last-minute route change."

Bill and Sue looked at each other meaningfully when they heard Joe was the one who made the last-minute change. They now both believed he was trying to set up Kim Lee to be arrested on drug charges. How would that information help them find Benjii? They were sure both incidences were connected.

Chapter 92

Lenny's phone rang again soon after he had made his last call to the drivers. He was confused about being given this responsibility but had followed the orders explicitly.

He recognized the voice as soon as he picked up the phone.

"You gotta check on the woman and the kid a couple of times a day. I just drove out there. Ruth was walking down the road with the kid."

"She can't get anywhere to get help. The area is too remote. There's no way she can walk that far, especially with the kid."

"There's always the possibility of someone driving by. When she saw me, she came up to the car window and asked if I had a cell phone to call 911."

"I doubt she'll walk that far again."

"Probably not, but we still have to be checking a couple times a day."

"Okay, I got another thing going on you need to know about. Joe Boccia called me and gave me a bunch of numbers to call."

"What for?"

"They are the drivers that deliver the merchandise to Max's storage unit. I call one number to tell the driver to move up the time he is to meet his contact. Sometimes I tell him to take a different route. When that contact is made, I call the next driver with the same kind of information. I just made the last call."

"How often do you do this?"

"I've never done it before. I didn't know anything about how deliveries were made. My job is to unload the merchandise then get it ready to be shipped to the retailers when I got the order from Max or Joe."

"Can't you see what is happening, Lenny? They are setting you up to take the fall if something goes wrong."

"Why do you think something may go wrong? Deliveries are just being made to a different address because of the fire at their old unit."

He didn't understand how Lenny could be so thickheaded.

"Because Max is having trouble with the cops watching him and Joe and is having problems with Kim Lee. I am willing to bet Kim Lee caused the explosion and fire. Max and Kim Lee have been meeting a lot lately. Kim Lee is mad, and Max is scared. That's a dangerous situation."

"How do you know all that?"

"I know everything. Just watch your back. I think you are being set up for a fall."

Lenny Butler was not as thickheaded as the man thought.

I got nothing to tie me here except my grandmother, he thought. *I never saw her until the other day, and she doesn't expect to see me again. I wonder where the old girl's money will go. Probably to charity. Besides, she's in great health. She is going to be around a long time. I hope she is. She seems very happy. There won't be much money left when she is gone. I've been broke all my life. Why change that?*

The guy says I am being set up by Max and Joe, but how do I know he's not setting me up? I've taken all the chances with the kid. I don't know anything about him. He's just a voice on the other end of the phone. I got the first five grand from him. That's more money than I've had in a long time.

I'll never see the rest of it, but I can survive without it. Survival is the key right now.

Lenny went to his apartment and threw all his belongings in his truck. He smashed his cell phone, planning on throwing the pieces in the river somewhere. He left what he owed for the month's rent in the mailbox. He didn't want someone searching for him because of a half month's rent.

I'll lose the deposit, he thought. *But I gotta get out of here.*

Once he was packed, Lenny Butler left for parts unknown. He thought briefly about the woman and kid he left in the cabin in the remote area Will they ever be found? What will the guy on the phone do? He expects Lenny is checking on them. Will he also go there?

Oh well, he thought, *they have enough food for the next few days.*
He pushed hard on the gas.

Chapter 93

Sue decided to call Max again to see if she could rattle him enough to get any kind of information at all that could lead to the whereabouts of Benjii. She just couldn't decide if she believed Max when he said he knew nothing about the child's disappearance. She vacillated between thinking Max had had Joe take the little girl or if he knew nothing as he claimed.

She called Max's house first, wondering if Ruth Carter had returned to the residence. When she received no answer at the house, she called Max's office.

"Max Bertolini."

"Hello, Max, it is Sue Patnode from the NRPD."

"I know where you are from. What do you want now?"

"I need some information about a couple of your employees."

"What information? What employees?"

"Let's start with Ruth Carter. Have you heard from her?"

"No, and when I do, I'm going to tell her to pack her bags and get out. I got to have someone at the house that I can rely on."

"Are any of her things still at your house?"

"Probably, I never go into the rooms that she lived in. I respected her privacy."

"I suggest you check out those rooms."

Max paused.

"Maybe I should."

"Now for the other employee. Where is Lenny Butler?"

"I'm not sure. I think he lives somewhere in an apartment on Franklin Street. He's probably listed in the phone book."

"I've been there, and he has gone. He cleaned out most of his belongings, paid his rent through yesterday, and left. He didn't even wait to get his deposit returned and didn't leave a forwarding address. That's three people connected to you who have disappeared. What's going on, Max?"

Max was confused. He had no idea what was going on, but he didn't want Sue to know how scared he was. Did all this have to do with Kim Lee and the problems with the drugs? Why would he? Max had paid back all the money Kim Lee lost on the diluted drugs. Also, Kim Lee never had to loan him the use of some of his men to watch Joe, Lenny, Ruth, and Jake. The fire and explosion at the unit had taken care of that. And what is going on with the shipment due in today? Lenny was supposed to be at the new facility to unload the cargo from the van.

"Max," Sue continued, "what happened to these people? Can you understand why we are a little concerned about your activities now?"

"I got nothing to do with any of that. I don't know any more than you do."

"Okay, here's another question. Maybe you can answer this one. Why did Joe Boccia divert your van with your drug shipment to Kim Lee's lumberyard?"

Max wondered how Sue knew about the van.

"I don't know anything about a van."

"You are not expecting a delivery today? Don't you wonder where the van is?"

"Yes, I am expecting a delivery today or tomorrow, but not in a van. All my deliveries come through freight."

"You are talking about merchandise for you legitimate business. I am talking about your drug deliveries."

"I don't know nothing about drugs."

"We have the van, Max. It was very clever of you to put the drugs inside sealed coffee cans. The shipment would look legitimate to an inspector. They wouldn't open the coffee cans, but we did. The packets in the cans contained heroin, ecstasy, and God knows what else. We have not analyzed everything else. We know the shipment was headed for your new unit on Parker Street until Joe, for some reason, diverted it to Kim Lee's lumberyard. We are going to have to get this all sorted out, Max. Then someone is going to jail. The question is, will it be you or Kim Lee? Don't try to leave town, Max. We will be watching your every move."

Sue hung up the phone.

Chapter 94

Jake was getting very nervous about the events of the last couple of weeks. He knew about the explosion at Max's unit and read in the newspaper about Laura's arrest and subsequent release on bail. He didn't know what Max or Joe would do about these events, but he intended to distance himself from the whole situation. He wasn't going to go to jail for anyone and especially not for Max Bertolini or Joe Boccia. He decided to make some phone calls.

"Hello."

"Joe, this is Jake Turner. I called to let you know that I am no longer going to work for Max. I have done everything he wanted me to. I located his kid and sister-in-law. I saw to it that she was harassed and made sure her coworkers were suspicious of her. I am sure her life has been miserable. There is nothing more I can do. I am terminating my contract with Max and will end my association with the kid I hired. I will send a final bill."

"Okay, I will let Max know your decision."

He was sure Max would be glad to be rid of Jake.

He was beginning to be a liability.

After speaking to Joe, Jake made another call before throwing out his phone. He called Dodie Mcintire's phone and was relieved that the kid was the one who answered.

"Hey, kid, I called to tell you that your work for me is over. I'm calling the rental on the post office box, so don't go back there."

"Did you get the information you wanted?" Dodie asked innocently.

Jake had to think for a minute. He had forgotten what he had told Dodie about why he wanted Laura harassed.

"Yeah, kid, you did a great job. Now it is best for you and for me if you forget you ever did this job, and don't mention it to anyone."

Dodie understood why the man did not want his work discussed and knew he was lying about Laura giving him information. He was disgusted with the whole situation he had let himself be drawn into and was glad he would not be hearing from this guy again. He hung up without another word and then called Bob.

When Bob heard this information from Dodie, he knew he was one step closer to finding Dodie's employer and hoped he was one step closer to locating Benjii. He knew post office boxes were never rented without proper ID. He went to the store and had the clerk look up the information about rental 413. He was shocked to find that it had been rented by Joe Boccia from New Rochelle, the prime suspect in the kidnapping of Benjii McKenzie.

Maybe the second kidnapping, he thought. *But I certainly hope not.*

He called Sue Patnode.

After speaking with Bob, Sue asked Bill to go with her to Joe's house. He was clearly unhappy about seeing them at his door again.

"What now?"

"We need to talk with you about the post office box you rented in Mapleton, New Hampshire."

"I never rented any box. Why would I do that?"

"To communicate with the kid you hired to harass Laura McKenzie before you kidnapped her little girl."

Joe knew he was getting in over his head. Survival mode set in. He decided to tell partial truths without saying anything about the drug business. He invited Sue and Bill into the house.

"Max decided to hire a private investigator to look for his kid and sister-in-law."

"Why now after over five years?"

"I don't know. You don't ask Max questions. You just do what you are told."

"Could it be to divert attention from his drug business?"

"I don't know anything about drugs."

"Do you know a Jose Santiago from the Adrian Roy Packaging Plant in Columbia?"

Joe tried to stay calm, but Sue could see his shocked reaction.

"I don't know anyone in Columbia. I've never been there."

"A worker from the Adrian Roy Packaging Plant says different."

"Look, I don't know anyone in Colombia, and I never rented a post office box."

"Joe, you are in deep trouble. All the evidence we find about drugs being packaged in coffee cans in the packaging plant in Columbia and all the evidence we find about the McKenzie child's kidnapping point to you. So far, we don't have anything on Max. The other person in his operation, Lenny Butler, has disappeared. You have been chosen to be the fall guy. You had better think about what you are going to do next and give me a call."

Sue and Bill turned and left Joe's house. Joe sank into his chair and put his head in his hands.

He was shaking violently.

Chapter 95

Sue couldn't help but notice how shabby Jake Turner's office was. There was no reception area and no secretary. When she walked in, Jake was sitting at his desk, sipping a beer.

Drinking on the job, Sue thought.

When Jake saw Sue walk into his office, he quickly tried to hide the beer. He did not recognize her. It would not do to have a potential client see him drinking during working hours.

"Can I help you?" he asked.

"I believe you can. Are you Jake Turner?"

"I am. This is my agency. Are you in need of a private investigator?"

Jake tried to sound very professional. The woman standing in front of him definitely had class. He could smell money.

Therefore, he was not too happy when she pulled out a badge.

"I'm Detective Patnode from the New Rochelle Police Department."

"Someone from your department was here a few weeks ago. I don't know anything about any police business."

"I believe you do. You investigated the disappearance of Max Bertolini's child. You claimed that you found the child living with Max's sister-in-law who disappeared at the same time that the infant did."

"No, I didn't."

"Look, Jake, Joe Boccia is pretty mad that you rented a PO box in Mapleton, New Hampshire, in his name. You had better tell the truth."

"Okay, okay, I am not taking a fall for either Boccia or Bertolini. Last summer Joe Boccia came to this office and hired me to find both the kid and the sister-in-law. I did that in just a few days' time."

"How?"

Jake was not about to tell Sue about Jim Fallon. He might want to use his services again someday.

"Just good detective work."

Sue knew better but was willing to let it go for the time being.

"How does the post office box come in?"

"Max wanted me to hire someone to harass the woman, so I hired a kid to do it. He left me notes telling what he did, and I left his payment in the post office box."

Sue knew that what Jake told her coincided with what Bob Cochoran told her. The kid must have been Dodie Mcintire.

"I am not involved with this anymore," Jake went on to tell Sue. "I just told the kid his job was completed, and I called Joe and told him I was all done doing their dirty work. I don't want anything to do with fires and kidnappings."

"Who do you think kidnapped the child?"

"Probably Joe Boccia."

"Why? What would be his reason?"

"Because he's stupid. He wants to take over Max's business. Just ask Carlos at the Blue Fin."

"Who is that?"

"I think he is Max's competitor in business."

"What business?"

"Drugs."

"What makes you think that Max and this Carlos deal drugs?"

"Everyone knows it."

"If Joe had the child, where do you think he'd keep her? We have been to Joe's house several times. She definitely is not there."

"I don't know. Ask Doris Abbott."

"Who is she?"

"She is Joe's part-time housekeeper. Her husband is real sick, and she had a lot of medical bills. She would probably do anything Joe asked her to do to get money to pay those medical bills."

"Where do I find her?"

"I don't know. She is probably in the phone book. I think her husband's first name is Ed."

As soon as she found the correct address, Sue went to the house. The place seemed deserted. She looked in the windows of the garage, but there was no vehicle there. The curtains were pulled down in the windows of the house. She rang the bell and knocked on the door, but there was no response. A woman stopped on the sidewalk and spoke to Sue.

"Are you looking for the Abbots?"

"Yes, do you have any idea when they may return home?"

"I don't know if they will ever be back."

"Why do you say that?"

"Something strange has been going on here. Ed, the husband, has been very sick. His wife, Doris, never leaves him home alone except for a couple of days each week when she does housekeeping for some guy that lives alone. But a while back she was gone for a couple of days, leaving her husband to fend for himself. I know because she asked me to call to see if he needed anything. Anytime I called, he said he was fine, so I did not go to see him. When she returned, they packed up and left without saying anything to anyone. I have not seen them since."

Sue showed the neighbor her badge.

"I am Detective Sue Patnode from the New Rochelle Police Department. Here is my card. If they return home, please call me."

"Are they in trouble?"

"I hope not. Please just give me a call if you see them."

Chapter 96

Sue had assigned a surveillance team to watch Kim Lee, but the team saw nothing until two days after the van was sent to Kim Lee's lumberyard.

Sue had no way of knowing that Kim Lee had received an anonymous call stating that Max had sent a van with drugs to the lumberyard and that the cops were there when the van arrived. The caller told Kim Lee that Max was trying to set him up.

"Kim, this is Detective Sue Patnode from the NRPD."

"I gave at the office."

"Very funny. I'm calling to let you know where your drug shipment is. You weren't at the lumberyard to accept the delivery."

"I don't know what you are talking about."

"I am talking about the cans of coffee with packets of heroin, ecstasy, and so on that Joe Boccia had delivered to your lumberyard. How did you know that the cops would be there? That would be the only reason you did not take delivery."

"I wasn't at the lumberyard because wasn't expecting any delivery there, and I don't deal drugs."

"Get back to me when you have something truthful to tell me."

Sue hung up and turned to Bill.

"I believe him when Kim Lee says he didn't know the van would be coming to his lumberyard. He wouldn't be stupid enough to have drugs delivered to him that obviously. He knows he is being set up to take a fall for Max. We will see what he does next. We need to set up surveillance. Make sure the teams rotate so they don't get too tired."

Kim Lee poured a Scotch for himself then one for Chico.

"Someone's trying to screw us," he said after telling Chico about the lumberyard delivery.

"Who, Max Bertolini?"

"He says no, and I can't imagine why he would. He just got me paid back for the lousy drugs he sent to me. And I am not even sure he was responsible for that. We sent him a message about what we would do if we are crossed."

"Are the FBI guys still at the unit?"

"Are you worried?"

"Nah, they won't be able to find anything. If it wasn't Max, who sent the stuff to the lumberyard?"

"Let's think about the people Max wanted watched, Ruth Carter, Lenny Butler, Joe Boccia, and Jake Turner."

"I think we can forget about Ruth Carter. She is just a middle-aged housekeeper. She wouldn't know anything about drug deliveries."

"Unless she listened to Max's business on the phone."

"True, but I got the impression that the caller that directed the van to the lumberyard was a man."

"Good point. That leaves Butler, Turner, and Boccia."

Just then Roberto walked in.

"Just got the newspaper. There is a big article about the Bertolini kid."

"What does it say?'

"Pretty much what we already know, except the cops believe that the child a woman named Laura McKenzie claims is hers is really Max's kid and that they are confused by the disappearance of two of Max's associates, his housekeeper and an employee named Lenny Butler."

"Do you think Max has anything to do with the disappearances?"

"Lenny Butler, maybe, Ruth Carter, I doubt."

After listening to this conversation, Chico said, "That leaves two. I doubt Jake Turner would know anything about deliveries. That leaves Joe Boccia."

"Time to make a visit."

Chapter 97

For some reason, Dave Howland decided to buy the daily newspaper.

It will probably be a waste of money, he thought. *But I am interested in what is being done to locate that kid from Mapleton, New Hampshire, since my former tenant's name keeps popping up.*

After reading the article written in the newspaper, he remembered the envelope Lenny left with the rent money in it.

I wonder if the scribbling on the envelope he put the rent money in means anything, he thought. *I think I'll look to see if I still have it.*

He searched through the old rolltop desk his grandmother left him when she passed away.

When he found the envelope, he decided to make a call.

Russ answered the phone.

"New Rochelle Police Department."

"Hello, my name is Dave Howland. I have something to tell you that may not be at all important. I hope I am not wasting your time."

"Talking to one of the citizens of New Rochelle is never a waste of our time, sir."

"Thanks. I recently had a tenant named Lenny Butler. He moved out of the apartment rather suddenly a couple of days ago. He left the rent money he owed me in an envelope. There was something written on the envelope that might be an address. At first I thought it was just doodling, so I ignored it, but now I am not so sure. I read his name in the newspaper linked to Max Bertolini and the story about the little girl that was kidnapped. I want to tell you what is written on the envelope."

"Just a minute. Let me get a pencil. Okay, shoot."

Dave read the information to Russ, carefully spelling each word.

"Thanks," Russ told him when he completed the information. "Be sure you don't lose that envelope. Better yet, can you drop it off here at the station?"

"I'm going by the station in the morning to check on a new tenant. I will drop it off then."

I know that address, Russ thought when he saw the envelope. *It is way across town in the boonies. Practically no one lives out there now. I can't imagine why Lenny Butler would write it on that envelope.*

He put the slip of paper away.

I'll show it to Bill when he comes in.

Russ answered the next call, throwing the envelope into his drawer.

Chapter 98

Joe was sick; everything was falling apart. He had planned so carefully. How could this be happening?

Who would ever imagine Jose Santiago would have the guts to go to the top honcho and report his part in putting the packets in the coffee containers?

Why didn't Carlos agree to buy his drugs? Kim Lee will probably be arrested because of the drugs sent to the lumberyard.

He wasn't surprised that Big Jake had spilled his guts to the cops. He would have done the same thing to save his own skin.

He wondered where the kid was. Would Doris Abbott tell all? Of course she would, especially if the authorities offered to help her with her husband's medical issues. He had no idea that Doris and her husband were missing.

I haven't heard anything from Max. He's in trouble himself, and he didn't believe it when I told him I did not have the van sent to Kim Lee's lumberyard.

He was not afraid of anything Max would do; he knew the cops would be watching him too closely.

I need to get out of here and fast, he thought.

He called the bank to close his account. He requested that they save cash for him to pick up and sent the rest of the money to his offshore account. He would never use his credit cards. They could be traced. He cut them up and put them in the trash.

He supposed the drugs he had stashed at his storage unit would eventually be found. He would lose all that money, but there was nothing he could do about it.

He packed what he could into his car and drove away. As soon as he thought it was safe, he would trade his car. He was a little sad at losing all his possessions.

Little price to pay to keep out of jail, he rationalized. *And everything could be replaced.*

One down and one to go, thought the man who watched Joe's departure.

About an hour after Joe left his home, Jimmy, one of Kim Lee's thugs, and two other men arrived at his house and rang the doorbell. They had been sent by Chico. When they received no answer, they banged on the door. Still no response. They looked through the window and saw the red light on the security alarm flashing, indicating that it had been set.

"Is there a window we can go through?" Jimmy asked. "If we can get inside, I can disarm the alarm system. It looks like a cheap one."

"Let's look near the patio."

They found a window near the kitchen door, and Jimmy smashed it with the handle of his gun. They were able to reach in and open the kitchen door, and Jimmy disarmed the alarm system. Then they went through the house from the basement to the upstairs level to be sure Joe was not at home.

They checked the bedroom.

"It looks like our friend flew the coop," Jimmy said. "There are just a few clothes left in the closet and bureaus. Shaving gear and all that kind of stuff are gone. Just in case he plans to return, let's show him he can't screw around with Kim's business."

They began to trash the place. Jimmy never touched a thing.

If they ever try to find who did this, he thought, *they won't find my prints on anything.*

Chapter 99

Max was not surprised when Laura showed up on his doorstep again. She had driven to New Rochelle again, knowing she was probably jeopardizing her freedom, but she just had to continue her search for Benjii. Max decided to prove to her once and for all that Benjii was not at Joe's.

"Follow me," he said as he got into his car.

Laura was absolutely exhilarated when Max finally agreed to take her to Joe's house. She still did not trust him, so she was glad to follow in her own car. When she parked behind him and got out of her car, she noticed he looked perplexed.

"Joe is not here," he said. "His car is not in the garage."

"Can you call him? Maybe he will be coming back home soon."

"Let me look around first."

It didn't take long for Max to find the broken window. He was able to gain entrance into the house through the door off the patio the same as Kim Lee's men had.

Laura waited briefly then followed Max into the house. She immediately saw all the devastation Kim Lee's men had left. She ran through the house, screaming for Benjii. When she realized no one was there, she collapsed.

Max called 911. He gave Joe's address then told the operator that he had a trashed house and a hysterical woman there.

"I need assistance," he said.

Sue had just received a call from the FBI saying they were just getting ready to take Kim Lee and Chico into custody for suspicion of arson that resulted in an injury to a police officer when the call from 911 came in.

"Bill, you had better go with the FBI agents. I will answer this 911 call. It came from Joe Boccia's address. The hysterical woman must be Laura McKenzie. I don't know who placed the call or why Laura would be there at this particular time."

When Sue arrived at Joe's, Max met her at the door. She looked at the security alarm questioningly.

"Someone has disarmed this. Was it you?"

"No, it wasn't. I don't know who did it. Whoever did this, I would guess." Max pointed to the destruction that was evident from the foyer. "Just do something about that woman. I am sick of listening to her."

"First things first."

Sue called her office for an investigation team to come search for prints and any evidence to determine who trashed Joe's house and what might have happened to Joe.

She then went into the living room, where Laura was sitting in a chair, her head in her hands, crying uncontrollably.

"Laura," Sue said, "this isn't the end of the world."

"It is the end of my world." Laura sobbed. "Joe Boccia is gone. He may not even be alive. He is the only one who knows where Benjii is. What if she is alone, cold, and hungry?"

"I don't think Joe knows where Benjii is," Sue told her. "Someone took her from the woman Joe hired to care for her. I believe she is safe and is being cared for."

"Where do we go from here?" Laura asked between sobs.

"First you and Max have to leave these premises so my investigative team can determine what happened here. You are in no condition to drive. I will have one of my officers drive you to your motel. Does Chief Cochoran know where you are?"

Laura shook her head.

"He and Tim think I am visiting a friend from the shelter."

"I want you to call him now," Sue said. "I will speak to him and tell him I am keeping you here. You did something very foolish, but I can understand why. I would probably do the same if it was my child that was missing."

Sue allowed Laura to listen when she talked to Bob Cochoran.

"What do you mean she is in New Rochelle? She is supposed to be visiting a friend who lives miles away from there. That could cause trouble with her release, if I report it."

"She understands that," Sue said. "I believe she stopped by here on her way home. I saw her, stopped her, and asked her to check into a motel here."

Sue knew this was not completely true but felt she needed to give Laura a break.

"There are events occurring here," she continued, "that may be connected to Benjii's disappearance. I think she needs to remain in New Rochelle."

"Okay, I'll go along with your request for a couple of days. Just be sure you know where she is at all times."

"Will do."

Sue hung up.

"I'll have the officer drive you to your motel now. We will bring your car to you when our work is completed here."

Laura walked numbly to the police cruiser.

I'll have a lot to tell Tim when I call him, she thought. *He probably won't have anything more to do with me when he realizes I lied to him again. I guess I can't blame him.*

When Sue returned to her office, she had a message to call the FBI agent.

"We have Kim Lee and his right-hand man, Chico, in custody. I think a third man, Roberto, somehow got away. He is a low-level player, so it is not a big deal. We think both Kim Lee and Chico are going to talk to try to save themselves. Chico will give up Kim Lee, and Kim Lee will give us Max. This is good for us."

Chapter 100

Max heard the doorbell ring. He was irritated that Ruth Carter was not there to answer the bell. She knew she was not to allow anyone in the house unless it was one of Max's associates. He lumbered slowly toward the door, hoping whoever was there would go away. He opened the door. At first, he did not recognize the man standing there.

"Hello, Max, long time no see."

"No way, it can't be," Max said, thinking aloud.

"It can be, and it is. Remember how you screwed me out of my business about twenty years ago? It is now payback time. Can I come in?"

"Why would I want to invite you into my house?"

"Because I have evidence I could share with the cops that would put you in jail for a long time."

"Really? Did you hear about the fire and explosion at my place of business?"

"Luckily, I had a sense that something was going down. I got the evidence I needed before the fire. I also got the goods on Joe Boccia. He wanted to get you in trouble with Kim Lee then take over your business. Nothing went right for him, so he tried to create a diversion by taking your kid."

"He hasn't got the kid. I've been to his house."

"He never took her to his house. He took her to a crummy apartment and hired some woman to stay with her."

"Tell me where he has her. It would get her mother and the cops off my back."

"Nope, I got her now. I had her taken to be sure she wouldn't get hurt. She's a cute little kid, and your sister-in-law is devoted to her."

"You got her now?"

"Not me. I am not stupid enough to put myself in a position that I could be sent to jail. Some of your employees have her."

"What the hell? Who?"

"I had Lenny Butler get the kid from Joe Boccia."

"Why would he do that?"

"People will do anything when they need money."

"How did you get to know Lenny Butler and where Joe had the kid?"

"Surveillance, sir, surveillance and patience."

"Where is the kid now? I heard Lenny left town."

"Don't you wonder where your housekeeper is?"

"Mrs. Carter? What does she have to do with all of this?"

"She is caring for the kid."

"Why would she leave here to do that? Are you paying her more than I am?"

"I am not paying her at all. It has to do with a threat to her sister's family—and with her good heart. Lenny left the kid alone. She was worried about that."

"She would be. What do you want from me, money? If that is true, you are out of luck. If you think you know so much, you must know about me giving most of my money to Kim Lee."

"From your Cayman Island account, sure, but you still have money in your account in the Swiss bank."

"How do you know about that?"

"I have a friend who can find out anything."

"Who is he?"

"No one will ever find that out from any of his customers. They may need his help again. He is probably the safest guy in America. And he will never divulge the name of his clients or what business he performed for them."

"Here is my bank account number." He slid a piece of paper with the information over to Max. "How will I know you won't keep coming back for more?"

"You will have to trust me the way I did you twenty years ago. I will let myself out."

Max tossed and turned all night, trying to decide what to do about Bob Durand.

I better pay the money then close the Swiss bank account. I'll have the rest of the money put in my account here.

There won't be enough left for anyone to question the amount. I'll have to transfer the money to a new account when I decide where to go. I know I can't stay in this town any longer. After I get settled somewhere, I will get a real estate agent sell this property. I'll sell it furnished. That will give me a couple of million to add to the coffer. The stuff at the storage unit can go to hell. I'm sure the FBI has probably confiscated most of it anyway. I'll pack what clothes I can take with me. The real estate agent can give the rest to Goodwill.

Max had taken two large suitcases to his car and was just going back to the house for the third when a black SUV drove up to his car. Two men got out and showed him their badges, stating that they were from the FBI.

"We would like to speak with you for a moment," they said.

"Why? Anything Bob Durand told you is a lie."

The FBI agents looked at each other puzzled.

"Who is Bob Durand?" they asked.

"Never mind. What do you want?"

The agents decided to let his comment go for minute and stated their reason for being there. They would file the comment in their brains and check the name Durand when they returned to the office.

"We came to talk to you about the fire and explosion at the warehouse where the merchandise for your business is stored. Can we come in?"

The agents took notice of the two suitcases in the trunk of Max's car and the third one in the foyer.

"Are you going somewhere, Mr. Bertolini?"

"Just on a short vacation. I can't conduct any business until you guys finish your investigation."

"We have good news for you. Our investigation is just about over. We have arrested the people responsible for that explosion and fire. It was Chico Hernandez. He was ordered to do it by Kim Lee."

"Who are they? Did they get the wrong unit?" Max tried to look puzzled.

"We don't think so. They did it for retaliation for problem they had that they blamed on you. Apparently, you sold them drugs that were mixed with cornstarch. That got them into trouble with their clients, and they lost customers."

"How could I? I don't know anything about the drug business."

"Would you be willing to meet with us at the NRPD to try to sort this out?"

Max nodded his head in assent.

Max was sweating as Sue and the FBI agents told him what Chico and Kim Lee had stated in their sworn statements. They made no mention of Bob Durand.

Must be he kept his word, Max thought.

He was surprised when he finally realized that Sue and the FBI believed that it was actually Joe Boccia that had compromised the drugs sold to Kim Lee. They believed this because of Jose Santiago's story.

Max didn't believe that Joe would have the guts to try to pull something like this on someone as dangerous as Kim Lee. Max had trusted all his contacts in Bolivia. He paid them well. They had no reason to work against him. He made no comments at all about this situation.

After about two hours of questioning, Sue knew she was not going to get more information from Max.

"Max," she said, "you can go home now, but you better unpack those suitcases. You are not going anywhere until we get all of this sorted out."

Chapter 101

Bob Durand checked out of the hotel and drove by the police station.

I think my work is done. The cops will take it from here.

He checked his bank account, smiled, then called his wife.

"Everything will be okay now," he said. "I will be home soon."

His wife cried tears of joy.

He had been angry twenty years ago when Max took his business away. Now he realized how lucky he was to have had that happen.

Max is looking at jail time, he thought. *I am not and never will.*

Bob had some money when he left New Rochelle nearly twenty years ago. It was enough for him to get a new start. He realized how dangerous and uncertain the drug business was. He saw how much he hurt the people he sold the drugs to. He watched as a beautiful young girl changed into someone who looked forty years old. He decided to look for honest employment. He got a job at an auto center. He quickly learned to do all kinds of repairs offered at the facility. His supervisor was so impressed he sent him an auto-repair school and gave him a raise.

He married a girl he met while repairing her car. She worked at a local hospital as a nurse.

They made a good living. They money he just got from Max will pay for college for his two children. The rest will go to a rehabilitation center for teen drug addicts. He wants to atone for the harm he did earlier in life.

He had been honest with his wife about his past as soon as he knew he wanted to spend the rest of his life with her. She was not happy about his going to New Rochelle but understood why it was something he had to do. He was happy that he would be able to tell her that Kim Lee and Chico would no longer be selling drugs to the young people in that town. Lenny and Joe are gone. He hoped they would not stay in the drug business, but at least they were no longer selling in his town.

My goal was to get drugs out of this town as much as possible. I have accomplished this for a while, but I am smart enough to know that someone else, probably Carlos, will take over. I sent him information on how I was able to get the others and told him I would be watching him. I won't be doing that, but I hope he is worried enough to stay out of the business at least for a while. I have one call to make, then I am going home to my wife and kids.

Chapter 102

That darn phone is always ringing, Russ thought. *I think I will just let it ring. I've got to get this paperwork done.*

As tempting as it was to let the phone ring, Russ knew he had to answer it.

"Police Department."

"I am going to give you an address," the voice said. "Check it out. A little girl's life may depend on it."

The voice relayed an address then hung up.

Where have I heard that address before? Russ thought.

Then he remembered the envelope that Lenny Gray's landlord had left a few days ago. He pulled the envelope from his drawer. The addresses matched. He immediately went to Sue's office and told her about the envelope and the phone call.

"This is something we need to tend to immediately. Russ, why don't you ride with Bill. The two of you can check on this address."

Sue knew how happy Russ would be to get out of the office. She radioed Bill, explaining the situation. He reported to the office immediately, and he and Russ were soon on their way.

Ruth Carter was getting worried. She had used all the material she had to make clothes for Benjii, and it was hard to keep them washed and dried. The child was good and compliant, but Ruth was running out of ways to keep her occupied. She was always asking for a new book to read and for new books for Ruth to read to her. She could not understand why they could not go to a store. Ruth did not want her to realize that they were being kept prisoners there. She would be too frightened.

Ruth's biggest worry was food. Their supply was running very low. She had very little money to buy more and no way to get to a store if she did have money. Possible she could walk the many miles necessary to buy food, but Benjii couldn't walk that far, and she certainly would not leave the child alone and go herself.

The man, Lenny, who took her and Benjii was good enough to them, but she had no confidence that he would return and bring more supplies. She still could not believe that he was her half brother. After the encounter on the road with a man a few days ago, she realized that more than just Lenny was involved. She did not understand the role of each man.

Ruth was sitting watching Benjii play with a cloth doll she had made for her when she heard a car in the driveway. She nearly fainted with relief when she saw that it was a police car. Then her relief turned to fear. Did the police think she had kidnapped Benjii? Will they arrest her?

She stepped outside.

"Are you Mrs. Carter?" one of the policemen asked.

"I am, and I have a child with me that has been missing for several weeks. I did not kidnap her. I am just caring for her. We have been kept here as prisoners. I have had no phone, no means of communication, no car, and no way of getting in touch with you."

Ruth was nearly hysterical. All she had gone through in these last few days hit her, and she sat down on the steps and cried.

Russ sat down beside her as Bill went into the house.

"Please take it easy, Mrs. Carter. We know you are telling the truth. Is the child inside? Is she safe?"

Ruth nodded.

Bill went inside and sat down beside Benjii quietly, trying not to startle her. She looked up and jumped up when she saw him.

"Hi," he said, "my name is Officer Bill. Is your name Benjii?"

She nodded quietly, not sure that she should trust this man even though he was wearing a police uniform.

"My mother always said if I have a problem and I can't talk to her, Tim, Marcy, or a teacher, I could always talk to a policeman."

"She is right, Benjii. Do you have a problem?"

He wanted to hear her version of what had happened while she was still calm.

Tears came to her eyes.

"Grandpa Mitchell picked me up at school and took me to his and Grandma Mitchell's house. I did not like it there, but they said I could not go home. Then I woke up here one morning, and Aunt Ruth was here. She is kind, but she said I can't go home right now, but maybe soon."

By then, Benjii was sobbing uncontrollably.

"I want to see my mama. I miss her. Why doesn't she come to get me? I want to go home."

Bill picked her up; tears were in his eyes also.

"Benjii, my friend Russ, who is outside with your Aunt Ruth, is going to take you and Aunt Ruth to the police station where I work and call your mother. She has been looking and looking for you. She did not come to get you because she couldn't find you. She has been very sad and has missed you a lot. We will get the two of you together as soon as it is possible."

As soon as Bill and Benjii came out of the house and Russ could see that she was fine, he got on the radio and called Sue.

"We have the child. She has been well cared for and is in good health. You better call her mother. We are headed in."

"I will pick her up. I am not sure I want her driving on the roads. She will be too emotional."

Laura was sitting in her motel room, crying silently. She had just talked to Tim. Although he tried to remain calm, she knew he was not happy that she was in New Rochelle. He was worried that it would affect her freedom. He wanted her to come home to Mapleton and was disappointed when she said Sue wanted her to stay in New Rochelle while she investigated the new developments in both Benjii's case and the events involving Joe and Max.

She was surprised to hear a soft knock on the door. Housekeeping had been in and completed their work, and no one else ever came to her door. She looked through the peephole and opened the door when she recognized Sue standing there.

She nearly fainted when she saw tears in Sue's eye.

"Please do not give me bad news." She sobbed. "I don't think I could take it."

Sue put her arms around Laura.

"These are tears of joy. We have Benjii. She is safe."

Laura stumbled to a chair. She was faint with relief and excitement.

"Where is she? I need to go to her immediately? Is she okay?"

"Laura, I came to drive you to my office. Benjii may be there when you arrive. If not, she will be there soon after."

Benjii was sitting in Bill's lap when Laura walked into the office. Benjii cried and sobbed when she saw her mother.

She rushed into her arms, crying, "Why didn't you come and get me at Grandpa Mitchel's? I didn't like it there."

Laura was crying so hard she wasn't able to respond for several minutes. There was not a dry eye in the police station.

After she had calmed down and was holding Benjii in her lap, she noticed Ruth Carter.

"What are you doing here? What did you have to do with all of this? Why didn't you tell me you had her the first time I spoke to you at Max's house?"

Laura's anger was palpable.

"Mommy, don't be mad at Aunt Ruth. She took good care of me."

"That is right, Laura," Bill said. "She was left miles away from civilization with no phone and no means of transportation. When she tried to walk for help, she discovered it was impossible, especially with Benjii."

"Also," Ruth added, "when we were on the road, a man came and picked us up, drove us back to the house, and warned me not to try to escape again. It was not anyone I had seen before."

"We need to contact the people in Mapleton and let them know we have Benjii and that she is safe. Then we need to take her to the hospital to be checked to be sure she has not been hurt in any way. After that, we can all sit down and try to sort everything out. Our talk will have to include Mr. Bertolini."

Laura flashed a visual warning not to have Sue say anything more about Max in front of Benjii then said, "I can get my car and take Benjii to the doctor to be checked."

"It is something this department needs to handle," said Sue. "But you certainly need to accompany us."

"Why do I have to go to the doctor's?" Benjii asked. "I'm not sick."

"You know how I had to take you to the doctor's to get weighed, have your eyes and ears checked to be sure you were ready to go to school? It is a checkup like that."

"Will I have to get a shot?"

"No, not this time."

Benjii seemed satisfied with Laura's answer and was willing to see a doctor.

"First things first," Sue said. "Laura, I will call Bob Cochoran first, then you can call Tim and the school."

"We certainly have one happy police chief," Sue said after talking with Bob. "You had better call Tim right away if you want him to hear the good news directly from you. I think Bob will get on the phone and let the whole town know what has happened."

Laura had to call the middle school to get in touch with Tim.

"I hope all is okay," Donna, the school secretary, said when she heard Laura's voice.

"I want to talk to Tim please, then he can speak with you."

"Of course, I will transfer your call to his office. I believe he will be there. It is between classes."

"Tim Atwood."

Laura burst into tears when she heard Tim's voice. He paled, fearing bad news.

"Tim," Laura said between sobs, "we found Benjii. She is safe and unhurt."

Tim could not believe what he was hearing. He began to ask a million questions.

"Tim, I will answer all your questions when I see you. I hope Benjii and I can start home soon."

Sue started to shake her head. She did not want Laura on the roads while she was in such an emotional state but decided not to say anything while Laura was on the phone.

Tim felt the same way.

"No way. Marcy and I will come to New Rochelle and drive you home."

"That won't work. We will have two cars then."

"I will rent a car and drive you back in yours. I need to make arrangements for someone to take my classes for the rest of today and for tomorrow. Then I will get Marcy out of school, rent a car, and head up. It will be a while before we can get to New Rochelle, but I will get there as soon as I can. I want you to know that Marcy and I love you and Benjii very much. In fact, I want you to know that I am very much in love with you."

Tim hung up before Laura could respond.

Chapter 103

Before the trip to the emergency room to determine that no physical harm had been done to Benjii, Max was summoned to a meeting in Sue's office. He was told to be there when they returned from the hospital. He showed no emotion when he was told that the child that may be his was found safe and unharmed.

Benjii refused to be separated from her mother, so everyone had to be careful about what was being said at the meeting. An officer trained to work with children was called in. Benjii did consent to sitting with that officer to play games and read stories. She was content as long as her mother was in the same room with her.

"Laura," Sue said as they waited for Max's arrival, "you know that DNA results determined that Benjii is Max's child. We cannot allow you to take her back to Mapleton without his signed permission. You also understand you still face felony kidnapping charges. For that reason, the Department of Child and Youth Services has the right to remove her from your care."

As frightened as she was, Laura tried to keep her composure for Benjii's sake, but she knew that at the end of this meeting, Benjii could be taken from her. She did not think the child could endure another separation from her.

"I will do all I can to help the situation," Sue said. "I truly believe Benjii is better off with you than anywhere else, at least for the time being."

Russ escorted Max into the interview room. He quickly noted that there were three police officers there as well as Laura and a child. He acknowledged the adults, ignoring the child. She looked at him fearfully, ran from the officer who was playing with her, and jumped up into her mother's lap.

"Give us a minute please," she asked the adults in the room. Then she turned to Benjii. "Benjii, remember I told you the adults in the room have things to discuss about where you have been these last three weeks? I explained it will be adult conversation that you will be bored with. That is why this police officer is here with games and books for you. I would like you to sit with her while the rest of us talk. Show her how well you can read for a child in kindergarten. I will be right here."

Reluctantly, Benjii climbed down from Laura's lap and went to the police officer who sat across the room.

"I will read *Green Eggs and Ham* to you," she said softly.

All the adults in the room, including the officer, were impressed with the way Laura handled the situation. Only Bill and Sue knew that the officer was also a representative from DCYS.

"Max," Sue said, "you realize that due to recent DNA tests, you have certain rights."

She wrote Parental on a card and turned it for all to see. She did not know if Benjii would hear or understand the word *parental* but did not want to take a chance.

Max did not answer. He was wondering how he could turn this information to his advantage. He glanced at the child. He could see so much of Lana in her. He could see nothing of himself but thought she had his mother's eyes.

Thank God she doesn't look like my father, he thought.

"There is something else you need to know that could affect your decision as to the outcome of this meeting. I have asked a judge to issue a warrant for your arrest on drug charges."

"I am not worried about that. You have no evidence against me. All you have is anything Kim Lee might say. He would say anything to save his own skin. No judge will issue a warrant based on what he has to say."

"Are you familiar with the Roy Import/Export Company in Bolivia?"

"That is one of the companies I import coffee from. What do they have to do with anything?"

"One of the factory employees went to see Adrian Roy the other day with an interesting story. Apparently, without Mr. Roy's knowledge, some packets were being placed in the top of the cans by second-shift people before they were sealed. This information came to light when someone called a third-shift employee and offered him a large amount of money to swap the packets with different ones and change the order number on the cartons so the new packets could be identified. Mr. Roy did a thorough investigation of the employees working the second shift. Careful observation uncovered the employees who were putting the packets in the cans. They confessed that they were being well paid to add the packets. Unfortunately, they are men who are poor and needed the money to support their families. They were fired from their jobs, and now they are looking at many years of jail time. Their families will have no means of support. The employee who found he could not accept money for doing something illegal has his job with a raise. I guess honesty is the best policy."

"What has this to do with me?"

Max knew the answer to this question but was hoping Sue did not.

"Money orders were sent to one of the employees at Roy's factory to pay the men who were placing the packets in the cans. Those money orders can be traced back to your office."

"It is not uncommon or illegal for businesses to use money orders in their business."

"Perhaps, unless they are used because the company has something to hide, like you do," Sue added.

Laura spoke up at that time. "Max, please do the right thing. I don't want anyone"—she looked toward Benjii—"to suffer any more trauma. I am not sure she could take it."

Max did not care about the child he had to admit was his; he just wanted to use her as leverage.

"So if I sign this little problem off, what do I get in return?"

"You know we can't promise you anything. The most you can hope for is a sympathetic prosecutor, judge, and jury when your defense attorney tells what a good person you were to see that your child was well cared for. I am sure a judge would take that into consideration if you plea bargain."

"Plea bargain?"

"Max, we want to get the person in Bolivia who arranged to have the drugs sent to you. We want to stop the flow of drugs into this country. If you sign this release and tell us all you know about the drug cartel in Bolivia, your sentence may be lightened."

Max knew his chances of missing jail time were slim to none, but he still had some hope of a short sentence.

One step at a time, he thought. "Give me the release papers," he said.

"Thank you, Max," Laura said softly as he was led from the room by Russ.

Max did not acknowledge her or anyone else as he left.

Laura was surprised when Sue spoke to Benjii.

"Benjii," she said, "you need to come to my office for a few minutes while your mom talks with this officer."

Benjii ran to her mother and clung to her tightly.

"No," she said.

"I am sure it is okay for Benjii to be here. I am not sure this officer and I have anything important to discuss."

"Well, you do, and the discussion needs to be done in private. Benjii, the sooner you do what I ask, the sooner you can head home to Mapleton."

Laura nodded to her, telling her to go along with Sue.

"I will be right here," she told the frightened child.

As soon as Benjii and Sue left the room, the officer introduced herself to Laura.

"Laura," she said, "I am Patty Gline, a social worker from DCYS. It will be my job to monitor Benjii's home situation and be sure she is in the placement that is best for her."

"I am a little confused that you would call her home a placement."

"I understand, but you must realize that the law considers you a kidnapper. You could become a convicted felon."

"But Max signed a release giving Benjii to me."

"I am afraid that is not enough. You will have to appear in family court and have a judge approve the release and possibly start an adoption hearing. During that time you will be monitored by a social worker from Mapleton. That person can show up at any time at your home or school to see how Benjii is doing. What that person says will have a strong influence on the judge who will make the final decision on who will have final custody of Benjii."

"School? I am not certain she can return to school."

"May I suggest that after a week or so, you return her to school, and return to school yourself. The sooner Benjii gets into a normal routine, the better. You may want to start off at a couple of hours at a time, then half day, and gradually work into a full day. Now you are free to meet Benjii in Sue's office. You can return to Mapleton but must contact Bob Cochoran as soon as you arrive home. You need to stay at your own apartment, not with another family."

How on earth does this woman know about Tim and Marcy? Laura thought.

She decided not to make a comment. She simply said thank you and left the room.

As soon as she entered Sue's office, a tearful Benjii jumped into her arms.

"I will have an officer drive you to your motel," she said. "It has been a log day for both you and Benjii."

She hugged Laura.

"Good luck," she said. She had tears in her eyes.

She did not tell Laura there might be a surprise for her at the motel.

Chapter 104

Sue had assigned a young officer who had just joined the force to drive Laura and Benjii back to Laura's motel after Benjii had the meeting with Max. She knew Laura was too exhausted to drive. The pediatrician who checked Benjii, after hearing her story, had insisted that she see a child psychiatrist before being released from the hospital. The entire process had taken several hours because the doctor had insisted that Benjii be put in a room and given food before the psychiatrist saw her. Benjii got grumpy, and Laura was restless but knew the procedure was probably necessary. She had been relieved when Benjii was finally released, but then they had to endure meeting with Max, which had taken another hour.

When Laura and Benjii got out of the back of the car, the officer got out also.

She squeezed Laura's hand and said, "Ms. McKenzie, I want you to know that the entire police department is thrilled that you found your daughter safe and sound. We have been praying for you."

With that, she got back into the car and drove away, waving. She did not want them to see the tears in her eyes.

Laura did not notice the car parked near her room. She unlocked the door, and both she and Benjii were grabbed and hugged before they had had gotten all the way into the room. Sue had called the motel and told the clerk to let Tim and Marcy into Laura's room if they arrived before Laura returned. She wanted their reunion to be private rather than in the motel lobby for strangers to witness.

The four of them hugged and cried for several minutes before speaking.

"How did you get into my room?" Laura asked.

Tim told her that the desk clerk had been given instructions to give them a key when they arrived.

"That was probably Sue Patnode's doing," Laura said.

"Can we go home now?" Benjii asked.

"Yes, we can," Laura answered.

Marcy and Tim looked at her questioningly.

"I have some papers to show you," Laura said as she removed them from her purse.

She showed Tim the release Max had signed and the permission from DCYS to return to Mapleton.

"We will be monitored carefully for a while then summoned to family court. Sue has sent a notice to Bob Cochoran stating that all charges from New Rochelle have been dropped. He is to monitor me carefully for one year. I need to remain in Mapleton for a year and make no significant changes in my lifestyle without his okay. If I am good for one year, all the records of my arrest will be expunged, and I will be in the clear."

"Well then, let's get out of New Rochelle as fast as we can," Tim suggested.

"We need to stop and shop somewhere. I must buy clothes and books and toys for Benjii. All she has is what Ruth Carter made for her."

"Who is Ruth Carter?"

"I will explain everything when I can."

Tim and Marcy knew they would have to be patient waiting for the answers they wanted. Laura did not want to discuss things in front of Benjii.

Six hours after their meeting in the motel room, Laura, Benjii, Marcy, and Tim drove into Mapleton.

"Look! There is my picture," Benjii said excitedly.

Tim and Marcy smiled. They knew that Laura and Benjii would see the pictures as they drove into the town. Dodie and Tom had organized a group of students to change the missing-child posters to welcome-home posters with yellow ribbons. Laura cried softly as Marcy and Tim explained what her students had done.

"Don't cry, Mom," Benjii said, patting Laura's arm. "Everything will be all right now."

Tim and Marcy brought Laura and Benjii to their condo. They helped her carry in the items they had purchased for Benjii.

"Perhaps I should have gone grocery shopping," Laura said. "I am not sure what I have in the house to eat. I have only been gone a few days, but it seems like weeks."

"Let's check your cupboards and fridge," Marcy said, smiling.

Laura could not believe her eyes. The cupboards were stocked with staples, and the fridge was stocked with perishables and casseroles.

"Compliments of both the middle and elementary school staff," Tim told her. "They wanted you and Benjii to have some time alone without worrying about anything. Why don't you check Benjii's room and see if everything is okay there, then Marcy and I will leave and let you and Benjii have some time alone."

They walked into Benjii' bedroom, and she squealed with delight as she saw her own bed, clothes, and toys. All the items Bob had removed had been returned.

"All charges against you were dropped in New Rochelle. There were never any charges filed here," Tim explained. "Bob had no reason to keep these items."

"He probably doesn't have the information from DCYS in New Rochelle. Why don't you and Marcy come back around eight if that is not too late."

"We will be here."

Laura would explain everything to Tim and Marcy at that time.

Chapter 105

Laura and Benjii stayed quiet for a couple of days. Laura did not ask Benjii questions about what had happened to her. She just listened as Benjii made comments about her stay with Joe and the woman who cared for her. Laura understood that they were as kind to her as they could be but just did not know how to deal with a child. Benjii had no idea how she got to the house where Ruth was.

Laura decided not to tell her what little she knew about that time.

Maybe later when she is stronger emotionally, Laura thought.

One morning, Benjii asked if she could return to school. It was just a week before April vacation.

"Maybe we can start tomorrow for just the morning," Laura told her.

She had spoken to Lila Ashton and her school principal. Lila had agreed to allow Benjii to return to class for a half day when she was ready.

The next morning, Laura and Benjii arrived at Benjii's school first. Laura was not ready to take her to the before-school program, so they arrived just as school was starting. When she walked in, Mrs. Clark, the secretary replacing Tammy Price, told her that Mrs. Ashton wanted to see her and Benjii in the office before going to the classroom. The students were well aware that Benjii had been missing.

There was no way to keep it from them. They had seen the posters everywhere. The teacher had spoken to the students the afternoon before, telling them to greet Benjii as they would any other student who had been absent from school for a while. They were warned not to ask questions about her absence. Lila wanted to escort Laura and Benjii to class to be sure all went smoothly.

When they walked in the classroom Ms. Colson told the students to say "Good morning" and "Welcome back" to Benjii. They did that as some of the students went up to hug her.

"We missed you," one of the students said.

Benjii noticed that one of the desks was empty.

"Where is Terry?' she asked.

"He moved," one of the students told her. "He is not in our class anymore."

Laura was happy to hear that. It meant Alex was doing well and that the family was together again.

I got so wrapped up in my own issues that I never got around to contacting Meg, she thought. *I will call her when I get home tonight.*

Laura was having a difficult time deciding when to leave the classroom. She was not sure how Benjii would react to the separation. Her teacher solved the problem.

"Benjii," she said, "it is time to go to the art room. Say good-bye to your mom so she can go to her school. I remember what a good line leader you were when you were here before. You can be line leader and walk with me."

Benjii hesitated for a moment, gave Laura a hug good-bye, took her teacher's hand, and went down the hall.

Laura had received permission from her school principal to visit her classroom. She would not be able to teach unless she was reinstated by the superintendent. When she was first absent from school, the other special education teachers helped with her caseload, but when the principal realized that she would be out for more than a week, he hired the retired teacher she had replaced to substitute for her.

When she walked into her classroom, she was greeted warmly by her students. She thanked them for the posters that greeted Benjii when she arrived in town. She couldn't find the words to express how much both she and Benjii appreciated their efforts. The students made it plain that she had done a lot for them during the school year, and they wanted to reciprocate. Mrs. Wade, the substitute teacher, asked Laura to stay for a minute when the students moved to another classroom when the bell rang.

"I was sorry to hear that you were assigned to team 6 this year," she said. "They are good teachers but want to do things their way. They don't give an inch if they don't agree with what is being done. They did not want special education students to be mainstreamed into their classes and did not want modifications made for them when they were. Tim Atwood asked me to meet with him and the team one day last week. They grudgingly admitted that the students were performing better than they expected and that you had done the bulk of the work to help them be successful. They also admitted that having the students in their classes had not caused them extra work as they had expected. Tim gave them quite a dressing down and told them he expected them to be kinder to you when you returned. I think you will find life easier when you return to school. I hope that happens soon. Your students need you. By the way, I think Mr. Atwood has a thing for you."

Laura thanked Mrs. Wade for her help and her comments and left the school to go to her lawyer's office.

"We have several things to deal with," Brenda Simpson told her. "First, we need to be sure that the courts in Mapleton realize that there are no charges filed against you anywhere, not from New Rochelle, not from here, nowhere. Then the judge needs to notify your school superintendent of that fact. You should be reinstated in your teaching position and receive back pay. Next we need to set up a system for your visits from DCYS. Some may be scheduled, but you will also have unannounced visitations. It should not take a year for them to assess whether you are a fit mother for Benjii. Anyone who knows the two of you knows she should be with you, and any different plan would devastate the child. I will start the process of getting witnesses to testify on your behalf when DCYS recommends your case to family court. First we have to go to district court to have your case cleared there. We go to court tomorrow morning at nine o'clock. I will meet you there."

Brenda did not tell her about the special phone call she had received regarding that court date.

When Laura picked Benjii up at school, she made arrangements for Benjii to attend a half day the next day also. Benjii was excited about being back to school and wanted to be there the next day.

"Ms. Colson said I could have sharing first tomorrow because I missed my turn one time."

Laura was relieved at Benjii's attitude. She did not want to have to take her to court with her the next day.

Chapter 106

When Laura got Benjii ready for school the next morning, Benjii asked her if she was going to her school again today. She had noticed that Laura was dressed up more than she usually was for school.

"No, not today," Laura said, "the students still have a different teacher that they are working with right now. Possibly I will go back after April vacation."

"Why are you dressed up?"

"I have errands to do."

"You look awfully dressed up to do errands."

"Some errands require a different kind of dress," Laura told her. Benjii looked puzzled but did not question her mother further. Laura met Brenda Simpson outside the courtroom.

"These proceedings shouldn't take more than a few minutes. Everything is pretty straightforward. It is mostly a formality. Because your first appearance was in this court, your case has to be cleared here."

Laura was surprised to see the people seated in the courtroom. Tim was there, but that did not surprise her. She was surprised to see Marcy, Dodie, and Tom there.

"Why are these kids here?" she asked Brenda. "They should be in school."

Brenda smiled. "Guess they're playing hooky," she said.

Laura continued to look around the room. She saw Chief Cochoran, which did not surprise her.

Officer Mary Kenyon was sitting beside him. Next, she spotted Pat Cook and Ruth Carter sitting together. Lila Ashton and Tammy Price were also in attendance.

"I had no idea my court appearance would create so much interest," she told Brenda.

The judge walked into the courtroom, and Laura's case was called by number.

"Are both sides ready to proceed?" the judge asked.

Brenda and the prosecutor both nodded.

"May I be allowed to speak first, Your Honor? I may be able to save the court a lot of time."

"Does the prosecution object to this request?" the judge asked.

When the prosecutor answered in the negative, the judge gave Brenda permission to proceed.

"Your Honor, charges brought against my client stemmed from an arrest in New Rochelle, New York. The New Rochelle Police Department has dropped all charges, so we request that charges be dropped by this court also."

"The charges are kidnapping," the judge said. "These are very serious charges. Kidnapping is a felony. On what basis do you request these charges to be dropped?"

"Your Honor, these charges were brought due to a complaint filed by a drug dealer in New Rochelle. He has since dropped that complaint."

"Who was kidnapped? I fail to see how so serious a charge can be dropped so easily."

Laura as was all as her friends in the courtroom was getting nervous.

"This was a very complicated situation that has been going on for over six years. The child in question has been well cared for and deeply loved by Ms. Mitchell, currently known as Ms. McKenzie. A full report has been sent to your office, but I don't believe it was sent in time for you to review it."

"Ms. Simpson, you should not have scheduled this court date until I had time to review this report. Court is adjourned for one half hour until I read the report."

The judge glared at Brenda as she left the bench.

"Has the prosecution read the report?"

The prosecutor nodded.

Forty-five minutes later the judge returned to the bench, and the proceedings were resumed.

"Does the prosecution object to or concur with the defense's request that charges against Ms. Mitchell/McKenzie be dropped?"

"The prosecution sees no reason to continue with these charges. Ms. McKenzie/Mitchell has proven to be an excellent mother to the child in question. Professionals who were interviewed, such as her teacher, the school counselor, and school principal, state that the child is very devoted to Ms. McKenzie. She has received excellent care, is in excellent health, is emotionally sound. The family, however, will be monitored by DCYS before decisions will be made about the child's permanent placement. Ms. Simpson has filed an adoption request on behalf of Ms. McKenzie, but we all know that action may be a little premature. We all know Ms. Simpson can be a little overexuberant."

Laura noticed a special look between the prosecutor and Brenda. *I wonder what is going on there*, she thought.

"The report I read," the judge stated to Laura, "outlines both your responsibilities and the responsibilities of DCYS. Do you accept these responsibilities? Are you okay with maintaining the lifestyle you are living now? You should not make any significant changes to the way you live. Do you understand you must stay in Mapleton, New Hampshire, until all issues regarding the best interests of the child in question are resolved?"

"Yes, of course."

Then the judge said something that Laura thought was very strange. She noticed that both Brenda and the prosecutor were smiling.

"Does anyone in the courtroom wish to make a statement or ask a question?"

"Yes, Your Honor."

Laura was surprised to see Tim walk to the judge's bench.

"If Chief Cochoran approves, would the court allow Ms. McKenzie to change her name?"

"With the chief's approval, the court could approve that change."

"In that case," Tim said as he walked to the defense's table with a ring box in his hand, "Laura, will you marry me?"

"Yes!"

Laura fell into Tim's arms as everyone in the courtroom stood and cheered. All eyes were moist, including those of the judge.

Epilogue

One year later

Laura had been allowed to return to school after April vacation the last school year.

She was happy to finish the school year with the students she loved so much. One month after school ended for summer break, Laura and Tim were married. They had a very simple ceremony with just a justice of the peace, Marcy, and Benjii in attendance. It was a far cry from the large church wedding Laura had always envisioned and Lana obviously had.

"Someday, we will have a big reception," Tim had promised her.

Now, one year later, a big reception was the last thing on Laura's mind. She and Tim were expecting their first child. The child would be born right after Marcy graduated high school. The money Tim had borrowed for Laura's bail had been returned to the fund set aside for Marcy's college tuition. Laura had allowed herself to be interviewed by Sonja Atwood as promised by Tim. Both Tim and Laura were satisfied with the story Sonja had written. It was professionally done.

John Breen had released the money left to Lana and Laura by their parents to Laura. Lana's portion of money was put into a fund for Benjii. It would pay for her college when she was of college age and would provide money for her future after college. Laura and Tim had used Laura's portion from her parents' estate to purchase a new home. It has four bedrooms.

"One for each of the kids and one for us," Tim said.

Marcy would be away at college part of the time, but it was very important to both Tim and Laura that she have a room to come home to.

Ruth Carter has been staying with her sister, Pat. They were trying to come to grips with the fact that they were related to Lenny and Joe.

"Lenny I can deal with," Ruth told Pat, "but I am having a difficult time accepting the fact that I am related to Joe. He was not a good person."

Pat had never known either man. She had more important things to think about. She had accepted the position of the head of the middle and high school food service program. Her income would be higher than it had ever been before. During the summer, she would be able to continue working as head cook for a local summer camp. Ruth will care for Tim and Laura's baby when Laura is in school.

Max had plea-bargained with the prosecutor with Sue and Bill's blessing. He will serve ten years in prison. His fortune made from drug money was confiscated and will be used to help fund drug-rehabilitation centers. Kim Lee will serve twenty years in prison, Chico thirty years to life. At this point, neither Lenny nor Joe had been heard from.

Bill, Sue, and Alex received commendations for capturing Max, Kim Lee, and Chico. Alex will no longer work undercover. He will spend more time home with his family. He will return to the force when he has fully recovered from his injuries. That should happen soon. He was surprised to learn that it was Bob Durand that had helped him achieve his goal of avenging the death of his brother, Bart. Ben also received a commendation for assisting with the capture of Kim Lee and Chico. With the help of Russ, he was able to prove that he was not a threat to his children. The accusations had been the work of his wife's boyfriend. That relationship had ended. Ben had full visitations rights with his children.

The team of teachers Laura worked with was assigned to different teams for the following school year, making things easier for Laura. No other teacher would have to endure what Laura had endured at the hands of this group of teachers.

At Laura's request, Tammy Price has been reinstated as secretary for the elementary school. Bob Cochoran often bragged about his part is locating Benjii.

No one ever knew the part Bob Durand and Jim Fallon had played in this story. They were both content to remain anonymous. Big Jake Turner would continue to struggle to keep his agency afloat.

What made Laura happiest was the fact that both Tom and Dodie were doing extremely well in school. Tim saw to it that Dodie was given an afternoon job working for the grounds crew. He no longer exhibited a tough-guy image.

Laura visited the shelter and told her entire story to the people there who had helped her so much. She also gave them a substantial donation.

She walked out of the shelter toward her car that would take her to her new home.

Everything has come full circle, she thought.

About the Author

Norma Wyman has lived her entire life in small communities in southwestern New Hampshire. She married young, and as soon as her two daughters started elementary school, she enrolled in Keene State College. She was awarded a Bachelor of Science degree in education and later a Master's degree in education. During her many years as an educator, she taught elementary and middle school students with behavioral difficulties. Norma also served as a title one coordinator and a learning disabilities specialist. She has worked with many children and adults on a volunteer basis, assisting them with developing reading and language arts skills. After retiring from teaching in the public school system, she worked for ten years with incarcerated adults in a local corrections facility. Norma has always had an interest in writing. Felony is her first novel. She currently lives in southwestern New Hampshire with her husband.

CPSIA information can be obtained
at www.ICGtesting.com
Printed in the USA
LVOW04s2103110816
499999LV00022B/828/P